lion down

Also by Stuart Gibbs

The FunJungle series
Belly Up
Poached
Big Game
Panda-monium

The Spy School series
Spy School
Spy Camp
Evil Spy School
Spy Ski School
Spy School Secret Service
Spy School Goes South

The Moon Base Alpha series
Space Case
Spaced Out
Waste of Space

The Last Musketeer

STUART GIBBS

lion down

A **funjungle** NOVEL

Simon & Schuster Books for Young Readers

New York   London   Toronto   Sydney   New Delhi

SIMON & SCHUSTER BOOKS FOR YOUNG READERS
An imprint of Simon & Schuster Children's Publishing Division
1230 Avenue of the Americas, New York, New York 10020
This book is a work of fiction. Any references to historical events, real people,
or real places are used fictitiously. Other names, characters, places, and events are
products of the author's imagination, and any resemblance to actual events or
places or persons, living or dead, is entirely coincidental.
Text copyright © 2019 by Stuart Gibbs
Jacket design and principal illustration by Lucy Ruth Cummins, copyright © 2019 by
Simon & Schuster, Inc.
Leaf art copyright © 2019 by Thinkstock.com

SIMON & SCHUSTER BOOKS FOR YOUNG READERS
is a trademark of Simon & Schuster, Inc.
For information about special discounts for bulk purchases, please contact
Simon & Schuster Special Sales at 1-866-506-1949 or business@simonandschuster.com.
The Simon & Schuster Speakers Bureau can bring authors to your live event.
For more information or to book an event, contact
the Simon & Schuster Speakers Bureau at 1-866-248-3049 or
visit our website at www.simonspeakers.com.
Interior design by Lucy Ruth Cummins
Endpaper art by Rickie Lee
The text for this book was set in Adobe Garamond Pro.
Manufactured in the United States of America
0119 FFG
First Edition
10 9 8 7 6 5 4 3 2 1
Library of Congress Cataloging-in-Publication Data
Names: Gibbs, Stuart, 1969– author.
Title: Lion down / Stuart Gibbs.
Description: First edition. | New York : Simon & Schuster Books for Young Readers,
[2019] | Series: FunJungle | Summary: Thirteen-year-old Teddy Fitzroy and his girlfriend,
Summer, investigate when a mountain lion is accused of killing a prized dog outside of
FunJungle Wild Animal Park in the Texas Hill Country.
Identifiers: LCCN 2017060160 | ISBN 9781534424739 (hardcover) |
ISBN 9781534424753 (eBook)
Subjects: | CYAC: Mystery and detective stories. | Zoos—Fiction. | Zoo animals—
Fiction. | Puma—Fiction. | Endangered species—Fiction.
Classification: LCC PZ7.G339236 Lio 2019 | DDC [Fic]—dc23
LC record available at https://lccn.loc.gov/2017060160

For my cousin Sheryl, who cares more about the animals of this planet than anyone I know

Contents

lion down

THE FISH CANNON

I got mixed up in all the cougar chaos the same morning I was shot with a herring.

The herring incident happened while I was helping feed the penguins at FunJungle Wild Animal Park, early on a Saturday morning in late May, before the park had officially opened for the day. My girlfriend, Summer, was also there. I was only thirteen, and Summer was fourteen, but since Summer's father, J.J. McCracken, owned FunJungle and both my parents worked there, we often got to go behind the scenes.

FunJungle's penguin exhibit was one of the largest in the world, with 416 birds on display: a mix of emperors, chinstraps, Adélies, macaronis, gentoos, and kings. Normally, I wasn't a big fan of being in with the penguins. Yes, they were cute, but all those birds generated a lot of poop, and penguin poop *reeks*. The exhibit smelled like a latrine full of rotten fish. However, Summer and I were braving the stench for two reasons:

First, a heat wave was frying central Texas. Normally, the temperature in late May should have merely been uncomfortably warm; instead, it was blisteringly hot. The day before, in science class, we had fried an egg on the school parking lot. Meanwhile, the penguin exhibit was chilled to twenty degrees Fahrenheit. It was the perfect way to beat the heat.

Second, we got to use a cannon.

It wasn't a *real* cannon. There was no gunpowder or anything like that. Instead, it was a pneumatic plastic tube created by the Zoom Corporation to move fish at high speeds.

Zoom had originally invented the cannon to help salmon get past dams in the Pacific Northwest. Salmon are born in mountain lakes, swim downstream to the ocean to mature, and then, years later, return to the exact same lakes where they were born in order to spawn. Unfortunately, dams often prevent the salmon from returning to their headwaters, and until recently, the only option had been to build expensive fish ladders, which were like giant concrete staircases the salmon could "climb" by jumping from one pool to the next. Firing the fish through a pneumatic tube over the dam was a lot cheaper—albeit somewhat ridiculous. J.J. McCracken had liked the idea, though. He had invested a good deal of money in Zoom, and while he was explaining the concept to Summer one night at dinner, she had suggested that maybe the tubes could be used for dead fish as well as live ones.

J.J. McCracken was a smart man, but he always claimed his daughter was even smarter; so when she made suggestions, he listened. (After all, Summer had come up with the whole idea for FunJungle itself when she was only seven.) Summer's logic went like this: FunJungle couldn't feed the penguins live fish, because it was hard to control parasites in a live food supply and we didn't want the penguins to get sick. So all their food was frozen and then thawed out for feeding time. In the case of the penguins, this amounted to over 700 pounds of fish a day. Normally, the keepers fed the penguins by tossing little chunks to each of them, which was very time-consuming and promoted abnormal behavior.

"That's not how penguins get food in the wild," Summer had told her father. "In the exhibit, they look like a bunch of pet dogs, sitting around, begging for treats. It's not natural!"

"It's still awfully popular," J.J. had argued. "At feeding time, I've seen crowds seven people deep at the glass."

"Well, imagine how much bigger the crowds would be if they saw the penguins actually *do* something," Summer said. "Suppose you shot the fish into the water and the penguins had to chase them down! It would allow the penguins to act more like they do in the wild, and it would be much more exciting for the visitors."

J.J. had pondered that for a bit, then grinned proudly. "All right," he'd said. "Let's give it a shot."

Which was how, two weeks later, Summer and I found ourselves in the penguin exhibit early on a Saturday morning, loading frozen herring into a fish cannon.

Getting there that early hadn't been any trouble for me; I lived in FunJungle's employee housing, which was a collection of double-wide trailer homes not far past the back fence of the park. J.J. owned ten square miles of property in the Texas Hill Country, of which FunJungle only took up a fraction. (So far, at least; J.J. was hoping to greatly expand his theme park empire in the future with additions to FunJungle and new resort hotels.) Out my door there was nothing but forest. Although I *liked* hiking in the woods, there was nothing else to do around there except visit FunJungle. I had my own employee pass that let me enter the park whenever I wanted, as both my parents tended to be there rather than at home.

My mother was the head primatologist at FunJungle, while Dad was the park's official photographer (though he still got away to take photos for *National Geographic* on occasion). Dad had accompanied me to the park that morning, but Mom had already been at work. Most animals wake up early, which means keepers have to be there early too—Mom was often on the job by five a.m.

Cindy Salerno, the head penguin keeper, lived a few trailers away from us. She was always cheerful and friendly and she baked a mean apple pie. (Although, as an occupational hazard, no matter how much she showered, she always smelled slightly like fish.) Cindy knew me well enough to trust me to help out with the cannon; she didn't know Summer that well, but J.J. had insisted Summer be there that morning because the whole thing was her idea. Cindy was excited about the fish cannon, but had felt we should give it a test run before the tourists arrived, just in case something went wrong.

This turned out to be a very shrewd idea.

At eight a.m. it was already sweltering outdoors, but inside the penguin exhibit we were dressed for winter. It was actually snowing in there. A special machine had been built for this. An enormous modified snow-cone maker shaved flakes of ice off giant cubes and blew them through vents in the ceiling. The snow then wafted down and piled up in drifts. The machine ran for a few hours every morning, generating over a ton of fresh snow a day. The penguins loved it. They were dancing in the shower of flakes, waggling their stubby wings in delight.

I enjoyed the snow quite a bit myself. I had never lived

anywhere it snowed, and even though I knew this was fake, it was still fun. The only drawback was that I didn't own any serious winter clothing and had to borrow ski clothes from Summer. The parka wasn't too girly, but it still had a fringe of pink fluff around the hood. Meanwhile, we were also wearing tall rubber waders to protect ourselves from the penguins. (Penguins aren't too aggressive, but if you crowded them, they would sometimes peck your shins to make you back off.) FunJungle had only purchased waders in adult sizes—no one had ever considered that thirteen-year-olds might be wearing them—so they rode ridiculously high on our legs.

"You are a serious fashion disaster," Summer informed me as we lugged the fish cannon into the exhibit.

"You don't look much better," I told her, pulling out my phone. "Maybe I should post your photo. . . ."

"Don't you dare!" Summer warned. As J.J. McCracken's daughter, she was famous without wanting to be; any embarrassing photos of her would instantly go viral. She dropped her end of the fish cannon and snatched a large, recently thawed herring out of a cooler. "Put that phone down, or I will smack you senseless with this."

"Aw, c'mon," I said. "Your fans would love it."

Summer brandished the herring with fake menace. "Don't make me use this, Teddy. I once killed a man with a halibut. Put the phone down."

One of my favorite things about Summer—besides her being beautiful and smart and surprisingly down-to-earth for a really rich girl—was that she had a great sense of humor. We spent a lot of time teasing each other.

However, the penguins had no idea Summer was wielding the fish in jest. Now that it was out in the open, 416 heads swiveled toward her at once. Sensing food, the penguins began waddling toward us en masse, barking for her attention.

"You ought to stow that herring until we're ready to go," Cindy warned. "Otherwise, we'll be overrun." She stepped between a particularly aggressive macaroni penguin and Summer and told it, "Back off, Fifty-Six. It's not breakfast time yet."

Summer quickly returned the fish to the cooler, setting it atop the hundreds of others stored there, then replaced the lid. The little penguin shifted its attention from Summer to the cooler, which it pecked at hungrily. "Why's he called Fifty-Six?" Summer asked.

"*She,*" Cindy corrected, then pointed to a tiny yellow band around the narrowest point on the penguin's wing. There was a "56" stamped on it. "That's why, right there. She's the fifty-sixth penguin we got here."

"You didn't name them?" Summer asked, surprised.

"*You* try naming four hundred and sixteen birds and

then keeping them all straight," Cindy challenged. "As much as I love these guys, it's awfully hard to tell them apart. Even when you work with them every day."

"Still," I said, "you haven't named *any* of them?"

"We named some of the king penguins, just for fun," Cindy said. "King George, King Arthur, B. B. King, Stephen King, Carole King, Chicken à la King. But to be honest, I still don't really know which is which without looking at the armbands."

Summer helped me pick up the cannon again and we moved it close to the edge of the water. The device wasn't too heavy, but it was unwieldy, especially the plastic tube. Dozens of penguins were now crowding around us curiously, and we had to be careful not to knock any of them over.

The exhibit was similar to virtually every other penguin exhibit on earth: The "land" portion of it was in the back, while the watery portion was up against the viewing glass, so that guests could watch the penguins swim. Swimming penguins were quite fascinating; they moved with amazing speed and grace. Meanwhile, penguins on land tended to be less interesting. Usually, they merely stood around in clumps, occasionally waddling from place to place or firing projectiles of poop into the water.

The representative from Zoom, a gangly, excitable man named Sanjay Budhiraja, was observing us on the other side of the glass. Cindy had invited him to join us in the exhibit, but Sanjay had been a bit skittish about being surrounded by penguins. "I'm not crazy about birds," he'd explained. Now he gave us a thumbs-up, signaling that the cannon was in the right place. We couldn't hear him through the thick glass, but we could read his lips well enough to see him say, "Fire it up!"

So we did. The cannon was a relatively simple device. The bulk of it was a small blower that created a differential in pressure in the plastic tube, sucking the fish through it. If we cranked the blower to the highest level, it could actually move the fish at twenty miles an hour, but for the time being, Sanjay had suggested we set it much lower. I flipped the power on and the cannon came to life with a low hum.

It was quiet enough that only the closest penguins took notice. The rest of them remained standing in their little clumps and squawking at one another.

Cindy pried the lid off the cooler. There were two kinds of fish in it: herring and capelin. The capelin were skinnier and more aerodynamic-looking, but for the first run, Cindy selected the herring that Summer had threatened me with earlier. "Let's start with this. Penguins really like herring."

"More than the capelin?" I asked.

"Oh sure, they have preferences, just like us," Cindy replied. "Capelin's like broccoli to them. But herring is ice cream. Aim that tube toward the water."

Summer and I grabbed the tube and directed the end of it at the aquatic portion of the exhibit.

Now that Cindy had a herring in her hands, the penguins' attention returned to us again. They all began waddling our way once more.

A small metal crate held the blower and the loading end of the pneumatic tube. Cindy placed the herring at the end, and it was instantly sucked inside.

The fish moved through the tube quickly, a small bulge rippling down the length of it. It looked like a python swallowing a large meal, sped up a thousand times. The fish shot past our hands and fired out the other end, plunging into the water.

Even though many of the penguins had been bred in captivity, the motion of the fish seemed to stimulate their innate instincts. A dozen of the penguins closest to the water's edge dove right in after the fish. A battle quickly ensued beneath the surface for it. A few of the smaller penguins got a morsel, but a big emperor labeled "99" won out and gulped the herring down.

"Did you see that?" Cindy exclaimed. "That was hunting behavior! It worked!"

In the viewing area, Sanjay Budhiraja gave a whoop of joy loud enough for us to hear him through the glass.

"Let's do some more!" Summer said.

Cindy grabbed another herring and fed it into the cannon. This time, I aimed the tube at a spot away from Ninety-Nine, since he'd already eaten. The second fish fired into the water. The penguins that were already swimming darted that way, while a whole new clump of penguins on land plunged in after it.

Cindy scooped up some capelin and we shot these into the water as well. Now all the penguins in the exhibit sensed the presence of food and began migrating toward the water's edge. Cindy was thrilled, Sanjay was still whooping, and Summer and I were cheering as we watched the penguins race around for the fish. The penguins either didn't know the fish weren't alive, or they didn't care. Whichever the case, it was great fun to watch, and we were all enjoying how well it was all working.

At which point everything took a turn for the worse.

The crowd of penguins along the water's edge was starting to get very big. They were so interested in the fish they didn't seem to care about us at all. They were congregating all around us. It was a little unsettling, especially when the emperors, which could be over four feet tall, shoved up against us. A particularly large one—335—actually tried to nudge Summer out of its way. Summer stumbled backward and stepped right on a poor little gentoo that was scurrying between her legs. The gentoo squawked in pain and Summer dropped the pneumatic tube in surprise.

The tube now snapped from my hands as well, just as a large herring was moving through it. Without anyone holding it, the tube whipped around on the ground, writhing like an angry snake among the penguins.

This now startled the birds, who stampeded away from it. Penguins aren't very adept on land, though. A stampede of them wasn't threatening so much as slow and clumsy. Dozens tripped and fell on their faces. Their fellow penguins either ran right over them or tripped over their prone bodies. Many who were waiting by the water's edge were shoved off and belly flopped into the pool.

The whole thing might have been comical if we had been watching it, rather than caught in the middle of it. A surge of panicked penguins knocked Cindy off her feet. She fell backward onto the fish cooler, which toppled, spilling its entire contents into the loading area for the fish cannon. The tube promptly began sucking up the fish and firing them out the other end.

Which might not have been a problem if a passing macaroni penguin hadn't bumped the dial for the blower, cranking it to top speed.

Now the fish came blasting out of the tube at twenty miles an hour in rapid succession. The fish cannon had become more of a machine gun. And without anyone holding it, the tube kept writhing around wildly, firing piscine projectiles in random directions. Frozen herring ricocheted off the fake icebergs and plowed into snowdrifts. A half dozen capelin slammed into the viewing glass and exploded on impact, leaving splatters of fish guts. A few unfortunate penguins got caught in the crossfire and were clocked by flying fish. None were seriously hurt, but each strike resulted in a cacophony of pained squawks and a slight burst of feathers.

Now the penguins grew even more panicked. They fled in every direction, unsure what was safe, a surging, chaotic sea of black and white. With their little tuxedoed bodies, it looked like someone had yelled "Fire!" at the Oscars.

Summer and I were scrambling about, dodging penguins as we tried to grab the tube, but as more and more fish shot through it at greater and greater speeds, it was thrashing about more wildly than ever. With one spasmodic jolt, it clotheslined Chicken à la King and sent the poor bird cartwheeling into the water.

Meanwhile, Cindy Salerno was trying to turn off the cannon, but a horde of penguins was crowded around the controls, gulping down the fish that hadn't been slurped up by the hose. In the midst of the crowd, one of the smallest penguins—a juvenile Adélie—got too close to the intake. With a sudden gasp of air—and a startled squawk—it was sucked inside. Since the little guy was equally as streamlined as the fish, he rocketed through the tube and fired out the other end, becoming the first penguin in history to fly.

Unfortunately, I was right in its path. The Adélie bore down on me, beak first, screaming in penguin terror and flapping its wings madly, as if desperately willing them to work. I dove for cover into a snowdrift and the penguin sailed over my head, soared the length of the exhibit, and plopped safely into the water.

A flock of frightened penguins quickly stampeded over my back. A few stepped right on my head, smushing my face into the snow. I flailed my arms, scattering them, and staggered back to my feet, spitting out ice flakes. . . .

Which was when the herring hit me.

It was an exceptionally large herring, and it caught me right in the chest.

Summer had finally managed to grab the tube and steady it, but not before realizing it was pointing directly at me. The herring hit me at full speed, hard enough to knock the wind out of me and throw me off balance. I stumbled backward, tripped over a chinstrap penguin—and fell into the water.

Penguins prefer their water very cold. At some places in the Antarctic, due to some interesting physics about ice and salt water, the ocean can actually be *colder* than freezing temperatures. The water in the exhibit wasn't quite that frigid, but it was close enough. It felt like my whole body had been slapped. Every one of my muscles tensed at once. And if the cold wasn't bad enough, I was also in a maelstrom of agitated penguins and half-eaten fish.

Many of the fish had been too big to eat in one gulp, so the penguins had torn them to bits instead, leaving clouds of white flesh and fish guts in the water. Penguins were darting through it all, gulping down what they could, moving far faster in the water than on land. It was like being surrounded by a swarm of fighter pilots, who dipped and whirled and corkscrewed around me.

My hip-length boots immediately filled with water and dragged me down, while Summer's ski jacket became saturated and heavy as an anchor. I shrugged everything off as fast as I could. Luckily, the water wasn't deep, so I quickly broke back through the surface.

Cindy was there, waiting for me, having finally turned off the fish cannon and waded through the penguins to my rescue. She grabbed my arms, hauled me back onto land, and wrapped her own parka around me to keep me from freezing solid. "Let's get you warm," she said, and hustled me toward the door.

Now that the cannon was off and the penguins had devoured all the loose fish, the birds had calmed down. The panic was over and they were now milling about, preening themselves as if nothing had happened.

I wasn't doing as well. The chill of the water had already sunk into my bones. My legs were trembling so badly I needed both Summer and Cindy to steady me as we hurried through the exhibit.

"I'm so sorry," Summer told me. "I didn't mean to shoot you!"

"It's n-n-not your f-f-fault," I said through chattering teeth. "It w-w-was an accident."

The door out of the exhibit was concealed behind a fake glacier. We passed through it into the keeper's area. This wasn't much warmer, but after the arctic temperatures I had just been subjected to, it felt like I had suddenly gone to the tropics.

Sanjay Budhiraja was there, holding a large blanket he'd found somewhere. Given the smell, I figured it had last been used to dry off a polar bear, but I didn't care. It was warm. Sanjay draped it over my shoulders and asked nervously, "Are you all right?"

"Y-y-yes," I said, shivering. "Just c-c-cold."

Sanjay heaved a sigh of relief, then said, "I just want you to know, this was not an insurmountable problem. Zoom can make alterations to ensure this doesn't happen again. And we can penguin-proof the intakes. . . ."

I suddenly realized there was another person in the room. She was a young adult—barely past college age, if that—and short but extremely fit. Her hair was cropped short, almost in a crew cut, and her nose was pierced. She wore a T-shirt and cargo shorts. There was something strangely familiar about her face, though I couldn't tell what. She was sitting in Cindy's chair, quietly observing everything.

Cindy seemed surprised by her presence too; she didn't appear to know the woman. "Are you with Zoom too?" Cindy asked.

"Zoom?" the woman asked, confused. "I don't even know what that is."

"It's a company that makes fish cannons," Sanjay said, as if that would make sense to anyone.

The mystery woman gave him a confused look, then told us, "I'm Lily Deakin. Doc's daughter."

I suddenly understood why she looked so familiar; she looked like Doc, the head vet at FunJungle. Not *exactly* like him, which would have been weird. But she was definitely the younger and more feminine version of him.

I had heard of Lily before, but never met her. Or even seen a photo of her.

Summer had apparently heard of her too. "Lily Deakin?" she repeated. "The ecoterrorist?"

"I'm not a terrorist," Lily said flatly. "I'm a warrior for animal rights. I fight for those who can't fight for themselves."

"What are you doing in my office?" Cindy asked.

Lily shifted her gaze to me. "I'm looking for you, Teddy. Something terrible has happened, and I need your help."

THE ACTIVIST

"I thought you were in jail," Summer said to Lily.

"No one ever pressed charges," Lily told her. "But I've been lying low for a while, just to be on the safe side."

We had left the Polar Pavilion so that Cindy and Sanjay could get things cleaned up before the park opened. Cindy still thought the fish cannon had potential, but it obviously needed some tweaking before it could be used in the exhibit.

We were following Adventure Road, the main pedestrian route that looped around FunJungle, not heading anywhere in particular. Even though the park wouldn't open for another fifteen minutes, there were still dozens of staff members around, making sure everything was in pristine condition before the tourists arrived: Every railing was polished; every piece of trash was cleaned up; truckloads of food were delivered to the animals before the concourses got too crowded to drive the trucks through. On that day, there were even more workers than usual: FunJungle's one-year anniversary was in four days and there was going to be a huge party to celebrate. A lot of decorating was underway. Work crews were hanging bunting, planting fresh flowers, and scrubbing the public bathrooms until they gleamed.

"So where have you been?" I asked Lily.

"Antarctica," she replied. "I did a couple months with Sea Shepherd, fighting illegal whaling."

A year before, Lily had been a member of a radical animal-rights group called the Animal Liberation Front and had attacked a meat-packing plant in West Texas. She and the ALF had believed that the plant was treating the animals inhumanely, and tried to burn the place down. From what I understood, they had failed pretty badly, only destroying a trash heap and leaving ample evidence that they were behind the crime. Several of the ALF members had gone to jail, but Doc had cut some sort of deal with J.J. McCracken to get his daughter off. I was pretty sure Doc was embarrassed about the whole thing. Doc was a gruff, taciturn guy to begin with, but he was even more guarded when it came to Lily. I hadn't heard him mention her name in months.

Sea Shepherd was a less radical animal-rights group than the ALF, though you had to be extremely committed to rights to join it. They sent boats out to prevent ships ___lling whales or capturing dolphins in international waters; its crews could be out on the sea in frigid climates for months at a time. I had heard it was a rough life, but a boat in Antarctica sounded like an awfully good place to lie low.

"Is there a problem with Sea Shepherd?" I asked.

"No," Lily replied. "I'm not with them anymore. I've done enough time on boats to last me the rest of my life."

It was already hot outside. Summer and I had ditched our sopping ski jackets, hanging them on a railing in the employee area behind the Polar Pavilion. I was now only wearing my damp clothes, but they were drying rapidly in the blazing sun.

"So what do you need our help with?" Summer asked.

Lily gave her a wary look. "I was really only looking for Teddy. I understand he's solved a few crimes around here."

"With Summer's help," I said quickly. I had noticed Summer was slightly offended by the idea that I had acted alone. "I couldn't have done any of it without her."

"Okay, so you *both* have solved some crimes," Lily said. "You figured out who murdered the hippo and who kidnapped the koala and who stole the panda. . . ."

"And we busted a rhino-horn smuggling operation too," Summer added proudly.

"Well, I have a crime that needs solving," Lily said.

Summer looked to me, her blue eyes gleaming with excitement, already prepared to accept the case.

I wasn't quite as eager. "We're not really detectives," I told Lily. "We're just kids who've gotten wrapped up in things."

Summer obviously wasn't pleased with my lack of enthusiasm. She turned to Lily and said, "But we still solved the cases."

"Even so," I added cautiously. "If this is a serious crime, you ought to be going to the police. Not us."

"The police don't think it's a crime," Lily said.

That struck a chord with me. The very first time I had gotten involved with a case at FunJungle, it had been because the police hadn't taken the crime seriously. Henry the Hippo, FunJungle's former mascot, had been murdered, but when I called to report it, the policeman I talked to thought I was just a dumb kid crying wolf.

"What happened?" I asked.

"Do you know who Lincoln Stone is?" Lily said.

"Of course," I said. "He's like the second-most famous person who lives around here, after Summer's dad."

"And he's a jerk," Summer put in. "A huge one. He tried to keep FunJungle from being built."

Lincoln Stone was a huge media personality who had a radio show, a TV show, and multiple bestselling books. I hadn't watched or listened to him much, but his basic premise seemed to be that everything the US government did was wrong. He was always complaining about something the government was doing, and millions of people tuned in every day to hear about it. Despite his hatred for the government, Lincoln always claimed to be the most patriotic American there was. He often dressed up like George Washington or Abraham Lincoln to deliver speeches about how disgusted they would have been by what our country had become, and the set of his TV show was festooned with American flags, portraits of the Founding Fathers, and stuffed bald eagles.

Lincoln had started out small, delivering his rants on YouTube and a tiny talk-radio station in southern Mississippi. He was quite a showman, and he seemed to legitimately believe what he was saying, even when it didn't make any sense. (Dad had often remarked that "Lincoln Stone is often wrong but never in doubt.") Lincoln had built a devoted following, which had led to his getting a show on a national cable channel. *Lincoln Stone Tells the Truth* had quickly become a hit, and suddenly, Lincoln was influential and rich. Shortly afterward, he had bought a large ranch in the Texas Hill Country ("where *real* Americans live") and moved his TV recording studio to San Antonio.

"FunJungle might be the one thing Lincoln and I actually agree on," Lily said, looking around the park with obvious distaste. "This place is nothing but a huge prison for animals."

"It is *not* a prison!" Summer said sharply.

"Really?" Lily asked. "So all these animals aren't here against their will?"

"Your father doesn't seem to think it's so bad," Summer replied. "My daddy pays him plenty to work here."

It seemed like the conversation was taking a bad turn, so I intervened. "Lincoln Stone didn't fight FunJungle for environmental reasons. He *hates* environmentalists. He only tried to stop this park from being built because he lives close by and didn't want all the tourists around."

"That's true," Lily admitted, dropping the argument.

Summer was obviously still annoyed, though. She kept glaring at Lily as we walked. "Stone cost my father a ton in lawyers' fees. And he *still* keeps suing every time Daddy tries to build anything. Like *that*." She pointed toward the back fence of the park, where the newest section of FunJungle, the Wilds, was under construction.

Lincoln Stone's lawsuits might have inconvenienced J.J. McCracken, but they hadn't slowed construction down much. Unlike the rest of FunJungle, the Wilds had no wildlife exhibits; it was all theme park rides, designed to lure tourists more interested in thrills than animals. It was going up with startling speed, thanks to the fact that J.J. McCracken owned a construction company and had made this project a priority. The Raging Raft Ride, a course of fake rapids built into a manmade mountain, was already mostly completed and loomed in the distance beyond the fence. We could see hundreds of workers scrambling all over it, looking like ants on an anthill.

Lily glared hatefully at the enormous construction project, like she was looking at something odious. Then she turned her back on it, continuing toward Carnivore Canyon. "Anyhow, Lincoln Stone claims that last night, a mountain lion ate his dog."

Summer and I were both caught off guard by this statement. Summer spoke up first. "A cougar ate King?"

"You know his dog's name?" Lily asked, surprised.

Even *I* knew about King, though, and I had barely ever seen Lincoln's show. "King is Lincoln's golden retriever. He was crazy about that dog."

"Lincoln talks about King all the time," Summer replied, then slipped into an imitation of Lincoln Stone's deep Southern accent. "King's the best dog there ever was. King's smarter than that pinhead we call a president. King could run this country better than anyone in Congress. King could do open heart surgery if there weren't laws against letting dogs be doctors."

"Well, King's dead," Lily said flatly. "He was killed last night."

"By a mountain lion?" I repeated. "I didn't even know mountain lions lived around here."

"There used to be lots of them in this area," Lily said. "Back before humans started tearing down every last tree to build shopping malls and golf courses and theme parks. They were all over Texas. That's why the University of Houston's mascot is the cougar. Heck, their range used to cover almost the entire United States. But they've been eradicated almost everywhere. I thought they were all wiped out in this area long ago. But I guess there's at least one left. For now."

I frowned, feeling embarrassed for not knowing any of this. I had spent the first ten years of my life in the Congo in Africa, where I had tried to learn everything I could about the local wildlife. And now I'd been in Texas over a year without even hearing about the mountain lions. We were passing Carnivore Canyon at the moment, and it occurred to me that I probably knew far more about tigers—which lived on the opposite side of the earth—than I did about an animal that lived right outside my door.

On the big wide lawn in front of Carnivore Canyon, an outdoor stage was being erected. This was the largest open space at FunJungle, so it was going to be where most of the celebrations would take place for the anniversary party. FunJungle's publicity department had revealed some of the events, like performances by famous local musicians and rare chances to get close to exotic animals, but they also had hinted there would be lots of surprises as well.

"What's all this have to do with us?" Summer asked Lily.

"I'm getting to that," Lily answered. "Whenever there's an incident like this, the US Department of Fish and Wildlife gets called in to investigate. I have a good friend there, and he was the one who got the call last night."

"A close friend like how?" Summer inquired. "Like he's one of your fellow activists?"

"No," Lily clarified. "He's not an activist like me. But he's a person who cares a lot about animals. Which makes sense, given that he works at Fish and Wildlife. Anyhow, he went out to Lincoln Stone's house, and while there was plenty of evidence that a mountain lion ate this dog, he saw a few things that were suspicious, too."

"Like what?" I asked.

"It'd probably be better if you saw them for yourself." Lily stopped near the Asian plains portion of SafariLand and stared out at a herd of muntjac deer. "I'd like you to come out to the scene of the crime, meet my friend, and hear what he has to say. Because if he's right, then something really strange is going on."

We stepped to the side of the road as a flatbed truck rumbled past. Not long before, it had been stacked high with bales of hay, but now all of that had been delivered to Safari-Land and the truck was heading back to the garage. A few stray pieces of hay fluttered in the air in the truck's wake.

"How strange?" I asked. "Are you saying your friend doesn't think the mountain lion killed this dog?"

"That's exactly what I'm saying," Lily answered. "My friend thinks someone else killed it and pinned it on the lion."

"Someone framed a mountain lion for a murder?" Summer asked, astonished.

"Yes," Lily said.

I gaped at her, dumbfounded as well. "That's crazy."

"That's exactly what my friend's boss said," Lily told me. "She doesn't believe it. Or maybe she's turning a blind eye for some reason. Which is basically condemning the mountain lion to death."

"How?" I asked. We all started walking again, moving along the edge of SafariLand.

"Normally, you can't hunt mountain lions," Lily explained. "They're protected under the Endangered Species Act. But if one gets too close to civilization and starts causing trouble, then it can be deemed a nuisance and the ban on hunting can be waived. Lincoln Stone is very upset about his dog, and he's already made it clear that he's going to petition for the lion to be put down. He wants revenge."

"So the lion could be killed even if it's innocent?" Summer asked, horrified.

"Not if we can prove it was framed," Lily said. "That's

what I was hoping you could help with. If we find out who *really* killed the dog, then we can save the lion."

I looked at my feet, unsure what to do. I was certain my parents wouldn't want me getting involved in another mystery: Each of my previous four had ended up putting me in danger. At the same time, I knew they'd be mortified to hear that an innocent lion might be killed—and that the proper authorities weren't even going to investigate. My gut instinct was to help, but I was concerned about my own safety as well. I didn't want to end up in danger again. Investigating the murder of a dog didn't *sound* hazardous, but maybe I was wrong about that.

Meanwhile, Summer didn't appear to have any concerns at all. She proudly put an arm around me and beamed at Lily. "You've come to the right place," she said. "No innocent lions are getting killed while we're around. We'll take the case."

THE SCENE OF THE CRIME

In the end, I weaseled out of making a decision right away. I agreed to go see the crime scene without actually agreeing to help investigate. I figured my parents couldn't get upset with me for that—it wouldn't be dangerous to visit the scene—and Summer probably would have been annoyed at me if I'd refused that much. Plus, there was a chance Lily's friend was totally wrong. He might have turned out to be a crazy conspiracy theorist who was inventing evidence to protect the lion, in which case I could simply refuse to help. I didn't want to be part of condemning a mountain lion to death, but if there really was one close by with a taste for pet dogs, then maybe putting it down would truly be the right thing to do.

However, Lily's friend wasn't a crazy conspiracy theorist

at all. Instead, he was an intelligent, likable guy.

His name was Tommy Lopez, and he met us at the end of Lincoln Stone's driveway. His Fish and Wildlife pickup truck was parked by the side of the road. There was a gun rack in the rear window with two rifles in it.

Tommy was built a lot like Lily: short but very fit. He wore his official Department of Fish and Wildlife uniform, a short-sleeved khaki shirt and dark brown pants with a DFW baseball cap pulled down low over his eyes. He also had a backpack with two reusable water bottles in the side pockets. There were big sweat stains under his armpits and around the collar of his shirt, indicating he'd been out in the heat a long time already.

Lily had driven us there in her car, an ancient hatchback that she had converted to run on vegetable oil. The engine worked fine, but the rest of the car seemed to be three minutes from falling to pieces. One rear window was missing and covered with plastic wrap, the front bumper was held on with duct tape, and I could see the road passing beneath us through rust holes in the floor.

Since I was thirteen, my parents didn't make a big deal about me needing to tell them everywhere I was going. They didn't want me heading off to San Antonio or Austin without permission, of course, but they were fine with me hanging out at FunJungle or exploring the woods around our trailer or going to Summer's house for the day. Lincoln Stone's ranch wasn't very far from the park, so it didn't seem like an issue to head out there.

In fact, Lincoln Stone lived even closer to FunJungle than I had realized. It was three miles by road, but much closer as the crow flew. It hadn't taken very long to drive there, which was a good thing, because I doubted Lily Deakin's car could cover much more distance before breaking down.

There was nothing about the driveway that indicated anyone famous lived at the ranch, which was probably the point; an unassuming entrance guaranteed more privacy. There was an electronic gate, but thousands of other ranches in the area had those too.

Tommy directed us to park on the gravel shoulder of the road. As we climbed out of the car, he introduced himself to Summer and me.

"It's nice to meet you," Summer said.

Tommy turned his attention to Lily and gave her a shy smile that said maybe there was more to their relationship than Lily had indicated—or that maybe Tommy *hoped* there'd be more. "Thanks for coming out here," he said.

"It's no big deal," Lily told him. "We're happy to help."

Tommy looked around skittishly, then said, "Lincoln's not here right now, which is good, because he's made it clear he doesn't want Fish and Wildlife pursuing this investigation any further. He just wants us to issue the permit to kill the cat. His housekeeper agreed to let me in, though. I told her I had to take a few more photos of the crime scene. But we need to be cool and not cause any trouble, okay?" He gave Lily a stern look, as though maybe he didn't quite trust her.

"We'll be cool," Lily assured him. Summer and I chimed in agreement.

A call box with a camera was mounted on a post to the left of the front gate. Tommy went over to it and pushed the button.

Someone answered in Spanish. The housekeeper, I figured.

Tommy replied in Spanish himself. I had been studying the language in school, but hadn't learned enough to follow the conversation yet. From Tommy's tone, I got the sense he had struck up a friendly rapport with the housekeeper. After a little back-and-forth, there was a buzz and the gate slowly swung open.

"We're good," Tommy told us, then pointed to his pickup.

We all climbed in. It was a tight squeeze, but since none of us were that big and we weren't going far, it wasn't too bad. Now that I was closer to the gun rack, I observed that one of the rifles fired bullets while the other fired sedation darts.

Tommy started the truck and we headed up the driveway. It snaked through a forest of live oak and cedar, climbing a small rise, and then Lincoln Stone's house came into view.

It was the ugliest building I'd ever seen.

It was a large, sprawling mansion, but it had been designed to look like a log cabin. The biggest log cabin on earth. Enormous tree trunks had been cut in half and cemented to the sides. A long wooden porch ran all the way along the front. Although the house had probably been built within the last three years, the wood had all been purposefully weather-beaten to make it look older. However, any sense of age the house was designed to convey was completely ruined by the array of high-end vehicles parked in front of it. There was a Bentley, a Maserati, a Ferrari, and a Ford pickup, all freshly washed and gleaming.

Tommy parked beside them and we climbed back out of the truck. Lily was gaping at the fake log cabin. "That is absolutely hideous," she said.

Tommy signaled her to keep her voice down. "Don't let the staff hear you say that! And from what I understand, Lincoln is trying to convey some sort of kinship with the original settlers of this country with this house."

"He's conveying that he's an idiot," Lily said under her breath.

An older woman in a maid's uniform emerged onto the porch, observing us warily, like she still wasn't sure if allowing us on the property was a good idea.

Tommy waved to her and flashed a smile. *"¡Hola, Elena! ¡Muchas gracias!"*

The woman pointed at her watch and said something in Spanish.

"¡Sí! ¡Sí!" Tommy said, then went on in Spanish. Whatever he said seemed to reassure Elena, who went back inside.

"Those trees Lincoln has stuck to his house aren't serving any structural purpose," Lily grumbled. "He's cut down old-growth forest and burned who-knows-how-much fossil fuel to have it trucked down here just so he can pretend to be Davy Crockett."

"I have to get a picture of this," Summer said, snapping a few shots with her phone. "It's unbelievably tasteless."

"Let me show you the crime scene," Tommy said quickly, like he was trying to change the subject. "Lincoln will be back in an hour and we want to be long gone before he gets home. It's right over here." He led us past the edge of the driveway and around the house.

On the back side, the architect had given up the notion of making the house look like a log cabin. Instead, it was completely modern, with huge windows and cantilevered patios, though it was still strikingly overdone. From here, there was a view of the surrounding Hill Country—although Lincoln Stone had leveled a large portion of forest to get it. It was immediately evident why Lincoln had tried to keep Fun-Jungle from being built: You could see the whole park from his house, and despite FunJungle's environmental mission, it didn't really blend in with its surroundings. The parking lots, in particular, were great black scars on the land.

I could also see the brown, dusty patch where the Wilds was being built and close to that, the trailer park where I lived with my parents.

Down the hill below Lincoln Stone's house were a swimming pool, an enormous hot tub, a wide lawn, and a lighted tennis court that looked like it hadn't ever been used. There was a layer of dust on it and the net sagged listlessly.

To the side of the tennis court was a private firing range. *This* looked like it had been used. A lot. A silhouette of a human being was tacked against some hay bales in the distance. Dozens of bullet holes perforated the chest. I knew that lots of people fired guns on their private property in the area—I had plenty of friends from school who did it—but the sight of the bullet-riddled silhouette made me uneasy.

The lawn butted up against a stand of trees. Tommy led us through them to a small clearing not too far from a barbed-wire fence that marked the edge of the property. Lincoln's house was still visible through the trees, but our view of it was obscured.

A small cloud of mosquitoes buzzed around the trees. Enough so that we could hear them. Thankfully, I had slathered on the bug repellant that morning. When you lived in the woods like I did, mosquitoes were a constant menace.

On the floor of the clearing, someone had tried to make a picture of something with masking tape. It hadn't worked very well, as the tape hadn't stuck to the dirt. It took me a few seconds of staring at it to realize what the point of it all was. "Is that an outline of the dead dog?" I asked.

"Yes," Tommy said sheepishly. "Mr. Stone has seen a lot of crime shows on TV, and he insisted that there ought to be an outline to show where the crime was committed. I tried to explain to him that we don't really do that sort of thing for animals, and he got very upset. So I did my best. Even though I didn't really have the right kind of tape. And there wasn't much of the body left to outline."

Summer snapped a picture of this with her phone too. "Is that why the outline's so small? Because that's all there was after the . . . uh . . ."

"Eating?" Tommy finished. "No. Mr. Stone wanted the outline to represent what King actually looked like."

"But King's a golden retriever," Summer said. "This outline looks like it's for a hamster."

"Oh," Tommy said. "You're thinking of the King from TV. Not the *real* King."

"There's two different dogs?" I asked, confused.

"The King from TV doesn't really exist," Tommy explained. "Lincoln made him up. The *real* King was a bichon frise."

Lily snorted with laughter. "A bichon frise? Mr. All-American Tough Guy had a lap dog?"

"A *French* lap dog," Summer added.

"Apparently he's allergic to most dogs," Tommy said. "But he knew having a bichon didn't really fit with his image. So he pretended to have a retriever for the cameras."

"That's why you never saw King on TV with him!" Summer exclaimed, putting things together. "Lincoln talked about him all the time, and showed photos, but the dog never came on the show."

I said, "So all those stories he tells about hunting and hiking and camping with King aren't true?"

"Almost *nothing* about Lincoln Stone is true," Lily informed me. "The guy's entire image was designed to attract a certain type of viewer. He's supposed to be a red-blooded, all-American alpha male. The kind of guy who likes to drink beer, race cars, and kill wild animals. But that's not what Lincoln used to be like. In fact, his name isn't even Lincoln Stone. It's Farley Turkmeister. And he was born in Beverly Hills."

I was awfully surprised by this, and from the look on Summer's face, it seemed that she was too.

"Anyhow," Tommy said, "there wasn't really much left of the dog to outline. Only the tuft of its tail—and the collar. It was right here." He pointed to a spot just south of the outline.

Both the tuft and the collar had been taken away, though. The crime scene itself looked like every other part of the clearing: a mat of dirt and cedar needles.

Summer snapped a few photos of it anyway. "Who found the body? Or, I guess, what was left of the body."

"Lincoln did," Tommy answered. "That's what he told my boss, at least. I wasn't there for the questioning. It was around eleven o'clock last night. Lincoln says he'd let King out to go to the bathroom, but the dog didn't come back when he called, so he came looking for him. He said he was searching for a long time, but he eventually found the remains here. And then he got sick over there." Tommy pointed to the edge of the clearing, where there was still a faint spatter of vomit.

"So, he didn't actually see a mountain lion?" Lily asked. "Or even hear one?"

"No," Tommy said. "But that's not really unusual. For a big animal, cougars can be extremely stealthy. There are plenty of cases of them getting into people's yards and eating a pet without anyone hearing or seeing anything. Sometimes the people are even out in the yard themselves, barbecuing or something, just a couple feet away. But there's plenty of other things that are suspicious about this case."

"Like what?" I asked.

"For starters, there *is* a mountain lion who lives in this area, but she wasn't anywhere near here last night."

"How do you know that?" Summer asked.

"Because she's collared," Lily answered.

"Right," Tommy agreed. "Her official number is T-38, but everyone at Fish and Wildlife calls her Rocket."

"Why?" Summer wanted to know.

"I'm not sure," Tommy admitted. "I think because the T-38 is a plane they use for training at NASA down in Houston, and NASA shoots off rockets, but that's just a guess. She's a five-year-old female, and this is part of her territory. We even know she's been on this property recently—"

"How recently?" I interrupted.

"Three days ago," Tommy said. "And she's been prowling around here on and off for the last two years. But last night, she wasn't anywhere near here. She was over by FunJungle."

"FunJungle?" I repeated, concerned. "Where?"

"Not anywhere close to the tourists," Tommy said reassuringly. "Over on the back side, near where they're building the theme park rides."

"I *live* right next to where they're building the theme park rides!" I exclaimed.

"Oh," Tommy said. "Then I guess she was near your house."

I must have looked worried, because he quickly added, "She's not really dangerous to humans, though. Probably. I mean, there's little kids at the house next door to here and she's never caused them any trouble. If Rocket's sniffing around FunJungle, it's because she's attracted to all the animals over there, not the humans. I mean, with all those exotic antelope in SafariLand, it must smell like a buffet dinner to her."

My heartbeat had sped up; I had to lean against a tree to steady myself. It surprised me that I was reacting like this to a mountain lion. After all, back in the Congo, I had grown up around plenty of dangerous animals. But it had been a few years since then. Maybe I was older and wiser, or maybe I had gotten a little soft in America; either way, the idea that there was a large predator on the loose in my neighborhood was unnerving.

"The point is," Lily said, "Rocket couldn't have killed King last night. And there's proof."

"So why didn't you tell Lincoln Stone that?" Summer asked.

"I *did*," Tommy said. "And I told my boss, too. They both said King must have been eaten by another mountain lion."

"And you don't think he could have been?" Summer said.

I knew the answer to this even before Tommy said it. I might not have known a whole lot about mountain lions, but I knew big cats pretty well. Still, I let him say it, rather than stealing his thunder.

"It's unlikely," Tommy said. "Because this is Rocket's territory. She's certainly marked it. Any other cougar would know they should find another place to hunt."

"Could Rocket have had kittens?" Summer suggested. "Maybe a little cougar did this."

Tommy shook his head. "She hasn't given birth recently. If she had, we would have known. She would have made a den and be spending time there, or at least staying close. But her radio transmitter hasn't shown movement indicating that has happened."

"What if it was a male lion looking for a mate?" I said.

"That's what my boss suggested." Tommy snapped a long dead twig off a cedar tree. "So that's what Lincoln thinks too. It's possible. But there are other things that don't add up. This doesn't look like a kill site at all." He pointed at the ground with his twig. "For starters, I don't see any tracks."

"The ground's pretty hard here," I observed. "Not great for tracks."

"I'd still expect to find *something*," Tommy countered. "But there's not. No signs of a fight, either."

"What kind of fight would a bichon frise put up against a mountain lion?" Summer asked. "It'd be like a piece of plankton trying to fight off a whale."

"Not exactly," Lily argued.

"Still, those dogs are tiny," Summer said. "It'd barely be an hors d'oeuvre for a big cat."

"Which is another problem," Tommy said. "If a cougar made a big kill, it might not be able to finish eating it and leave something behind, but a bichon frise? The whole thing should be gone. So why leave the tuft of the tail?"

"It's mostly hair, right?" Summer asked. "Carnivores don't eat the hair of their prey so much as the meat."

"True," Tommy admitted. "But still, I wouldn't expect the tuft to be left *here*. A mountain lion doesn't want to hang out near humans any more than it has to. If it killed a small dog like that, chances are, it'd take off with it and eat it somewhere safer. Not right by the house."

"Wouldn't King have made some noise?" Lily asked. "If he was being attacked by a cougar, he probably would have been barking up a storm. Or crying in pain. You'd think Lincoln would have heard it."

Tommy considered that for a few seconds. "Maybe not. Rocket could probably take down a bichon awfully fast. King might never have seen her coming. So I don't think the lack of noise counts as evidence."

"What if it was some other predator?" I asked. "There's coyotes around here, right? Could one of those have eaten King instead?"

"That was actually my first thought." Tommy flicked away a mosquito that was feeding off his forearm. "But this doesn't look like a coyote kill either. A coyote would have made a mess of a bichon. There'd be pieces of it everywhere. Or at least a lot of blood. Honestly, I don't think *any* animal did this. I haven't even told you about the collar yet. My boss took it as evidence, along with the tail, but I have a photo of it." He took out his phone and brought it up.

Summer and I leaned in to see it.

The photo showed the collar lying on the ground we now stood on. The collar was hot pink with King's name spelled out in rhinestones. The buckle was still fastened; the collar had been torn in the back. There was a smear of blood on it, dulling some of the rhinestones.

"That's a butt-ugly collar," Summer observed.

"The cat bit through it?" I asked.

"That's what it's *supposed* to look like, I think," Tommy said. "But to me, it just looks all wrong. I'm not saying the cougar wouldn't have bitten through it, but again, there's no sign of a struggle here. The ground's a little scraped up, but still . . . I'd expect the cat to attack the dog fast, snap its neck maybe, and then take off with it. Not eat it here and leave the tail and the collar behind." He paused, like he was gathering the nerve to say something. "This doesn't look like a mountain lion attack to me so much as someone trying to make it *look* like a mountain lion attack."

I surveyed the small clearing, thinking about that. My theory that Tommy Lopez might turn out to be a conspiracy nut hadn't come true. His analysis of the crime scene all made sense. It didn't completely explain away the possibility that a mountain lion had killed King, but it indicated that possibility was slim, at best. I was pretty convinced Tommy was right.

"And you think this was done to get the cougar declared a nuisance?" I asked. "So someone could get permission to kill it?"

"There's lots of people around here who aren't crazy about Rocket," Tommy said sadly. "Ranchers who are worried she'll kill their livestock. Hunters who just want the chance to take a cougar down. Families worried about their kids. Even the staunchest environmentalists can freak out when they find out there's a predator living near *them.*"

It occurred to me that I'd had a very similar reaction when I learned about Rocket living close to me.

"And your boss isn't backing you up on any of this?" Summer asked. "Doesn't she believe you?"

Tommy chose his words carefully before answering. "My

boss seems to be more concerned about politics than the lion."

"How so?" I asked. As I spoke, something in the clearing caught my eye. To the side, not far from the mangled outline of the dead dog, was a tiny chunk of something white, which stood out against the brown dirt. I knelt to examine it.

"My boss would like to move to another, more powerful job someday," Tommy explained. "And Lincoln Stone has a lot of political clout. If he doesn't like you, he can ruin your career."

"So your boss is willing to let an innocent cougar die if it means advancing her career?" Lily asked angrily.

"I don't know," Tommy replied.

"What are you looking at?" Summer asked me.

"I'm not sure," I said.

The white object was less than an inch long and oddly shaped. There was a perfect ninety-degree bend in it and the edges were totally straight, indicating it hadn't formed naturally. I poked at it with a stick. Whatever it was made out of was solid but chalky.

"Looks like it came off the bottom of someone's boot," Tommy observed.

"Like how?" Lily asked.

Tommy lifted his foot, showing us the sole of his own boot. The tread was thick and heavily ridged. There were ninety-degree angles in many of the ridges. "Someone steps in something wet, like mud—then it dries out and gets left behind in little bits and pieces."

Summer said, "So maybe whoever killed King left this here!"

"It's possible," Tommy agreed cautiously. "But there's been a lot of other people around here since last night. Any one of them could've left that behind."

"It still might be a clue, though," Summer said.

Tommy nodded, then set down his backpack and took out a plastic evidence bag and tweezers.

"That doesn't look like mud to me," Lily remarked. "It's *white*."

"There can be white mud." Tommy knelt by the small object and picked it up with the tweezers. "Places where there's lots of limestone in the soil. And there's plenty of limestone around here."

I watched him closely as he carefully bagged the object. He was right about the white mud, and yet, I didn't think that's what the object was made of. The chalkiness of it reminded me of something else, but I couldn't recall what.

Suddenly, someone shouted my name.

This caught all of us by surprise. We should have been far away from any other humans, let alone anyone who knew me. The voice was a young boy's, somewhat high-pitched.

We all looked around, trying to place where it had come from.

"Teddy!" the kid called again. "Over here!"

I spotted him through the trees, downhill a bit, on the other side of the barbed-wire fence. He was about ten years old and he was waving frantically for my attention. Next to him stood a younger brother, maybe seven, who looked much more shy. They were dressed for an afternoon in the woods, with hiking boots and cargo shorts and wide-brimmed hats. For some reason, both were carrying croquet mallets.

"Do you know those kids?" Summer asked.

"Yeah," I said. "I do. Their mom's a keeper at the park. Works with wolves, I think."

I had met the whole family at a barbecue one of the other keepers had thrown at our trailer park a few weeks before. There hadn't been many other kids there, so the boys had tagged after me most of the time. One of them had impaled my soccer ball on a prickly pear cactus and ruined it. Their names were Grayson and Jason Mason. Or possibly Jason and Mason Grayson. I couldn't quite remember.

The older one was waving much more frantically now. "Hi, Teddy!" he called. "It's me! Grayson! Grayson Mason!"

Lily snickered at the name.

I waved back at him.

"Looks like you have a fan club," Summer teased.

"You're just jealous because someone recognized me for once and not you," I teased back. Summer *hated* being recognized in public. She didn't like to go out much because of it, and when we did, she always wore sunglasses and a baseball cap pulled down over her eyes.

Now that I'd seen him, Grayson was waving even more frantically. His arm was moving so wildly I feared he might bop his brother in the head.

"You should go say hi," Summer said.

"But the crime . . . ," I said.

"The dog's not gonna get *more* dead," Summer told me, then gave me a shove in the kids' direction.

I headed down through the trees to the barbed-wire fence.

The Mason kids looked a lot alike, even though there were several years between them. Red hair. Lots of freckles. Perpetually sunburned skin. According to their mother they had moved there from somewhere in the northern US— Minneapolis, maybe—and were having trouble adjusting to the heat. Grayson beamed excitedly as I approached.

"Do you guys live right here?" I asked, pointing over the fence.

"Yeah," Grayson said enthusiastically. "But it's not really our house. We're just renting it."

"We're renting the *guest* house," Jason corrected quietly.

I wasn't too surprised to hear this, even though my parents, as FunJungle employees, got their housing for free. The FunJungle employee trailer park wasn't big enough to house every single employee; the free housing had been an incentive to get a famous primatologist like my mother to sign on. And frankly, the trailers weren't that nice. They were freezing in the winter and sweltering in the summer. I would have been happy to live somewhere else.

"Right," Grayson agreed. "The guest house. But it's plenty big for our whole family. The real house is *huge*. Are you here because of King? Are you investigating?"

I was taken aback by these questions—and the suddenness with which they'd been asked—until I remembered the Mason boys had been well aware of my reputation for solving crimes when they met me. Their mother had introduced me as "the kid who figured out who killed Henry."

I thought about denying that I was there because of King, but I didn't see much point to it. "That's right. Did you guys see or hear anything strange last night?"

"You mean, like a mountain lion?" Grayson asked.

"Yes."

"No," Grayson answered. "But Mom says mountain lions can be really quiet. She also says there's been a couple prowling around here lately."

"A couple?" I repeated. "She's seen them?"

"She's found tracks." Grayson held up his croquet mallet. "That's what this is for. Mom told us to stay together and not go far from the house, but if we *do* see a lion, we should make a lot of noise to scare it off, and if it comes too close, we can fight it off." He swung the mallet like a club, trying to look tough. Unfortunately, the mallet was in bad shape. The head popped off, flew over the fence, and nearly nailed me in the face. I ducked and it sailed over my head and clonked off an oak tree behind me.

"Oops," Grayson said.

"Don't worry about it." I picked the mallet head off the ground. It was old and weather-beaten, with black dye from the croquet ball smeared on the end.

Jason suddenly burst into tears. Like everything else, he did it quietly. There was barely a sound, but he was obviously very upset.

"What's wrong?" I asked him. "Are you scared of the lion?"

He shook his head and sniffled.

"He's upset about King," Grayson told me, then looked to his brother. "Isn't that right?"

Jason looked at him with red-rimmed eyes and nodded.

I handed the head of the croquet mallet over the fence to Grayson.

He shoved it back onto the handle. "King was a nice

dog. We liked him a lot. Even if Mr. Stone didn't."

"What do you mean by that?" I asked.

"He didn't treat King very nicely," Grayson said. "He was always yelling at him. Calling him stupid and stuff. We could hear him all the way at our place." He gave the croquet mallet a practice swing. The head flew off again and landed in a copse of trees on the Masons' property. Grayson sighed sadly.

"Mr. Stone yells *a lot*," Jason said softly.

"Hey!" a voice boomed from behind me. It was deep and distinctive; I recognized it immediately. Lincoln Stone was home earlier than expected. "What'd I tell you kids about coming onto my property?"

"See what I mean?" Jason asked me.

I turned around to see Lincoln Stone storming across his lawn toward us, his face mottled with anger. He was dressed in his standard good-old-boy outfit: jeans, boots, a blue button-down shirt, and a cowboy hat. His voice had a Southern twang to it. If he was really from Beverly Hills, he had gone to great lengths to hide it. He was also carrying a shotgun. It wasn't aimed at us, but it was still scary. "This here's my land, not yours!" he shouted. "Now, get back on the other side of that fence!"

Grayson and Jason took a few steps back, cowering in fear.

"They *are* on the other side of the fence," I told Lincoln. "And they have been the whole time."

"I'm not talking to them!" Lincoln snapped. "I'm talking to *you*! Get your butt back over there with your friends!"

"I'm not here with them . . . ," I began.

"Then you're trespassing?" Lincoln asked before I had a chance to finish. "You know what the law here says I can do to trespassers? It says I can shoot your sorry butt."

"Whoa!" Tommy rushed out of the trees and into Lincoln's path, waving his arms desperately. "He's not trespassing! He's with me!"

Lincoln stopped and glared at Tommy. He looked even more annoyed to see the Fish and Wildlife agent than he was to see me. "What on earth are you doing here with a kid? This isn't a day care. It's my home!"

"Teddy isn't just any kid," Tommy said. "He's really smart. I brought him in to help with the investigation."

Lincoln shifted his attention to the crime scene. He had been so focused on me and the Mason boys he hadn't noticed everyone gathered in the trees. Now that he saw Summer and Lily, he grew even more annoyed. "Crap on a cracker, Lopez, you brought a couple of girls here too?" The way he said "girls" made it clear he meant it as an insult.

Lily bristled at this. "I'm not a girl. I'm a woman."

"Same here," Summer said angrily.

Lincoln didn't even bother responding to them. He kept on speaking to Tommy, like Lily and Summer weren't even worth his time. "This isn't a tourist attraction, it's a crime scene!"

"And we are treating it as such," Tommy said deferentially. "These folks are helping me gather more evidence. . . ."

"Evidence?" Lincoln exclaimed scathingly. "What more evidence do you need, you dimwit? A mountain lion ate my dog, pure and simple. It's a blatant case of feline caninicide."

"Caninicide?" Summer repeated.

"Yeah," Lincoln said. "It's like homicide, but for a dog. And that cougar's guilty of it. So instead of poking around here, you should be out trying to find that dang cat before it eats someone else's pet. Or a child!"

Tommy reddened around the ears, though I couldn't tell if this was due to embarrassment or anger. He did an impressive job of restraining himself, though. "Mr. Stone," he said calmly, "it's imperative that we don't make a mistake here. . . ."

"I'll tell you what'd be a mistake," Lincoln said, getting right in Tommy's face. "Saying one more word to me. Unless it's 'Yes, sir.' Because I can call up your boss right now and have you busted down so low you'll have to look up to look down. *¿Comprendes, amigo?*"

Although Lincoln hadn't said anything overtly racist to Tommy, there was something mocking in the way he said the last two words that certainly *seemed* to be disdainful of the fact that Tommy was Latino.

Tommy stayed right where he was, glaring hatefully at Lincoln. He looked like he wanted to punch Lincoln Stone in the nose. And Lincoln looked like he wanted Tommy to try; he was spoiling for a fight, and my guess was, he probably wouldn't fight fair.

Lily placed a hand on Tommy's arm. "Let's go," she said.

Tommy kept his eyes locked on Lincoln's, but it was evident that Lily had gotten through to him. His glare softened and he seemed to come back to his senses. "All right."

"That's right," Lincoln taunted. "Listen to your girl there. Sounds like she actually has some sense to her."

Tommy didn't take the bait this time. He broke his stare-off with Lincoln and turned toward where we'd parked. "Come on, kids. We're going."

Lily, Summer, and I fell in behind him as he led the way around the house and back toward the car.

Lincoln wasn't the kind of guy who'd just let us walk away without getting in a last taunt, though. "Lopez, next time I see your sorry butt, you'd better be holding a warrant to hunt that lion." He cocked his shotgun to punctuate his point.

None of us looked back. It seemed best not to reward his behavior with any more attention. The same way we were told to handle bullies at school.

I did look toward the Mason boys, though, intending to wave good-bye. But both of them had run off during our showdown with Lincoln. I couldn't blame them.

"I can't believe it," Summer said under her breath. "I thought his whole dirtbag image was an act for television. But he's an even bigger jerk in real life."

"I've met a lot of bad people," Lily added. "And that guy is definitely in the running for the worst. I'll bet he killed his own dog just so he could have an excuse to shoot Rocket."

I wondered if that was possible. "Even if he didn't, he obviously doesn't want us investigating this anymore. We probably aren't going to be able to come back here."

"We won't," Tommy agreed. "But we can manage. I've taken tons of photos of the crime scene."

"I took a bunch too," Summer said, then cast a sideways glance at the giant log cabin. "Looks like Lincoln has lots of security cameras around this property. Has anyone looked at the footage? Maybe the killer is on there."

I looked at the house. Sure enough, there were several security cameras mounted prominently under the eaves of the roof, aimed all around the house. They were much bigger than they had to be, which I figured meant that Lincoln *wanted* people to see them. Most of the time, the mere existence of cameras was enough to deter thieves. Though they wouldn't deter a mountain lion.

"I didn't even notice those," Tommy said, sounding annoyed at himself. "That's a good idea."

"Lincoln Stone should have known about them," Summer said. "He didn't suggest looking at the footage?"

"If he did, I didn't hear about it," Tommy replied.

"That's because he's the killer," Lily said, then looked to Tommy. "I told you these kids would be helpful."

Tommy gave her a shy, appreciative smile. "Yeah, you did."

As we neared Tommy's pickup, I glanced back across the property. Lincoln Stone had walked out of the trees to a place where he could keep an eye on us. He was watching us like a hawk, making sure we were getting right into the truck and leaving. He had the shotgun tucked under his arm and a disdainful look on his face.

I shuddered. I didn't know if Lincoln could have killed his own dog or not, but I *was* sure of one thing: He wasn't the kind of person you wanted to get angry at you. If we did, he could cause all kinds of trouble for us.

And yet, even though he didn't want us investigating the crime, I realized I was going to help do it. I believed Tommy Lopez was right that someone had framed Rocket. My parents wouldn't be happy about my getting involved, but I knew they wouldn't want an innocent lion to be killed either. I would simply have to be careful and hope things didn't work out as dangerously as they had for me in the past.

Unfortunately, that wouldn't turn out to be the case.

And bizarrely, this was only the *first* investigation I would get asked to be a part of that day.

THE ASSIGNMENT

"We're having a problem with the giraffes," J.J.
McCracken said.

We were eating dinner at his house, along with Summer and her mother, Kandace. As we had been driving down Lincoln Stone's driveway in Lily Deakin's car, Summer had received a text from her father inviting me to dinner that night. I had immediately called my parents and asked them if I could go. I always enjoyed dinners at the McCrackens'. They gave me more time with Summer—and they were usually much better than dinners I had at home. My parents weren't bad cooks, but they rarely had the time or energy to put much effort into it. Meanwhile, the McCrackens had a gourmet chef on staff.

We were eating grass-fed filet mignon fresh from the

McCrackens' ranch along with béarnaise sauce, farro, and a ragout of roasted spring vegetables. I hadn't even known what farro or a ragout was until a few minutes before, but they were both delicious.

"Oh, for crying out loud, J.J.," Kandace said with a sigh. "Please tell me you didn't invite Teddy here to talk about work."

I didn't know Summer's mother as well as her father, because I saw J.J. a lot more. He had an office at FunJungle, and he was there all the time. Kandace was at least twenty years younger than J.J., and almost everyone on earth believed she had simply married him for his money. J.J. wasn't a very attractive man, but he was rich, while Kandace had been a relatively famous professional model at the time. She was also six inches taller than him. From my experience, though, they seemed to really love each other, despite being very different people with very different interests. For a rich person, J.J. didn't seem to care much for luxuries, while Kandace made no secret of how much she enjoyed them. They often took separate vacations, with J.J. going camping or fly-fishing, and Kandace going to fancy hotels and fashion shows.

However, the biggest difference between them might have been how they felt about FunJungle. It was J.J.'s passion project, and while he had originally started the park to make money, he had become more and more invested in his animals and now spent much of his profits protecting endangered species in the wild. Meanwhile, Kandace didn't really seem to like the place. She liked certain animals, such as horses, quite a lot. But she had zero interest in most others.

Since Summer *loved* FunJungle—after all, it had been her idea in the first place—she spent much more time with her father than with her mother. This was a sore point for Kandace, who was constantly looking for ways to better their relationship and give them more "girl time" together—as long as those activities didn't involve wild animals.

"I didn't invite Teddy here for shoptalk at all," J.J. said. "But it so happens, this giraffe thing just came up, and I figured I'd get the kids' thoughts on it." He deliberately looked at Summer and said, "*Both* of your thoughts. You two have been very helpful solving mysteries at the park."

I froze, a forkful of filet halfway to my mouth. "Mr. McCracken . . ."

"For the hundredth time, Teddy, you can call me 'J.J.' When you say 'Mr. McCracken,' I think you're talking to my father."

"Okay. J.J., you *know* my parents don't want me investigating any more crimes, seeing as I keep ending up in danger."

J.J. raised a hand, palm forward. "Hold on there. I never

said this was a crime. It's a *mystery*. Which is different."

"How so?" Summer asked, excitement in her eyes.

"Something's happening to the giraffes," J.J. explained, "but I don't necessarily think someone's doing it to them on purpose. Or that anyone's even doing it at all."

"What do you mean?" Now that I'd been told this wasn't a crime, I felt comfortable enough to return to eating my dinner. Summer might have been thrilled by the prospect of two crimes popping up in one day, but I wasn't. Investigating one was plenty for me.

"The giraffes keep getting sick," J.J. told us. "Not badly sick, but sick enough. Something's getting into their digestive systems and giving them diarrhea."

Kandace gasped, upset this had even been mentioned at the table. "J.J.! That's disgusting!"

"You're telling me," J.J. agreed, missing the whole reason for his wife's reaction. "When most animals get the squirts, you can't even tell, 'cause they do their business two inches above the ground. But when it happens to a giraffe, all that stuff's shooting out from six feet up in the air. Looks like a poo waterfall."

Kandace turned greenish. "Do we really have to talk about low-class things like this at the dinner table?"

"It's not low-class, Mom. It's science!" Summer said, though it was obvious she found her mother's nauseated reaction amusing. "Dad, does the giraffes' diarrhea look kind of like this?" She took a mouthful of chocolate milk and spit it back into her glass.

"Summer!" Kandace groaned in disgust, clutching her stomach.

"It sort of does," J.J. said, oblivious to Kandace's discomfort. "And then it splatters all over the giraffe's legs and the ground. Half the tourists who see it look like they're gonna lose their lunch."

"And now I'm going to lose my dinner," Kandace said, shoving her plate away.

"Do the giraffes ever vomit?" Summer asked her father. "Because that'd be *really* gross. Can you imagine something eighteen feet tall puking? It'd look like this!" She stood up, made a retching noise, and hocked a mouthful of ragout into her napkin.

"Summer!" Kandace cried.

J.J. chuckled at Summer, then said, "I was worried about that myself. But it turns out giraffes can't vomit. No animal that chews its cud can. So when they get sick, everything just comes out the poop chute."

"Enough!" Kandace declared, exasperated. "I don't want any more talk about poop at the dinner table! We have a guest!"

"Teddy doesn't care," Summer said. "We talk about poop all the time."

"What do you think is making the giraffes sick?" I asked J.J. quickly, hoping to change the subject before Kandace ended dinner and sent me home.

J.J. answered, "The keepers think they're probably getting poisoned by something. Not badly enough to kill them, but getting the trots like this on a regular basis isn't good for them either. We were thinking it might be either the water supply or their food, but unfortunately, the evidence indicates there's probably human involvement."

"You mean, someone's *trying* to poison the giraffes?" Summer asked, horrified.

"That's where we're in kind of a gray area," J.J. said. "We don't know if someone's trying to do it—or if they're doing it by accident somehow."

I popped another piece of steak into my mouth. "Why do you think it's definitely a human?"

"A couple reasons," J.J. said. "First of all, the giraffes are only getting sick on Mondays."

This was strange enough to even provoke a response from Kandace, despite her distaste for the subject. "Only Mondays? Really?"

"Really," J.J. confirmed. "Which the vets say means the poisoning is probably taking place on Sundays. If it was happening on Saturdays, they'd be getting the runs on Sunday."

"How long has this been happening?" Summer asked.

"Every Monday for the past four weeks," J.J. replied.

"Definitely sounds like a pattern," Summer said.

"But that doesn't mean a human is necessarily behind it," I said. "It could still be something in the water supply or their food."

"True. So we've taken steps to eliminate those possibilities." J.J. ticked them off on his fingers. "First, we brought in water from other sources and they still got sick on Monday. Second, we changed the food supply. Once again, sick on Monday. That leaves some kind of random environmental factor or human involvement, and my money is on humans. Someone's probably feeding them something that's bad for them. It happens all the time at the park, just not usually on a regular basis."

I knew this was a sad fact of the zoo business. No matter what steps any zoo took to discourage people from feeding the animals, on any given day dozens of people did. There were signs posted on every exhibit at FunJungle warning guests that feeding the animals could make them sick, and yet, almost every day, I saw some idiot standing right in front of the signs and feeding the animals anyhow.

My guess was, very few of the guests meant any harm, but the act was still dangerous. Many people assumed that an herbivore such as a giraffe could eat any plant at all, but that wasn't the case. Most animals had extremely specialized diets and any variation from those could be unhealthy for them. Meanwhile, there were plenty of morons who tried to feed animals things that weren't remotely good for them. Usually, this was food they had purchased at FunJungle, and a staggering amount of the food FunJungle sold wasn't even that good for humans. I had seen people offering animals almost any type of junk food imaginable: lollipops, candy corn, chili fries, potato chips, churros, soft-serve ice cream. I had even seen people offering sips of their sodas to animals ranging from monkeys to elephants to okapis. It was startling that the same people who complained about the exorbitant cost of the food at the park would then turn around and give it to an animal, even after being warned that it would make the animal sick.

And then, there were some people who really did seem to be acting maliciously. They would offer animals things that weren't food at all, like napkins or plastic toys. Back when Henry the Hippo had been alive, the FunJungle mascot had usually kept his mouth open, eagerly waiting for guests to throw food to him, and people had often thrown garbage instead, thinking it was funny. Plastic drinking straws were particularly dangerous to animals, as they got stuck in their digestive systems and caused all kinds of medical emergencies; for this reason, most zoos in America didn't even hand out straws with drinks.

"FunJungle lets the public feed the giraffes on Sundays," Summer observed.

"Right," J.J. said. "Well, we let them feed the giraffes most days, but there's a good chance our culprit could be doing it at the Sunday event."

FunJungle had a giraffe feeding program, where guests could pay five dollars to give the giraffes a few leaves of lettuce. A great many zoos did this. Giraffes were docile, friendly, and extremely popular. Furthermore, with giraffes, if you ran the feeding properly, there was little chance of a tourist getting bitten by accident. To feed most animals, you had to hold the food dangerously close to the animals' mouths—and thus, their teeth—but giraffes have eighteen-inch-long prehensile tongues, with which they can grab food from up to a foot away.

"But aren't the keepers monitoring the feedings?" I asked. "Just so something like this doesn't happen?"

"They are," J.J. said. "So, to be honest, if someone *is* slipping the giraffes something, it's probably happening at some other point during the day. The best way to tell, though, would be to have a team set up to watch the giraffes all day. Which is where you two come in." He aimed his pointer fingers at Summer and me like they were the barrels of six-shooters.

Summer sat up in her chair, excited. "You mean, you want Teddy and me to do a stakeout?"

"In a way," J.J. said.

"No!" Kandace exclaimed. "J.J., I don't want you dragging our daughter into something that could be dangerous."

"It's not going to be dangerous . . . ," J.J. argued.

Kandace said, "The last time Summer got wrapped up in an investigation, she nearly fell into the crocodile pit! And poor Teddy almost got eaten by a polar bear!"

"This is different," J.J. said. "All I'm asking them to do is help keep an eye on the giraffes for a day. They won't be going up against poachers or animal smugglers or anyone dangerous. And they'll have my security force there to back them up."

"Then why not just have your security force do this in the first place?" Kandace demanded. "Don't you pay them to handle things like this?"

"Yes," J.J. said. "But to be honest, I think these kids could do a better job."

"Really?" I asked.

"There's no need for modesty here, Teddy," J.J. told me. "If it hadn't been for you and Summer, I'd never have known who bumped off my hippo or kidnapped my koala or stole my panda. The truth is, I've had my security force out at the giraffe paddock the past two Sundays, trying to catch this culprit, and they've come up dry."

"That's no surprise," Summer said. "No offense, Dad,

but most of the people you have working FunJungle Security couldn't find a hole if they were standing in it."

J.J. frowned at this, but he didn't argue the point. Summer might have been exaggerating, but FunJungle Security was mostly made up of people who couldn't get law enforcement jobs anywhere else. Chief Hoenekker, who ran the operations, was a smart guy, but he couldn't do much on his own.

"I'd pay you for your time," J.J. said. "Ten dollars an hour."

That got my attention. J.J. had never offered to pay me to help him before. And the park was open sixteen hours on Sundays. A full day's stakeout would bring in $160, which was more money than I'd ever had.

Summer wasn't as impressed. "Ten dollars?" she scoffed. "I could get twice that working at the mall."

"The most you could make at the mall is minimum wage and you know it," J.J. said.

"It doesn't matter what the offer is," Kandace said. "*I* still think this is a bad idea."

Summer ignored her and kept negotiating. "You want us to find out who's poisoning the giraffes? It'll cost you twenty dollars an hour."

"Twelve," J.J. countered.

"Eighteen," Summer said.

"Stop negotiating right now," Kandace ordered.

"Fourteen," J.J. said. "And I'm not going any higher."

"Then I guess the park guests on Monday are going to be seeing a lot of giraffes with the runs," Summer replied.

J.J. sighed. "All right. Sixteen."

"Plus food and beverages," Summer said.

"Deal," J.J. agreed. He seemed to be impressed by Summer's negotiating.

"Why is no one listening to me?!" Kandace shouted.

J.J. and Summer both turned to her, looking surprised she was there.

"As far as I'm concerned, you spend way too much time at that park as it is," Kandace told her daughter. "If you want to make money, there are easier ways to do it. You're famous. There are plenty of companies that would pay you thousands of dollars just to tweet about their products."

"That's not *work*," Summer said dismissively. "That's just trading in on our family name."

"Darn straight," J.J. concurred. "I got my first job when I was Summer's age, putting up fences for local ranches, working four hours a day after school in a hundred degrees. This won't be nearly as tough. But it'd still be good for these kids to do a little real work and learn the value of money."

I was quite pleased with the idea of earning money for investigating a mystery, which I had always done for free up until that point. But one thing still bothered me. "I really appreciate this, J.J., but before I agree to anything, I need to check with my parents."

"It's already done," J.J. told me. "I took care of it."

I set my fork down, surprised. "Really?"

"I know I've been a little bit"—J.J. paused to come up with the right word—"weaselly about how I've gone about seeking your help before. That hasn't exactly put me in good stead with your parents. So I figured I ought to be completely aboveboard on this one. I called them up before I invited you over here. Told them everything that was involved, and they signed off on it. Of course, I told them it was only going to be ten dollars an hour, not expecting that my own daughter would bleed me dry. . . ."

"Like *you* wouldn't have negotiated in that situation," Summer taunted.

J.J. chuckled at this. "So, what do you say, Teddy? Are you in?"

I asked, "All you need us to do is watch the giraffe exhibit tomorrow?"

"That's right. Though I'd like you as clandestine as possible. Act like you're two kids hanging out at the park for the day, not junior detectives on the lookout for criminals. It's possible that, if someone really *has* been poisoning those animals on purpose, they've been keeping an eye out for security. But they won't expect a couple kids to be on the job."

"And what happens if we catch someone doing something wrong?" I asked.

"Not *if*," Summer corrected. "*When* we catch them. Because we're going to find them."

"You won't have to get involved," J.J. explained, glancing at Kandace as he said this. "I don't want you two taking any risks at all. You'll be in constant contact with security. The moment you see anyone up to no good, you call my people and they will take care of the situation. Is that understood?"

"Fine," Summer said, sounding disappointed. It was clear she'd been hoping for a little more action.

For my part, I was happy with those orders. I had ended up in enough danger over the past year. "Sounds good to me."

J.J. now turned his full attention to his wife. "How about you, darling? You okay with this?"

Kandace sighed heavily. "I suppose so. As long as you can guarantee the kids won't get in any trouble."

"I promise they'll be safer then baby birds in their mama's nest," J.J. said.

With that, the conversation turned to other topics, and I finished the dinner feeling excited about the idea of investigating the giraffe poisonings and eager to catch the culprit behind them.

I would have been wise to remember that baby birds *aren't* always that safe in their mothers' nests. As usual, things at FunJungle worked out far worse than anyone expected.

TRACKS

Since I had eaten dinner at the McCrackens', my parents hadn't rushed home from work. None of us was ever in a hurry to get to our home.

FunJungle's PR department referred to the employee housing area as "Lakeside Estates"—but it was neither lakeside nor estates. Instead, it was a trailer park next to a muddy sinkhole that occasionally had water in it. J.J. had recently come through on a long-delayed promise to replace our old, crummy trailer with a new, deluxe double-wide, but my parents still didn't like being there much. At certain times of year, it was nice to sit outside, but now we were deep in the midst of mosquito season and the sinkhole was a perfect breeding ground for the horrid little insects. For every few minutes you sat still at Lakeside Estates, you'd lose a pint of blood.

Mosquitoes were far less of a problem inside FunJungle, which was a mystery. J.J. claimed there was a large colony of bats nearby that kept the mosquito population in check, but I had never seen that many bats around the park, nor could I understand why they would eat the mosquitoes at FunJungle but not Lakeside Estates. My parents figured that J.J. was secretly dousing the park in insect-repelling chemicals late at night, but had no proof of this. My parents didn't complain, though, because while they loved pretty much every single creature alive, insects included, they hated mosquitoes with a passion. When we had lived in the Congo, mosquito-borne diseases were the number one cause of death. Technically, mosquitoes were the most dangerous animals on earth, indirectly killing millions of people a year by transmitting malaria, yellow fever, chikungunya, and other fatal sicknesses.

For their dinner, Mom and Dad had ordered takeout from a park restaurant and picnicked at a lookout over the African section of SafariLand, pretending like they were back in the Masai Mara. J.J. had his driver drop me off at the front of the park. FunJungle was closed when I got there, but I had my ID badge and everyone in security knew me anyhow, so I came in through the nighttime employee entrance, crossed the park, and met up with my parents for the rest of the walk home.

Lakeside Estates was located beyond the rear of the park.

Our route home took us out the back employee entrance, and then along the edge of the construction site for the Wilds. Even after dark, lots of people were still at work. J.J. was so determined to have the rides open as fast as possible that he had construction underway until well after nightfall most days. This was another reason that being at home wasn't so nice; we could hear the heavy machinery from our place. Even my mother, who slept so soundly that she had once napped through an elephant stampede, had resorted to wearing earplugs at night.

On the far perimeter of the construction site, where no tourists ever went, there was only a cheap chain-link fence looping the Wilds. While the project was slated to be beautifully landscaped in the future, at the moment it was a big, barren eyesore. Every living thing over twenty square acres had been scraped off the ground, leaving only dirt and rocks behind. What would eventually be buildings were now only cement slabs and wooden frameworks. The future Black Mamba roller coaster was a jumble of iron beams, while the Falcon Strike ten-story plunge was only three stories so far. The Raging Raft Ride was the closest to being done, but its skeleton of steel bars was still only partially crowned with fake rock.

"You're really okay with me working for J.J.?" I asked my parents.

"Why would we have a problem with that?" Dad replied.

"Besides the fact that the man's a sneak, a cheat, and a liar," Mom said.

"Charlene!" Dad gasped, mock offended. "You're talking about Teddy's future father-in-law!"

"That's not funny," I said, feeling my face turning red.

"Yes, it is," Mom teased.

Dad grew serious. "J.J. may have handled your ability to solve cases poorly in the past, but we really appreciated that he called us before he even talked to you this time."

"We were certainly concerned when he suggested bringing you in to investigate another case," Mom added. "However, this one sounds different from the others. Far less dangerous. And, to be honest, I think you could really help."

"You do?" I asked, surprised.

"Of course I do!" Mom exclaimed. "You're a very smart kid, Teddy. You have a gift for seeing things that other people don't. And I'm not only saying that because I'm your mother."

"J.J. obviously sees it too," Dad said. "That's why he wants you on this case."

Mom said, "If you can figure out what's happening to the giraffes and make some money doing it, then everyone wins. Just don't take any risks this time. If there really is a criminal, leave catching them to FunJungle Security."

"Okay," I agreed, then noticed that my father was no longer walking with us.

He had stopped a few feet back and was staring at the ground.

"Jack?" Mom asked. "Did you drop something?"

Dad looked up at us, seeming startled, as if he had somehow already forgotten we were there. He paused a bit before replying, like he was trying to decide whether or not to tell us the truth about what he'd seen. "Uh . . . no."

Mom started back toward him, her interest piqued. "What's going on, then?"

Dad pointed to the ground. "Mountain lion tracks."

Most people wouldn't have been able to spot an animal track at night when they weren't even looking for it, but Dad was a professional wildlife photographer and a master when it came to tracking animals. Even so, this one stood out particularly well. It was right along the chain-link fence, in a patch of whitish limestone clay. The same type of clay Tommy Lopez had suggested the tiny white object at the crime scene might have been made of. The clay was part of a large patch that extended far on the other side of the chain-link fence. With the trees and plants scraped off in the construction site, the topsoil had eroded, leaving only the bare limestone beneath. Being white, it practically glowed in the moonlight, making the track much more obvious than it might have been otherwise. And yet, it wasn't *that* obvious. Mom and I had walked right past it without noticing.

Mom was a good tracker herself, and my parents had both taught me enough about tracks over the years so that I could easily tell this one had been made by a large cat, rather than a coyote or even a stray dog. Canines show claw marks in their tracks, while cats retract their claws, and the pads of a cat are bigger and closer together than dogs' pads are.

There were three clear tracks in the mud. Dad knelt and placed his finger along one of them, crudely measuring it. "Four inches across. That's an adult. A little dried out, so not too recent. Though it might have been made last night."

I crouched beside it as well, partly to examine the track—and partly to take a closer look at the clay, which I prodded with a finger. On closer inspection, it was definitely not whatever the white object I had found at Lincoln Stone's was made of; that had been more crumbly. For a moment, I wondered if the mystery object could have been clay of a different consistency, or clay that had dried out more, but that didn't seem right. I was now quite sure that the item wasn't clay at all, but some other substance entirely.

The lion tracks were heading the same way we were, away from the park, following the fence line. Mom moved ahead, scanning the ground carefully. The patch of clay quickly gave way to an area where the topsoil hadn't eroded yet, which was better environmentally but made finding tracks in the darkness more difficult. Mom switched on the penlight that she kept attached to her key chain. Two dozen feet along, she gave a cry of excitement. "I've got another one! Only partial, though."

Dad and I hurried to catch up with her. We both had penlights on our key chains as well; when you lived on the far edge of civilization, you often found yourself wandering around in the dark. The beams from the lights weren't wide, but they still made a big difference.

If either of my parents was concerned about the lion being close to our home, they didn't show it. Both had spent much of their lives around wild animals, predators included. Most of the time, the carnivores weren't nearly as dangerous as the herbivores. In Africa, hippos and Cape buffalo killed far more people every year than lions or leopards did, while in the Americas, you were much more likely to be attacked by a bison in a national park than a bear. My father had obviously been wary about mentioning the tracks to me, but now my mother and I were both caught up in the thrill of tracking the big cat.

My parents leapfrogged ahead of each other, so neither was searching the same section of trail, picking up more partials as they went along. The tracks continued along the fence line, following the trail we used to get to Lakeside

Estates, until the trail veered off toward the trailer park. Then, the tracks stayed with the fence, moving through a small meadow of spear grass, until a point fifty feet past the turnoff, where a large oak tree stood. The branches of the oak extended far out over the chain-link fence.

We all stopped to inspect the bark of the tree. Even I could see that there were multiple sets of long, vertical claw marks in it.

"The cat climbed the tree to get into the construction site," I deduced.

"More than once," Mom said. "I'd say at least five times, probably more."

"Why would it want to do that?" I asked. "There's no food in there for it. And there's a lot of people."

"I'll bet the cat isn't climbing over when the humans are there," Dad said. "Mountain lions don't like humans much. I know everyone's working late here, but they're not working around the clock."

"I think they stop around midnight most nights," Mom observed. "That's when the noise dies down. And cats are nocturnal anyhow."

"As for food," Dad told me, "there might not be any animals inside the construction site, but there's thousands in the park, and a cat could smell them from here for sure."

"Plus, there's *that*." Mom pointed through the fence to

the Raging Raft Ride. At the base of the manmade mountain was a large fake lake for the rafts to plunge into. It had been completed only recently, and was now full of water, which shimmered in the moonlight. "First you house all the potential prey at FunJungle. Now J.J. has built the largest freshwater source for miles in every direction. Of course the lion's going to come sniffing around."

I stared at the fake lake, wondering where the next-closest water source even was. The "lake" of Lakeside Estates had dried up weeks before, as had many of the seasonal streams in the area. The lion wouldn't have known the Raging Raft Ride was manmade; all she would know was that, suddenly, there was a lot more water in her territory.

"Do you think the lion can get into the rest of FunJungle?" I asked.

Dad thought about that before answering. "The fence around the park would be tougher to get over than this one, because it has barbed wire strung at the top, but there are probably places where there's a tree that could be climbed. There wouldn't be branches hanging over the fence like on this one, because J.J. doesn't want people climbing over, but a lion could climb trees that people couldn't."

"So the animals could be at risk," I concluded.

"Possibly," Mom replied thoughtfully. "In the main part of the park, most of them are housed at night, but in

SafariLand, it's a different story. And that's the closest area of FunJungle to the water supply."

"We should probably let J.J. know." Dad turned away from the fence and started through the woods toward our house. As I fell in beside him, he said, "You already knew there was a mountain lion around here?"

"Why do you say that?"

"You didn't seem very surprised when I pointed out the tracks."

I thought back to my reaction and realized Dad was right. But then I realized that his own reaction had been a little odd. "Did *you* know there was a lion around here?"

"Yes," Dad admitted. "I found some tracks a few days ago, closer to our house."

"Where?" I asked.

We arrived at Lakeside Estates, rejoining the path from FunJungle. Dad pointed to the far side of the "lake." "Over there. Heading toward the park."

"And you didn't tell me?"

"We didn't want to alarm you," Mom said. "We thought it might be a one-time thing, the cat just crossing through. But now it appears she's spending more time around here."

That was why my father had hesitated about mentioning the tracks at first, I now realized. Because he was unsure how Mom would feel if he let me know.

"How did *you* know about the lion?" Dad asked me.

I considered making up a story, wary about telling them the truth, because that would open up a whole can of worms. But I figured lying would only cause more problems down the road. So I said, "A guy from the Department of Fish and Wildlife told me. His name's Tommy Lopez."

We were crossing through the trailer park now. Lakeside Estates was slightly nicer than the original trailer park for employee housing had been, but not much. The trailers were arranged in a more orderly fashion, but no landscaping had been done, so we were forced to wind our way through large patches of prickly pear cactus to get to our home. At other times of year, when it wasn't as humid and there was less construction noise and fewer mosquitoes, some of our neighbors might have been outside, barbecuing or simply enjoying the night sky. Now they were all inside their trailers. Air conditioners were humming loudly everywhere.

Mom and Dad exchanged a wary glance. "How do you know this Tommy Lopez?" Mom asked.

"He's a friend of Doc's daughter, Lily. She introduced me to him today."

"Lily was here?" Mom asked, surprised. "I thought she was in Antarctica."

"She's back. Doc didn't tell you?"

"Doc doesn't say much about his daughter," Mom said.

"But I thought you were friends."

"I think Doc is embarrassed by Lily," Mom explained. "She obviously cares a lot about animals, but her recklessness has caused her father a lot of problems. I think he's had to bail her out of trouble on a regular basis."

"Why did she come see *you*?" Dad asked.

"Because Tommy Lopez thinks that a mountain lion didn't really kill Lincoln Stone's dog. He thinks someone framed the lion so they'd have an excuse to kill it."

Dad frowned at the thought of this. "You mean someone's looking to have the lion declared a nuisance?"

"Yes."

"That's crazy," Dad said.

"And yet, I wouldn't put it past people." Mom sighed heavily. "There's a lot of folks out here who don't want that lion around. I'm actually kind of shocked that someone's looking for a legal reason to hunt it rather than just killing it illegally."

"Really?" I asked.

Mom said, "People do it all the time. Especially with predators. They hunt them, trap them, poison them. Whatever it takes to get rid of them."

We arrived at our trailer. It wasn't locked. We lived too far out for thieves to bother us, and we didn't have anything worth stealing anyhow.

The moment I opened the door, I was hit by a wave of

heat. My parents didn't like leaving the air conditioner on for the large part of the day we weren't home because it wasted electricity and was expensive. But our first few minutes upon returning home were always miserable.

I flipped on the lights and the AC as my parents followed me inside. The main area of our trailer was a living room–kitchen furnished with a cheap table, chairs, and a sofa.

"Teddy," Dad said gravely. "Did Tommy and Lily come to you for help figuring out who killed the dog?"

"Yes," I said.

"And what did you say to them?" Mom asked.

"That I'd think about it."

Dad opened the fridge, grabbing beers for Mom and himself, taking a little extra time to enjoy the cold air before he shut the door again.

"I don't want you doing that," Mom told me.

"Why not?" I asked. "You said it was okay for me to help J.J. find whoever was poisoning the giraffes!"

"That's different," Mom explained. "J.J. is going through a lot of trouble to make sure that all you are doing is observing the giraffes. That's the limit of your involvement in that case. But I don't know this Tommy Lopez one bit, and all I know about Lily Deakin is that she has a knack for getting herself in trouble. If you get mixed up with them, you could end up in trouble too."

"Or worse." Dad popped the cap off a beer and handed the bottle to Mom.

"But if no one does anything, that lion will end up dead!" I argued.

"That may be true," Mom said. "But it doesn't mean *you* have to be the one who gets involved. It's Tommy's job to investigate this. Not yours."

"Tommy's boss doesn't want him to investigate," I said defiantly. "And Lincoln Stone doesn't either. They *want* the lion dead."

Dad and Mom looked to each other, saddened by this information. Mom placed the cold beer against her head to cool herself off, while Dad propped himself right in front of the air-conditioner vent.

"Even so," Dad said, "this still isn't your fight. When you've gotten mixed up in things like this before, you've ended up in serious danger."

"Not as much danger as that lion's in," I argued.

"You've nearly been killed before," Mom reminded me. "More than once."

"This time is different," I said, hoping that it was true.

My phone buzzed in my pocket. I fished it out and found a string of texts from my friends that had suddenly arrived all at once. This was a common occurrence. The cellular reception at Lakeside Estates was terrible, so J.J. McCracken had souped up the Wi-Fi in all our trailers. Almost every time I got home, I was deluged with outdated messages. I scrolled to the last one, which was from Summer:

TURN THE TV ON NOW!!! CHANNEL 3.

"Summer says something important's happening on TV," I said, grabbing the remote.

Our TV was about twenty years old, but then, we barely used it. I couldn't remember the last time it had been on.

The local news was showing on channel 3, and the mountain lion was the lead story. Lincoln Stone was having what appeared to be a live press conference in front of his home. Several reporters were clustered in the driveway where I had been only a few hours before, pointing microphones at him, while his ugly fake log cabin loomed in the background. The news scroll at the bottom of the screen read: "Live: Local celebrity Lincoln Stone makes big announcement in cougar case."

As we tuned in, Lincoln was in the middle of a rant, red-faced in anger, the same way he often was on his show. "The mountain lion that killed King is a threat to this community! Next time it might not be a dog that gets eaten, but a child. Or maybe even an adult. Now I know that all the tree huggers out there think this cat should have more rights than I do, but that's just plain idiocy. I'm not going to sit here while a vicious, bloodthirsty predator menaces the lives of my fellow citizens! Therefore, I am putting a bounty on its head. I will pay fifty thousand dollars to whoever brings me the carcass of the cat that killed King."

The announcement caught my parents and me by surprise. The reporters had the same reaction. There was a moment of stunned silence, and then everyone started shouting questions at once. Lincoln didn't answer them. Instead, he said, "If anyone wants to know anything else, the full details are on my website, LincolnStoneForAmerica.com." Then he turned his back on the cameras and headed toward his house.

The news returned to the studio, where the anchors seemed floored by Lincoln's announcement as well.

I looked to my parents. Both were dumbstruck.

"That fool," Mom said. "He has no idea what he's done."

"Oh, I think he knows perfectly well what he's done," Dad said. "He just turned this entire county into a war zone."

OPERATION HAMMERHEAD

The hunters didn't even wait until the next morn-
ing to start combing the area for Rocket.

Word of Lincoln Stone's bounty spread like wildfire.
Fifty thousand dollars was a lot of money. Hundreds of
people who were about to go to bed suddenly pulled their
clothes back on, grabbed their guns, and headed out to kill
the cougar before anyone else could.

Almost all of them figured the cat would still be somewhere near Lincoln Stone's home, and the biggest piece of
wilderness around that was the FunJungle property. Most
of it remained undeveloped, and very little was even fenced.
Thus, right outside our door were several square miles of vir-
gin forest.

It was possible that the hunters had no idea they were

trespassing on J.J.'s land, but then, it was equally likely that they knew and didn't care. After all, they were already willfully attempting to break one law: It still wouldn't be legal to kill the lion until the Department of Fish and Wildlife officially declared it a nuisance and issued the permit, but everyone was hunting it anyhow.

Mom and Dad had rushed out immediately after the news ended to scuff out the lion tracks we'd found, hiding even that slight bit of evidence that the cat was around, but lots of hunters still came poking through Lakeside Estates. Most of them had used FunJungle's entry road to get there, as it provided the easiest access to the wilderness. The road was gated off to cars at night, but the hunters were obviously parking on the edge of the property and then following the road on foot. Our home sat directly between where the road ended at the employee parking lot and the wilderness. So throughout the night, I heard hunters tromping past our place, as well as several heated arguments between rival groups declaring that they had gotten there first and thus deserved dibs on the cougar.

I also heard quite a lot of gunshots. None were inside Lakeside Estates itself, but they were close enough to rouse me from my sleep. Once awake, I had trouble going back to bed, fearing an errant bullet might pierce the cheap walls of our trailer. My parents had the same concern; we laid out sleeping bags in the living room, keeping ourselves close to the floor, but I remained nervous through the night.

Thankfully, Rocket survived. Possibly, no one even saw her—although there was ample evidence that, in their haste to earn the money, several hunters had shot at things that they mistakenly *thought* were the lion. Even if many of those things didn't look anything like a mountain lion at all.

Bulldozers, for example. Hunters shot two different ones that had been parked close to the fence of the Wilds. In addition, overzealous hunters also shot several trees, many prickly pear cactuses, four PRIVATE PROPERTY: NO HUNTING signs, three large boulders, and one windmill. One man, who turned out to have been drinking, quickly got turned around in the woods and shot his own car. There were at least ten accounts of different hunting parties opening fire on one another, but miraculously, no one was hurt, save for one idiot who rested a loaded gun on his foot and accidentally blew off three of his own toes.

J.J. McCracken was terrified that, sooner or later, some fanatical hunter would mistake one of the park animals for the lion and shoot it. But even with all his political clout, he couldn't get the police to start rousting hunters from his property until dawn. (The local sheriff had argued—probably correctly—that anyone wandering out in those woods at night stood a decent chance of being mistaken for a mountain lion themselves and shot by accident.) At first light, though, law enforcement arrived en masse, arresting people by the dozens for trespassing.

Lincoln Stone then issued an angry press statement against J.J. McCracken, claiming that he was "harboring a fugitive varmint" on his property.

The local division of the Department of Fish and Wildlife didn't issue any statements at all.

With all the commotion, I didn't get much sleep. So when I showed up at J.J.'s office in the morning to get my orders for the stakeout, I was frazzled and groggy. J.J. wasn't in much better shape, having spent much of the night on the phone with everyone from the local police to the FBI, trying to deal with the onslaught of hunters. Chief Hoenekker, the head of FunJungle Security, was also in a testy mood, although his wasn't due to lack of sleep; he seemed annoyed that J.J. was forcing him to use Summer and me to investigate the giraffe mystery.

No one except J.J. knew where Hoenekker had worked before coming to FunJungle, but given the secrecy and the fact that Hoenekker always dressed and acted like he was in the military, a lot of people figured he'd come from some highly classified special ops division. Unfortunately, no matter how competent and qualified Hoenekker was, his security force was equally incompetent and unqualified. This was a major source of frustration to Hoenekker, who was constantly pestering J.J. for more money so that he could hire people with IQs above those of the animals.

Our assignment was rather easy: Summer and I would hang around the giraffe paddock for the day, acting like tourists, but keeping an eye out for anything suspicious. We would be aided in this by FunJungle Security personnel Marge O'Malley and Kevin Wilks. The way Marge and Kevin had been selected for the job was very simple: No one else in FunJungle Security had wanted to do it.

Neither Marge nor Kevin was very bright, but Marge was at least exceptionally committed to her job. Until recently, she had been a nemesis of mine, convinced that I was up to no good, and determined to prove it. However, in the course of recovering FunJungle's stolen panda, I had finally earned Marge's respect. She had been downright kind and friendly to me ever since.

Technically, Marge wasn't even FunJungle Security anymore. She had been kicked out after a disastrous incident in which she had ruined the FunJungle Friends Dance 'n' Sing Parade while in pursuit of a criminal, destroying two floats and the instruments of an entire high school marching band in the process. For the past month, she had been working as a director of crowd control operations, which was basically making sure people didn't cut in lines; she was essentially a glorified hall monitor. Marge had been good at this—she liked yelling at people who were breaking the rules—but she had started to find the job tedious and was bucking to get back into security. The giraffe stakeout seemed like a decent way to give her a test run.

As for Kevin Wilks, he was a decent person and he had always been nice to me, but he had the deductive skills of a dead muskrat.

Then again, Marge and Kevin weren't being asked to do much deduction. They were merely supposed to stay in the vicinity of the giraffe exhibit, in radio contact with Summer and me, in case they were needed. They were going to be undercover themselves, in standard tourist garb, which at FunJungle meant shorts, baseball caps, and souvenir T-shirts. Even so, J.J. didn't want them lurking *too* close to the giraffes, recognizing that neither was really a master of blending in, and he didn't want the presence of law enforcement to spook any screwball who was trying to poison the giraffes on purpose.

The radios were pretty cool, with little buds that fit in our ears and microphones that clipped to our shirts. The wires that went to the earbuds were extremely thin and nearly impossible to see, so you had to look really closely to tell that we were wearing them. The one big drawback was that, if you weren't careful, you could forget you were wearing the radio and broadcast something private to everyone else. So Summer and I opted to not wear them most of the time, putting them in only when we needed to be in contact.

In theory, Summer should have been the biggest hindrance to our undercover work, as she was famous, but Summer was extremely adept at blending in when she wanted to. The trick was that, when she went out to public events where she was supposed to be noticed, she always wore pink. It was her trademark, although the truth was that Summer didn't like it much. Her fans associated the color with her, and, therefore, when she wasn't wearing pink (which was most of the time), she was almost invisible. For our stakeout, she was wearing her standard incognito outfit: a baggy T-shirt, sunglasses, and a baseball cap tucked down low over her eyes.

Marge, who had always fancied herself the closest thing FunJungle had to a commando, felt that we needed an official military name for the stakeout.

"What's wrong with 'the stakeout'?" Summer asked as we were all heading out to our posts in the morning.

"It's lame," Marge argued. "And it's not specific enough. If we don't name the operation, it might get confused with other operations over the radio."

"That's right," I said. "There's also a platoon of marines staking out the platypus exhibit today."

"Really?" Kevin asked, surprised. "Why? Is someone trying to steal the platypuses?"

Marge bopped him on the back of the head with an open hand. "He's joking, you idiot." Then she thought for a moment and said, "What about Operation Deathstalker? That sounds cool."

"It sounds psychotic," Summer said.

"How about Operation Giraffe?" Kevin asked eagerly. "You know, because we're watching the giraffes?"

"We can't call it that!" Marge told him, aghast. "It's too obvious. Then anyone who's eavesdropping on our communications will know exactly what we're talking about!"

"Why would anyone be eavesdropping on our communications?" I asked.

"We don't know what kind of fiends we're up against here," Marge warned me. "This giraffe poisoning situation might just turn out to be the tip of the iceberg. Maybe there's a whole criminal organization at work up to some nefarious purpose here and we're merely scratching the surface."

Summer gave me a look that said agreeing to the stakeout with Marge might have been a big mistake.

"Operation Kangaroo!" Kevin suggested triumphantly. "This way, it's a misdirection, right? If the criminals are eavesdropping on us, and they hear Operation Kangaroo, they'll think we're staking out the kangaroos and not the giraffes."

"I really don't think there's a criminal organization at work here," I said.

"We're not calling it Operation Kangaroo," Marge said dismissively. "That's too cute. If we're going to use an animal, it needs to be an awesome one. Something that's deadly, maybe."

"Ooh!" Kevin said excitedly. "Like a blowfish?"

"Those aren't deadly," Marge said. "All they do is inflate themselves when they get scared."

"They're deadly if you eat them," Kevin told her. "They're poisonous."

"That's not exactly intimidating," Marge said. "I mean something that can kill you without needing to be dead first. Like a tiger. Or a wolverine. Or a hammerhead shark."

"Operation Hammerhead!" Kevin exclaimed.

Marge broke into a smile. "I like it," she said. "It sounds cool *and* deadly. Like us." She mimed whipping out a gun and blowing away her enemies.

Summer rolled her eyes. "We're not getting paid enough to put up with this," she told me.

We arrived at the giraffe paddock just as the park was opening. The paddock was located directly next to the African Plains in SafariLand; the giraffes could be released into the plains if the keepers wanted. The giraffe feeding area was a round platform that extended out into the paddock. It was raised ten feet above the ground, as was much of the viewing area for the giraffes, as this allowed guests to look the beautiful creatures in the eye, or to hand food directly to them without forcing the giraffes to bend down to get it. It was accessed by a small wooden bridge, at the front of which was a turnstile. To pass through the turnstile, you had to show the receipt proving that you had paid for the experience. Despite the five-dollar cost, the line to feed the giraffes was often more than fifty people long.

There were six different feeding stations on the round platform, each run by a separate person who would advise the tourists about the proper way to feed the giraffes and then give them a few leaves of lettuce. Running a feeding station was hot and repetitive, but the people who worked there all seemed to enjoy it; they had proudly named themselves the Giraffe Staff.

Summer and I posted ourselves on a bench in a shaded area close enough to the giraffes to keep a close eye on the entire paddock. It was only a few minutes before the first park guests arrived, eager to feed the giraffes before the lines got too long. Marge and Kevin milled about, doing their best to look like tourists. To Kevin's dismay, Marge felt they ought to act like a couple on their third date, even though Marge was at least ten years older than Kevin. She insisted that they hold hands and stare at each other lovingly, which Kevin was having a hard time with. Marge wasn't unattractive, but she was a slob, and she never used deodorant; somehow, she'd gotten the idea that it caused cancer. Thus, on a hot day like this one, she sweated a lot and smelled bad.

I soon discovered that a stakeout wasn't as easy as I had expected. As much as I loved seeing giraffes in the wild, watching people feeding them for hours on end wasn't nearly as fascinating. No one was doing anything remotely sinister. The tourists appeared excited, fascinated, and occasionally grossed out by the long, slobbery tongues—but no one seemed to be up to no good, which was boring. Plus, the heat was brutal, even in the shade. Combined with my lack of sleep from the night before, I was having an extremely hard time staying awake. Even after Summer got us jumbo 72-ounce souvenir cups of highly caffeinated soda, I kept nodding off.

At one point, somewhere around noon, I snapped back awake to find Summer in the midst of reading something off her phone to me. ". . . which would mean that *any* mountain lion could be killed. That's horrible!"

"What?" I asked, trying to shake the cobwebs from my head.

Summer looked up from her phone at me. "You fell asleep again, didn't you?"

"I'm sorry. Last night was awful." I realized I had nodded off with the radio in my ear. Marge was rambling on about a new initiative she wanted to start at FunJungle to fight pickpocketing. I noticed that Summer had removed her own earpiece, so I plucked mine out too.

"I was reading the laws about depredation permits for mountain lions," Summer said. "If I'm understanding this right, they're insanely stupid. Apparently, if Lincoln Stone gets this permit to allow a nuisance animal to be killed, it doesn't actually specify that you have to kill the exact same mountain lion that you consider a nuisance. It allows you to kill *any* mountain lion."

I rubbed my eyes, wondering if I had misunderstood Summer due to my exhaustion. "So you could kill a lion that *didn't* eat the dog, and the law would be totally fine with it?"

"Yes!"

"That's crazy."

"Tell me about it. How could a law like that even exist?"

I stared out at the giraffes, wondering if I had missed

anything while I was napping. But nothing criminal appeared to be happening. The tourists kept changing, but the scene remained almost exactly the same. "Lincoln Stone has people all over the county trying to kill a lion now. There's a really good chance one of them will get the wrong one."

"*Any* lion will be the wrong one! Because no lion killed that dog in the first place."

"Have you heard anything from Tommy yet? About the video from the security cameras?"

Summer checked her email for what was probably the thousandth time that day. Not that I could blame her; we didn't have much else to do. "Nope."

I fished my phone out of my pocket to do the same thing.

"Do you think Marge asked Kevin to pretend to be her boyfriend because she thinks he's cute?" Summer asked.

I looked up to find that Summer was watching them. They were strolling along the exhibit, trying to act normal. Marge was holding Kevin's hand and smiling happily. Kevin looked like he'd rather be holding a dead sea slug.

"Maybe," I said.

"He's a good-looking guy," Summer observed. I must have looked upset, because she quickly corrected, "Not as good-looking as *you*, though. And he's dumb as a box of rocks."

My phone started to ring. According to the caller ID, it was Lily Deakin.

Before I could answer it, though, Marge O'Malley called over the radio. Even though I was holding the earpiece in my hand, she was loud enough for me to hear her. "Eagle Eyes, come in," Marge said. In addition to naming our operation, she had also insisted on giving us all code names. "This is Mamma Bear."

I reluctantly flipped off my phone, figuring I could call Lily back, then made sure there weren't any tourists watching before sticking the radio earpiece back in and turning my radio microphone on. Summer did the same thing.

"Eagle Eyes, this is Mamma Bear," Marge repeated impatiently over the radio. "Do you read me?"

"Yes, Mamma Bear, we read you," I begrudgingly replied. "And we have visual contact with you too."

Marge and Kevin were now off to the side of the giraffe paddock, in a spot without too many tourists, where Marge felt it was safe to check in. Even so, she wasn't doing a great job of being inconspicuous, bending her neck at an unnatural angle to speak directly into her microphone. "Any suspicious activity to report in Operation Hammerhead?"

Summer said, "If there was any suspicious activity, we would have reported it."

"We have a potential bogey in the feeding area at nine

o'clock," Marge informed us. "Requesting visual confirmation."

The feeding area was circular, which allowed six groups of tourists to feed the giraffes at once. As part of her determination to make our stakeout as military as possible, Marge had broken the area down into twelve zones, each corresponding to an hour of time on a clockface.

I had brought one of my father's cameras with a big telephoto lens to help with our reconnaissance. A surprising number of people brought cameras like that to FunJungle, allowing them to zoom in on distant animals in SafariLand or get extreme close-ups of animals that were closer by. So it didn't look too suspicious for me to peer through it at the giraffe feeding area. After all, no one could tell I was using it to focus on the tourists, rather than the giraffes.

I zoomed in on the far left of the feeding area, where nine would have been on a clock. A middle-aged couple wearing Harley-Davidson T-shirts was gleefully feeding a giraffe. The man had a big, thick beard, while the woman was as skinny as the legs of a flamingo. They didn't look threatening or mean-spirited in the slightest. "Marge, are you talking about—"

"Use the code names, Eagle Eyes."

"Sorry. Mamma Bear, are you talking about the people in the motorcycle shirts?"

"That's affirmative. Shirts like that are a red flag. I'm thinking they might be members of a biker gang. And biker gangs are often involved in the drug trade. Especially crystal meth."

"So your theory is that a biker gang is drugging the giraffes?" Summer asked skeptically.

"Possibly," Marge replied. "Meth addicts are capable of extremely depraved behavior."

I zoomed in closer on the couple in the T-shirts. FunJungle got a fair share of serious bikers. There were lots of windy roads in the Texas Hill Country that motorcycle enthusiasts enjoyed cruising, and FunJungle was the biggest tourist destination in the area. I had been a bit suspicious of the first bikers I had seen in the park, as many looked awfully mean and imposing in their leather riding outfits, but they had turned out to be as enthusiastic and excited as any other tourists. I had actually witnessed one burly, heavily tattooed biker squeal with delight upon seeing a baby zebra. The couple I was watching now seemed like more of the same. They might have looked tough when seated astride their motorcycles, but at the moment, they were laughing giddily as the giraffe ate lettuce leaves from their hands.

"I don't think they're drug addicts," I reported. "They look like normal tourists."

"Well, keep a close eye on them anyhow," Marge ordered.

"See if maybe they have any suspicious tattoos."

I thought about arguing that this was ridiculous, but it was easier to just pretend to do it.

Next to me, Summer's phone rang. She checked the caller ID and reported, "It's Violet. I'm gonna take it." Then she popped her earpiece out, flicked off her microphone, and answered, "Hey! What's up?"

Through the telephoto, I saw that the man in the Harley T-shirt *did* have a tattoo. But it was of Mickey Mouse, which I didn't think counted as suspicious. I reported this to Marge, who didn't seem convinced.

"Mickey Mouse?" she asked cynically. "Is Mickey doing anything unsavory in the tattoo?"

"You mean, like poisoning a giraffe?" I said. "No. Mickey's smiling. I think these people are theme park fanatics, not criminals."

Summer paused her conversation to tell me, "Violet, Ethan, and Dashiell are going to be at the park today. Think they can swing by? It won't ruin the operation, will it?"

"No," I said. As far as I was concerned, the more Summer and I looked like kids hanging out with our friends, the less we looked like junior detectives on a stakeout.

Summer returned to her call. "Sounds good. We're going to be here all day. When do you want to come by?"

The biker couple fed their last lettuce leaf to the giraffes and reluctantly gave up their spot to some other eager tourists. I shifted the telephoto lens away from them, sweeping it across the feeding area. . . .

When I *did* notice some people behaving suspiciously. A couple in their twenties was looking about furtively, making sure the staff at the feeding area wasn't paying attention to them. Both were dressed unusually formally for FunJungle tourists. The man wore khakis and a button-down shirt with a tie, while the woman wore a very pretty dress. In all my time at FunJungle, I couldn't recall ever having seen a tourist wearing a tie before. Since I was looking at them with a camera, I snapped a few photos. As I did, the woman quickly pulled something from her purse and turned toward the giraffe.

I didn't get the chance to see what it was, though, because a group of tourists stepped into my line of sight. It looked like the woman in the dress was holding something out to the giraffe, maybe even feeding it, but I couldn't tell what. "Marge!" I exclaimed, forgetting to use her code name in my excitement. "There's some suspicious activity in the feeding area!"

"Where?" Marge demanded.

Before I could answer her, Summer told Violet, "Great! See you at two o'clock!"

"Two o'clock?" Marge replied, mistakenly thinking Summer had been talking to her. "I'm on it!"

"Wait!" I pleaded, but Marge had already bolted for the feeding area.

"You can't hesitate in the face of crime!" she told me, bowling over a gaggle of little kids on a church field trip.

Kevin trailed right behind her, blindly following her lead.

The tourists who were blocking my line of sight moved out of the way. Whatever the young, formal couple had done to the giraffe already seemed to be over. The woman was slipping the suspicious object back into her purse, while the man was now making a show of feeding the giraffes for the staff there. I quickly snapped a few more photos of them.

They were standing at what would have been twelve o'clock. I shifted my focus to two o'clock. To my dismay, a family was gathered there. They appeared to be tourists from eastern Asia: two parents, three young children, and two grandparents.

Marge had now reached the entrance to the feeding area. She barreled her way through the line of guests waiting to go in, then flashed her badge to the startled woman working the entry gate. "FunJungle Security!" Marge bellowed, shoving through the turnstile. "We have a situation!"

Summer hung up with Violet, staring in astonishment at Marge. "What's she doing now?"

"She's supposed to be going after those people," I said, pointing to the well-dressed couple, then I indicated the

Asian family. "But she's going after them instead."

Summer rolled her eyes, then shouted into her microphone. "Marge! Don't! Stop!"

"Don't stop?" Marge asked. "Roger that!" She bore down on the unsuspecting family.

"You're heading for the wrong people!" I yelled.

But Marge didn't respond. Later on, I would learn that she had knocked her earpiece loose while shoving aside yet another Giraffe Staff member, but Marge was so gung-ho in the midst of a mission she might have ignored me anyhow. Her microphone was still in place, so I could hear her as she yelled at the hapless family, "Put your hands in the air and step away from the giraffes! I have a taser and I am not afraid to use it!" She snapped the taser from her belt and flipped it on, allowing electricity to crackle between the prongs.

The tourists did not speak English. And since Marge was not wearing her official FunJungle uniform and had pocketed her badge to grab the taser, she did not look like a security guard. Instead, she looked like a deranged park guest wielding an electronic weapon.

Thus, the Asian tourists did what they probably thought was the sensible thing: They ran. So did most of the other tourists in the feeding area. The children and grandparents fled for the exit, while the father protectively placed himself in between Marge and his family.

Marge mistakenly perceived the family's flight as proof of their criminality, rather than self-preservation. She lunged with the taser, catching the poor father in the arm. He trembled in pain as the electricity jolted his body, while his family screamed in horror.

And then, the biker with the Mickey Mouse tattoo and the Harley T-shirt came to the rescue. He body-slammed Marge, knocking the taser from her hand and driving her into the railing.

Marge now mistook the biker as a fellow giraffe-poisoning conspirator, instead of a good samaritan trying to protect some innocent tourists from a crazy woman. She shifted her attention to attacking the man, rather than trying to maintain her balance while being shoved up against a railing with a ten-foot drop on the other side. She tried to clobber the biker with a right hook, swinging at him with all her might. The man deftly sidestepped the assault—and Marge's momentum carried her over the railing. Marge pitched into the paddock, dropped the ten feet, screaming the whole way, and landed flat on her back in a pile of hay.

Several tourists gave the biker a standing ovation.

The giraffes paused to inspect the loud, screaming woman who had plummeted into their paddock, then went back to eating.

Kevin Wilks didn't have any idea what to do. His whole

plan that day had been to simply take orders from Marge, but now even his dim brain seemed to realize that following Marge's lead at this point would be a bad idea. So he simply backed away from the feeding area and acted as though he had nothing to do with Marge at all.

In the chaos, I lost sight of the suspicious well-dressed couple. They had fled the feeding area with everyone else, falling in right behind the Asian family, but then dispersed into the crowd.

"C'mon!" Summer shouted, leaping to her feet. "Let's go after them!"

I stayed rooted to my spot. "We're not supposed to get involved this time."

Summer gave me an annoyed look. "They're getting away!"

"They could be dangerous," I argued.

"They might have poisoned the giraffes!"

I knew this was true. But I also knew that the last time I had gone after a criminal, I had ended up in the polar bear pit. So I hesitated.

"Fine," Summer said angrily. "I'll go after them myself."

"Summer, wait!" I yelled.

But she didn't listen. She ran off anyhow, while I stood there, staring after her impotently.

Summer had already wasted too much time waiting for me, though. By the time she got down to the giraffe paddock, she couldn't find any sign of the well-dressed couple.

Our best lead in the giraffe poisoning case was gone.

BAD BEHAVIOR

Summer and I had never had a fight before. Sure, we had been annoyed at each other at times, but never really angry. Until Operation Hammerhead.

After failing to find the well-dressed couple, Summer returned to our spot under the tree near the giraffe paddock. At the time, everything was even more chaotic than it had been when she left, so we didn't have a chance to talk right away—but it was obvious Summer was upset with me.

The Giraffe Staff had temporarily closed the feeding area while they tried to make sense of what had happened, which created a lot of exasperated tourists; they had already paid their money and waited patiently in the hot sun, and now they wanted to finally feed some darn giraffes. Meanwhile, the FunJungle paramedics had arrived to deal with

Marge. While FunJungle had one of the finest medical teams on earth for animals, the medical care for humans wasn't so impressive. When my mother had injured her ankle earlier that year, she had chosen to go to the veterinarian to have it fixed, rather than the regular doctors.

Given that Marge had fallen ten feet, she hadn't injured herself too seriously, thanks to landing in a pile of hay. Instead of breaking her neck or getting a concussion, she had escaped with only a broken leg. Unfortunately, Marge was a very bad patient. She howled in pain so loudly that tourists were showing up at the giraffe paddock expecting to find a pack of wolves on the hunt. The giraffes were unsettled by her wailing; they kept getting spooked and stampeding around their enclosure. The Giraffe Staff was seriously considering shooting Marge with the tranquilizer gun until the medics finally sedated her.

When Summer got back, Chief Hoenekker was grilling me about what had happened. He had arrived on the scene with six FunJungle security guards, who had immediately been put to work calming angry tourists and trying to restore order. Pete Thwacker, the head of Public Relations, had also shown up, along with a few other people who I assumed were lawyers, because they were all wearing suits. (No one who worked at FunJungle wore suits except Pete and the lawyers, not even J.J. McCracken himself.) They had caught up with the Asian family and were talking to them and the bikers, probably figuring out what they could offer to keep them from suing FunJungle.

"Did you find the suspects?" Hoenekker asked Summer.

"No," she said, then glared at me. "No thanks to Teddy."

I was hurt that Summer had said this, but I didn't think it was worth arguing about at the time. Hoenekker seemed to have very little patience left as it was.

"I took some photos of the suspects," I said. "And we know exactly what time they were in the feeding area. Are there security cameras around here?"

"Of course," Hoenekker answered. "There's security cameras pretty much everywhere in this park."

"It shouldn't be hard to identify them, then," I said. "You can check the footage and see what they were doing."

"And if you act fast, you can probably put out an alert to everyone in security around FunJungle," Summer added. "The suspects shouldn't be too difficult to spot, given what they're wearing. You could catch them before they leave the park."

"Let me see the photos," Hoenekker told me.

I brought the photos up on the screen of Dad's camera and easily found one that showed the suspects clearly. Hoenekker took a photo of that with his own phone, forwarded it to his entire staff, and then called his video supervisor to have her examine the giraffe paddock footage from 12:05 in the afternoon. After all that, though, he still questioned Summer and me for another fifteen minutes, learning exactly what had gone wrong. Every once in a while, he would groan in frustration at something Marge had done— or at Kevin's complete failure to do anything at all.

"Why did you even assign *them* to this job?" Summer asked. I got the sense her annoyance with me was making her annoyed about everything else, too. "They can't possibly be the best people you have."

"You'd be surprised," Hoenekker replied. Summer started to respond, but he quickly cut her off. "If you have an issue with that, bring it up with your daddy. If he wants a better security staff, he needs to pay for it. Because right now, he's paying my people less than he pays the janitors. Marge and Kevin might not be the sharpest tools in the shed, but they both follow orders and try their best—which is more than I can say for most of my employees. I have guards that I wouldn't trust to mail an envelope, let alone go on a stakeout."

Eventually, Hoenekker seemed satisfied that he'd learned all he could from us and left to deal with other business. The FunJungle paramedics got Marge onto a stretcher, brought a small truck into the giraffe paddock, and drove her to the hospital. Pete Thwacker and the lawyers bought off the family and the biker couple with offers of ten years' free admission to FunJungle, three complimentary nights at the FunJungle Safari Lodge (redeemable at any time), and vouchers for $500 worth of free food and FunJungle merchandise. Since the giraffes were still skittish after all Marge's howling, the giraffe feeding was closed for the rest of the day; the angry tourists who'd bought tickets for it had their money refunded and were given free limited-edition anniversary souvenir soda cups and Li Ping panda bobbleheads.

Even though the feeding was canceled, the giraffes were still on exhibit, so Summer and I resumed our stakeout. Hoenekker assigned two new guards to help us. (Marge was obviously out of commission, while Kevin went to the locker room to take a nap, as he had to work a late shift that night.) Sadly, the new recruits were proof of Hoenekker's complaint about how incompetent his staff was. They were locals who had failed to graduate high school, and both could barely figure out how to work their radios, let alone help us hunt for criminals. One actually stuck the microphone in his ear and tried to talk to us through the earpiece, while the other somehow accidentally dropped his down his pants.

I finally got around to checking the message Lily Deakin had left for me before all the chaos had started. She said that she and Tommy had learned something important, and that I needed to call her back immediately, but when I did, all I got was her voicemail, so I left a message.

By the time everything was settled enough for me to talk to Summer about why she was upset with me, Violet, Ethan, and Dash showed up. Summer sprang for lunch and they hung out with us on our stakeout for an hour until the heat got to them. The heat was getting to Summer and me too, and things were still weird between us, so Summer suggested we work shifts for the rest of the afternoon. She went off to the Polar Pavilion with the others for an hour, then came back and let me go join them, and we switched on and off like that for the rest of the day, avoiding spending any time with each other on our own.

The hours alone on the stakeout were boring, but the breaks with our friends made the day go much faster. And sadly, given how annoyed at me Summer seemed to still be, it was better to not be forced to sit next to her all afternoon. I spent my time on duty trying to be as vigilant as possible, though I also compulsively checked my texts and email every minute, hoping for word from Lily or Tommy or Hoenekker about either of our investigations.

It wasn't until nearly six o'clock that I finally got a text from Lily: Sorry I didnt get back to u. Crazy day. Can we meet up 2morrow?

I have school tomorrow, I wrote back. Can you update me now?

Cant, she wrote. Ill meet u after school?

I was sure my parents wouldn't want me to agree to this, but I was desperate to know what Lily and Tommy had learned. So I texted back: Ok.

Great, Lily wrote. And then I didn't hear from her again.

When FunJungle closed at eight p.m., I was exhausted. Except for the excitement with Marge, the day had been a bust. I had witnessed plenty of people doing dumb things to the giraffes, like trying to pet them or get them to lick their ice-cream cones, but the giraffes had shrewdly kept their distance and thus, none of the behavior seemed like it could have resulted in poisoning. A startling number of people had dropped things into the paddock by accident. By my tally, there were four phones, twelve pairs of sunglasses, eight baseball caps, and too many park maps to count. Two morons almost dropped their own children while posing them on the railing. However, the Giraffe Staff was apparently used to all this; they convinced the idiots to take their kids off the railing and fished all the dropped items out quickly before the giraffes could get to them.

Summer came along as I was packing up my father's camera. Since I had the last shift, I was surprised to see her.

I thought she might have left the park. "What are you doing here?" I asked.

"My father paid us to stay here all day," she said coldly. "So I stayed all day."

I considered pointing out that her father had paid us to watch the giraffes for the whole time the park was open, not to switch off every hour, but I figured she was irritated enough with me already. I simply zipped up the camera bag and slung the strap over my shoulder.

"We ought to download about what we both saw here today," Summer said, then started down Adventure Road. "Besides that well-dressed couple, did you notice anyone doing anything suspicious?"

I dropped in beside her. "No, but I guess someone might have poisoned the giraffes by mistake. Like, by accidentally dropping something into the paddock."

"We're not looking for accidents." There was a slightly icy tone to Summer's voice, indicating she was still upset with me. "We're looking for a pattern. The giraffes couldn't be getting poisoned every Sunday by people making mistakes."

"Maybe it's the same person. Someone who visits the park every Sunday and accidentally drops something dangerous into the exhibit each time."

Summer gave me a disapproving stare. "That's ridiculous."

Her tone was now starting to get to me. "Do *you* have any better ideas?"

"Yes! It was obviously the well-dressed couple!"

"We can't just assume it was them. We don't have any proof that they poisoned the giraffes. . . ."

"We would have, but you let them get away."

"I did not!" I exclaimed.

"You certainly didn't help try to catch them."

"We weren't *supposed* to help catch them! That was Marge's job!"

"Well, Marge was busy screwing up. And then you turned chicken."

"Hey!" I exploded, getting really upset now. "The last time I went after a criminal here, I got thrown into the polar bear exhibit! I almost got eaten!"

"And I nearly fell into the crocodile pit," Summer shot back. "But I didn't wimp out just now."

"Fine," I said angrily. "You want to play this game? Here's what has happened to *me* on investigations here: In addition to nearly being eaten by the polar bear, I've almost been trampled by Cape buffalo, elephants, and every antelope in SafariLand. I've been chased by a rhino. I nearly drowned in the shark tank. I got held at gunpoint by a man in a panda costume. Someone freed the black mamba when I was by its exhibit. And I was nearly squashed by a plummeting dead hippo. So I think that maybe I've earned the right to be a little cautious where bad guys are concerned!"

Summer stared at me a bit. She seemed to be aware I had a good point, but not ready to admit it. Finally, she said, "I wasn't asking you to do anything dangerous. I just wanted to follow those people before they got away. And guess what? They got away."

"Nobody has ever *thought* they were asking me to do anything dangerous," I reminded her. "But I've ended up in plenty of danger anyhow."

Summer didn't have a response to that. She just kept on walking.

It occurred to me that we were heading in the opposite direction of the front gates—or the administration building, where J.J.'s office was. "Shouldn't we be going the other way?" I asked. "Isn't your dad waiting for you?"

"Probably," Summer replied. "But there's someone I want to talk to first."

"Who?" I asked.

"Her." Summer pointed down Adventure Road, toward Carnivore Canyon. A woman in the standard FunJungle keeper's uniform—khaki shirt, shorts, and boots—was leaving the exhibit. Even in the fading light, I could see she had freckles and red hair like her sons, Grayson and Jason. "That's Natasha Mason, right?"

"Right. How'd you know . . . ?"

". . . what she looks like? There's a database of all the keepers online. I looked her up last night."

"Is she expecting to talk to you?"

"Nope. This is an ambush." Summer waved and yelled, "Mrs. Mason! Do you have a few minutes?"

Natasha turned toward us, startled to hear her name, but then smiled upon recognizing me. "Hi, Teddy! I heard you ran into my boys yesterday."

"I did," I said, then started to introduce Summer. "This is—"

"I know exactly who you are," Natasha told Summer. "It's very nice to meet you. I hear you were at our neighbor's yesterday too." The way she said "neighbor" made it very clear she didn't like Lincoln Stone one bit.

"That's right," Summer said. "We were hoping we could ask you some questions about what happened last Friday night."

"I'm trying to get home before my boys go to bed. But if you don't mind walking to my car with me, we could talk on the way." Natasha didn't give us a chance to answer. She just started down Adventure Road toward the employee parking lot.

So Summer and I walked beside her.

"Did you see or hear anything strange at Lincoln Stone's house on Friday night?" Summer asked.

"You mean the night the cougar supposedly ate King?"

"You don't think that's what happened?" I asked.

"Do *you*?" Natasha returned.

"Our friend at the Department of Fish and Wildlife doesn't think so," Summer replied. "Why don't you?"

"Because I don't think the cougar was anywhere near our place that night," Natasha said. "I know she's been around, of course. I've seen her tracks and found scat. But I haven't seen anything fresh in at least two weeks."

"That doesn't prove she wasn't nearby," I pointed out.

"True," Natasha conceded. Then she looked around furtively to see if anyone was close by. Once she confirmed we were alone, she lowered her voice and said, "I *did* hear something strange Friday night. But it wasn't a cougar."

"What was it, then?" Summer asked. "A coyote?"

"No, it was a man. A bunch of men, really. Friends of Lincoln's, I guess. It sounded like he was having some kind of stag party at his place."

"A party?" I repeated, looking to Summer. "Tommy didn't say anything about Lincoln having a party that night."

"Well, he did," Natasha said. "It wasn't big, but it was still loud. I couldn't hear anything they said specifically, because they were way over on Lincoln's property, but I'm sure there was alcohol involved. They were all drunk and rowdy. And they were firing guns as well."

Summer asked, "You mean, like hunting?"

"No, I think they were just out on that blasted gun range of Lincoln's. Which he doesn't even have a permit for, by the way. The family we're renting from told me."

Summer looked to me, intrigued. "I'll bet Lincoln didn't even tell Fish and Wildlife about all this."

We reached the rear employee exit, which led to the employee parking lot. Passing through it was the complete opposite direction that Summer needed to go, but she was too interested in what Natasha was saying. We followed her through the gate.

"Do you think one of Lincoln's friends shot King?" Summer asked.

"It's possible," Natasha answered. "When people with guns drink, bad things happen. I can't say what really happened to King, but I'll tell you what *didn't* happen. No mountain lion would have come anywhere near a bunch of loud, drunken men shooting off guns. Mountain lions don't like humans, they don't like noise, and they're probably savvy enough to know that guns mean trouble."

Once we exited the park, the construction site for the Wilds was to our right, the path that led to Lakeside Estates was straight ahead, and the employee parking lot was to our left. Even at that hour, the parking lot was still quite full and the heat of the day was radiating off it. I figured we'd get to Natasha's car soon, so I hurried to get to the next question while we still had time. "Your sons indicated that Lincoln wasn't very nice to his dog?"

"He certainly yelled at King a lot. I can't say if he abused the poor thing or not, but I'd say he definitely wasn't a good owner."

"Why not?" I asked.

"Lincoln left that dog outside all the time," Natasha explained. "And that crummy barbed-wire fence wouldn't hold him. We found King sniffing around our place a couple times, but Lincoln just kept letting him run free."

"In the woods?" Summer asked, horrified. "King was a bichon frise! Wouldn't the woods be dangerous for a little dog like that?"

"Definitely," Natasha agreed. "And Lincoln knew that cougar was around. He was always complaining about it. Plus, there are coyotes in the area too. And rattlesnakes and cottonmouths and copperheads, for that matter. So if Lincoln really cared about King like he says, why didn't he keep that dog locked up safe inside?"

We arrived at an old, banged-up minivan that looked like it hadn't ever been washed. Natasha fished her keys out of her bag.

"One last question," Summer said. "Have you told any-one else about any of this?"

"No." Natasha unlocked the van and climbed into the front seat. "I thought maybe some investigator would come by, but no one did. And I simply haven't had the time to track down the right people. Speaking of which . . ." Natasha glanced at her watch. "I really have to go."

"Thanks for your time," I said.

"Sure thing." Natasha started to close the van door, then thought better of it and said, "By the way, you didn't hear any of this from me. Lincoln Stone is already a pain in my rear as it is. The last thing I need is for him to hear I've been talking about him behind his back."

"Understood," Summer said.

Natasha shut the door, backed out of the parking space, and drove out of the lot.

Summer and I started back toward the employee gate.

"Man," she said. "Lincoln Stone's even worse than I thought. Not only is he a jerk to people. He was a jerk to his dog, too." There was no longer an icy tone to her voice. It seemed that, in the excitement of learning this new informa-tion, she had forgotten all about being angry at me.

"Assuming Mrs. Mason is telling the truth," I said.

"Why would she lie to us?"

"To protect herself."

Summer gaped at me. "There is no way that woman framed a mountain lion for killing King. She works with carnivores! She doesn't want anyone to hunt them! If anything, she likes that lion a million times more than Lincoln Stone."

I thought about that a moment, then conceded, "I guess so."

"Plus, we *know* she wasn't lying about how Lincoln Stone treated that dog. Because it was definitely killed outside his house. Even if a mountain lion *did* eat it, it only happened because he was letting his little bichon frise run around unattended. At night. In the woods. When he knew there was a mountain lion around. He might as well have put that dog on a plate and covered it in barbecue sauce."

"But the cat didn't do it. . . ."

"No. Someone else did. But if they hadn't, it was probably only a matter of time until that dog got eaten." Summer's phone buzzed with a text message, and she pulled it out of her pocket to check it. "It's from my father! He has news about the giraffes."

"What's he say?" I asked.

"He wants me to call him. Unfortunately, the coverage out here's garbage."

"No kidding."

We were almost to the employee gate, skirting along the chain-link fence of the construction site.

A loud pop echoed through the Wilds. Then there was another.

Summer turned to me, her eyes wide with worry, which was exactly what I was feeling. "Those were gunshots!" she exclaimed.

We pressed up against the fence, peering into the construction site. Sunday was the one day of the week J.J. McCracken didn't have the construction teams working late, so for once, the site was eerily devoid of noise and activity, save for the Raging Raft Ride in the distance, where a test of the water flow was underway. Water was churning through the chutes into the big, fake lake.

Something darted past the lake. It was only a silhouette against the shimmering background, but I could tell it had four legs, it was rather large, and it was moving fast.

The mountain lion.

Another gunshot rang out. This time, I saw the muzzle flash, up at the top of the Raging Raft Ride.

Someone was hunting the lion inside the park.

The next thing I knew, Summer was scrambling over the chain-link fence. "Come on!" she yelled. "We have to stop this!"

I knew that going with her was potentially dangerous, but at the moment, the lion was the one whose life was hanging in the balance. Plus, I really didn't want Summer to think I had chickened out twice in one day. If Rocket ended up dead, she would never forgive me.

So before I could think things through, I followed her over the fence and into the construction site.

THE WILDS

The construction site was difficult to run across at night because there were obstacles everywhere: piles of construction supplies, giant spools of cable, heaps of dirt and sand. Most dangerous of all were the deep trenches dug into the earth. They were for water mains and sewers and electrical wiring, and there was a staggering amount of them. In the darkness, they were almost impossible to see until we had nearly fallen into them.

I was yelling at the top of my lungs, trying to scare off both the hunter and the lion. I doubted either could hear me over the roar of the rapids, but I figured it couldn't hurt to try. It didn't seem to matter what I yelled, really, so I was mostly shouting, "Hey!"

Meanwhile, Summer speed-dialed park security on her

phone. "This is Summer McCracken!" she said to the dispatcher. "There is a hunter firing a gun in the Wilds right now! Tell Hoenekker and everyone else on duty to get out here now!"

She hung up, then suddenly paused beside a dormant bulldozer.

"Are you going to drive that thing?" I asked.

"I wish. But I'll bet there's no keys." Summer scrambled up onto the treads, opened the door, and grabbed what she had noticed slung over the driver's seat: two Day-Glo orange construction vests. She tossed one down to me. "Might as well put these on. So the hunter doesn't shoot us by mistake." She slipped hers on, then leaped back down and started running again.

I raced after her, pulling my vest on as well. Even though it was flimsy, it glimmered in the moonlight, making us stand out, which made me feel a tiny bit safer.

I realized I was far more worried about being hurt by the hunter than the lion.

I had done some research on mountain lions the night before. While there had been cases of them attacking humans, those were extremely rare—especially when you considered that millions of people lived surprisingly close to mountain lions. Several of the largest cities in America were located in mountain lion territory, including Houston, Dallas, San

Antonio, and Denver. Los Angeles, the second-biggest city in the country, had at least twelve lions living in the mountains around it. A lion had even lived smack in the middle of LA in Griffith Park for years without a single attack; few people had even seen it, even though thousands of people hiked in the park every day. So I wasn't expecting Rocket to attack us.

Plus, Rocket was already on the run, heading away from us. It didn't seem likely to me that she would double back our way. I was hoping she had kept on running in the direction we had seen her going, jumping the fence and continuing on into the woods, moving far away from the hunter.

As for the hunter, I hadn't seen any sign of him since the last muzzle flash from his gun. It made sense that he might have remained at the top of the Raging Raft Ride, as that offered the best view of the construction site, but then again, he might have come down to chase after the lion. Or maybe he had heard me yelling and fled the park. Still, Summer and I raced on toward the Raging Raft Ride, hoping to scare him off or at least determine where he was so we could point him out when FunJungle Security arrived.

Summer suddenly froze in front of me, so fast I almost ran into her.

"What's wrong?" I asked.

"That smell." She sniffed the air and wrinkled her nose. "It's awful. What is that, a kill?"

I inhaled. There was a distinctly putrid scent blowing toward us, and for a moment, I thought she might be right; Rocket might have killed an animal close by, possibly even one of the exotics in SafariLand.

But then I noticed which way the wind was coming from and realized what the scent was. "It's not a kill. It's the FWAP."

"Ohhh." Summer nodded understanding, then started running again.

FWAP—the FunJungle Waste Appropriation Plant—was the facility that handled the incredible amount of poop at the park. The thousands of animals at FunJungle generated several tons of it every day—the elephants alone could produce up to 300 pounds each—and it couldn't simply be left where it was. Obviously, it was unsightly and smelly, but more importantly, there was simply too much of it to break down and return to nature the way it did in the wild. Even in the vast space of SafariLand, all the poop couldn't be left where it dropped. FunJungle had actually experimented with leaving it in place, back before the park was officially open, but within a few days the stench was unbearable.

So FunJungle, like all zoos, needed a treatment facility. During the day, all the poop was collected from the exhibits and discreetly moved to the plant, which would then combine the poop with other recyclable waste from the park to create high-grade compost, which was then sold to local farmers. The compost was extremely cheap, but since the ingredients for it were all being generated for free, it barely cost anything to make in the first place, and thus, J.J. McCracken turned a tidy profit.

Unfortunately, J.J. had made one serious mistake with the location of FWAP. At first, putting it on the most distant side of the park had made plenty of sense. After all, no tourist wanted to see it—or smell it. But now that J.J. had decided to expand FunJungle with the Wilds, FWAP sat within sight of several of the rides. And, as we had just discovered, when the wind shifted, it was also within smelling distance. So FunJungle was in the process of building a new waste treatment facility, FWAP 2.0, but it wouldn't be completed for another few weeks.

"I think I see the hunter!" Summer announced, pointing as she ran.

We were closing in on the Raging Raft Ride, near enough that it loomed against the dark sky and the sound of the churning water was now significantly louder. At the very top of the "mountain" was a craggy peak of fake stone. I could make out the silhouette of a man standing on it, the long shaft of a rifle gleaming in the moonlight by his side.

"Hey!" I yelled again, as loud as I could.

The hunter didn't flinch. He probably hadn't heard me over the roar of the rapids.

"Where the heck is security?" Summer asked angrily. "*Someone* should have been here by now."

I glanced at my watch as I ran. It had only been a few minutes since Summer had called the dispatcher, but at least one security guard should have been stationed close to the Wilds, if not inside the construction site itself. J.J. had recently told me he was concerned about thieves looting his construction supplies—as well as radical environmental groups angry about the expansion of the park who might vandalize the rides to slow their construction. Plus, after the night before, it shouldn't have been a surprise that there would be hunters around. I would have expected J.J. to have *more* guards than usual.

We were almost at the Raging Raft Ride, but now a new obstacle appeared in our path. Thousands of black plastic tubes were arrayed in long racks, angled into the air. The tubes were all four feet long, but ranged in diameter from three to six inches. The racks themselves were thirty feet long and bolted to the ground. It looked like some sort of medieval barricade.

"What the heck is that?" I asked.

"They're for the fireworks!" Summer exclaimed, starting to thread her way through the racks.

"What fireworks?" I asked, following her.

"Daddy wants to have a big show for FunJungle's anniversary party."

"Really? I never heard about any fireworks."

"They're supposed to be a surprise."

"Oh." I wondered if that was the truth. I was sure Summer *thought* it was—she was probably only repeating what J.J. had told her—but J.J. might have lied to his own daughter about this. According to my parents, J.J. had originally wanted fireworks at FunJungle every single night, but many of the animal specialists, including my mother, had argued that long series of loud explosions would distress the animals. So it made sense that, if J.J. wanted fireworks for his party, he would arrange for them covertly. Out in the Wilds, the launching tubes weren't hidden, but they blended in with all the construction, so it was possible none of the keepers had noticed them yet. My mother certainly hadn't; if she had, she would have been livid.

Summer and I wound through the fireworks racks and finally arrived at the Raging Raft Ride. The ride was similar to that of many theme parks, where guests would go down a fake river in large, round rafts that held eight passengers. The basic idea was to provide some thrills and soak the riders—which would provide welcome relief during the long, hot Texas summers. At the edge of a fake lake, there was a loading area that was designed to look like a backcountry ranger station, beyond which the rafts would be hauled to the top of the mountain on a giant conveyor belt. Once there, they would careen through a series of manmade waves, whirlpools, and chutes until they reached the grand finale: a three-story slide down LoseYerLunch Falls into a standing wave designed to drench everyone.

To make the ride more appropriate for a zoo, there was a vague ecological theme to it. Full-size animatronic models of American animals like beavers, wolves, bobcats, moose, and grizzly bears were hidden in facsimiles of their natural habitats along the river. (J.J. had toyed with the idea of having *real* animals in exhibits along the ride, but all of his biologists had resoundingly vetoed the idea.) The models were designed to *look* as real as possible, though, so that young children—and maybe even gullible adults—would think they had really spotted a wild animal.

Meanwhile, there were also nods to landmarks in many national parks along the way: a smaller version of Half Dome from Yosemite, the weathered hoodoos of Bryce Canyon, the delicate rock bridges of Arches, and a tunnel through the trunk of a giant fallen tree like the ones in Sequoia. At the base of LoseYerLunch Falls, right before the rafts reached the exit dock, an enormous, Old Faithful–like geyser would erupt, soaking all the riders—again.

Tourists weren't supposed to ever walk on the mountain, but there had to be access for maintenance workers, so a path ran along the course of the "river." In keeping with the theme, it was designed to look like a rustic mountain hiking trail, complete with wooden direction markers and rock cairns. Summer led the way to it and I stayed right on her heels.

The trail quickly rose five stories up a series of fake stone steps alongside the giant conveyor belt. After our sprint through the construction site, I was wearing out, and the stairs left me gasping for breath by the time I reached the top. Summer didn't seem nearly as tired. If anything, she seemed a bit annoyed at me for slowing down. "Come on!" she implored me, then raced ahead, disappearing behind a hoodoo.

"Summer!" I yelled. "Wait for me!"

She didn't respond. So I tried to ignore the pain in my side and soldiered on after her.

Now that we were atop the fake mountain, it was evident that much more had to be done until the ride was completed. The entire back side of the mountain was unfinished; it was only a skeleton of iron beams. In several spots, there was a sheer drop down five stories and the railings hadn't been installed yet; there were only a few loose ropes to prevent us from tumbling off the path. Most of the decorating had yet to be done. The rocks weren't painted; the fake trees weren't installed; woodland creatures were strewn haphazardly all around. I quickly discovered that there are few things as disconcerting as rounding a corner in the dark to find yourself facing a pile of badgers.

The river itself was operating perfectly, though. Water gushed through the chutes at thousands of gallons a minute, creating waves and eddies and sending great sprays of mist into the air. There were moments when it felt like I was racing through an actual mountain gorge, rather than a fake one. At many spots, water had sloshed out of the chute, making the surface of the path wet and slippery, so I had to watch my step to make sure I didn't slip and go flying over the edge.

And yet, I didn't slow down. Summer was still ahead of me somewhere, on her way to face a hunter in the darkness, and I didn't want her to do that alone.

"Summer!" I yelled into the night, trying to be louder than the rapids. "Where are you?"

Again, there was no response.

I was almost at the craggy peak where we had seen the hunter. To reach it, the trail crossed over a steep, narrow gorge through which the ride churned below. At some point in the future, there was probably going to be a bridge over it, most likely designed to look like one that you might see in the wilderness, with ropes and wooden slats, but at the moment, it hadn't been built. Instead, there were only a few long wooden boards laid across the gorge, with a spindly wooden railing built on one side. Although the water was twenty feet below, the spray had made the boards wet, so crossing them looked to be treacherous.

Still, I grabbed the railing and set across. The boards jounced worryingly and the railing trembled in my grasp. Even though the gorge below my feet was manmade, it was still deep enough to make my heart pound. Except for the peak ahead of me, the makeshift bridge was the highest point for miles. I could see all of the construction site around me and the great dark swath of wilderness directly beyond it, dotted only with the occasional light of someone's home in the surrounding hills. Lakeside Estates was merely a smattering of lights in the woods down far below.

At the edge of the fake lake, two pairs of headlights sliced through the night. The vehicles were big and blocky: the Land Rovers that FunJungle staff used to get around. Security had finally arrived.

The boards groaned and shuddered beneath my feet, reminding me to focus on the task at hand. I gripped the wobbly railing tighter and took the last few steps to the opposite side of the gorge.

A lot of water had collected there, creating a puddle that soaked my shoes, but at least I was on solid ground again.

I heard the sound of scuffling from the darkness nearby. Someone—or some*thing*—was coming around the craggy peak, not following the official trail. I spun that way to look for it . . .

And found myself staring directly into the eyes of a mountain lion. It was crouched in the shadows, ready to pounce, its mouth open in midsnarl, revealing its fangs.

I recoiled in fear and stumbled over the boards that formed the bridge behind me. My shoes slipped in the puddle, my feet shot out from under me, and I pitched backward. I grabbed the railing to steady myself, but it tore free under my weight.

Somehow, in the midst of that terrifying moment, I caught another glimpse of the mountain lion and realized it was only a model. Sooner or later, it would be moved into position where the riders could see it, but for now, it had been abandoned in the shadows.

But that revelation came too late. I was already falling into the gorge.

THE RAPIDS

As I fell backward off the rock, I spotted some-thing else in the shadows beyond the lion. A human form, quickly circling the craggy peak, coming my way.

And then it was gone, replaced by a blur of images as I tumbled downward: rock and mist and sky and rock again.

I plunged into the water. It was bracingly cold and moving fast. My feet glanced off the bottom of the gorge, and then the current caught me and whisked me downriver.

I had once fallen out of a raft while with my father on the Zambezi River below Victoria Falls. That had been frightening, but the fake river was moving even faster than the Zambezi did because it was specifically designed for speed. This was very different from the other times I had found myself in trouble in the water at FunJungle. On those occasions, the water had been still, so I simply had to remain calm and swim for the surface—although I had sometimes needed to fend off sharks or polar bears while doing it. Now I was at the mercy of the water itself. I was sucked downward, dragged along, bounced off the walls of the fake gorge, and flipped head over heels. I was desperate for air, but in the darkness, it was hard to even tell which way was up.

Finally, I broke through the surface, managed a desperate breath, and then got yanked right back down again.

Something plunged into the river behind me. I didn't see it. I only felt and heard the impact in the water, and then the bottom seemed to drop out from under me.

I had come to a slide. It was smaller than LoseYerLunch Falls, but the idea was the same: The raft would career down this part quickly and crash into a standing wave at the bottom. The water here was shallow in order to make the slide work better—only a few inches deep—so I was able to breathe again as I skimmed downward. Unfortunately, I had hit the slide while moving backward, so I plunged down it headfirst.

On the Zambezi trip, my father had told me what to do in case I fell into the river, and I figured the same rules made sense here: I needed to get my feet in front of me, so they were leading the way downriver. That way, if I slammed into any obstacles, my feet would take the brunt of the impact. (On the Zambezi, there were also crocodiles, and you wanted to hit them feetfirst too, so you could kick them in the snout, rather than having them bite your head off. Thankfully, that bit of advice wasn't necessary here.)

I dug my left elbow into the slope as hard as I could. The concrete base of the slide scraped my skin, but the maneuver worked decently well. I quickly spun around so that my feet were in front of me, then took a deep, gasping breath as I plunged through the standing wave.

It was surprising how hard water could be. Hitting the wave was like running into a wall. It knocked me flat against the bottom of the chute. But now I had my bearings and I was turned in the right direction. Even in the dark and the tumult of the rapids, I could use my arms and legs to keep myself oriented so I was facing downriver. It was hard work, and I was already tired from my run through the construction site, but adrenaline was coursing through me, giving me the strength to carry on.

I shot through a fast-moving patch of rapids, my feet caroming off a few fake boulders that might have split my skull if I'd hit them headfirst, then whipped through a large whirlpool and fired down a narrow slot canyon.

At one point, I caught sight of three fake moose perched on the edge of the river above me, implacably watching my journey with their glassy eyes.

There was a tremendous rumble ahead of me. I figured it had to be the final falls, but it sounded like every wildebeest in the Serengeti stampeding at once. The entire river seemed to vibrate around me.

I hurtled around a corner and was plunged into darkness. It took me a moment to realize I was passing through a tunnel. The water slowed here, creating a calm before the final storm of LoseYerLunch. Manmade stalactites jutted down from the ceiling while fake bats wheeled about them on hidden wires. Ahead of me, a curtain of water rained down over the tunnel's exit.

Rafters on the Raging Raft Ride didn't start at the very top of LoseYerLunch Falls. Instead, you came *through* the falls, emerging from the tunnel and getting drenched before sliding down the chute. If I had been in a raft, it probably would have been really fun. But now, on my own, without the protection of any sort of vehicle, the approaching drop was terrifying.

I tried digging my feet and hands into the bottom of the chute to stop myself, but the water was moving too fast and I couldn't gain purchase. The exit was coming up quickly. So I took a final deep breath, wrapped my arms tightly around me, and pointed my feet straight ahead.

The water pounded me as I punched through the falls, and then I was racing downhill. The standing wave at the bottom of the falls was significantly larger than the one I had hit before. I closed my eyes tightly and braced for impact.

This wave hit me much harder than the first one had. Guests in the inflatable rafts would have crashed through it and bounded along the surface, but an undertow yanked me downward instead. The bottom of the fake lake was concrete, rather than mud, and I rolled along it for a few feet before the water calmed enough for me to try surfacing. I kicked off the bottom.

But my foot caught on something. Underwater metal fences flanked me on both sides. They were there to make sure that the rafts followed the proper course back to the exit dock, instead of floating aimlessly across the lake. However, they hadn't been designed with swimmers in mind. My shoe got snagged in the gap between the fence and the bottom of the lake, keeping me from surfacing. Only the top of my head broke through the water, and then the current shoved me down again. With my foot caught, I was forced face-first against the concrete. I kept trying to wrench myself free, but the current was too strong and now the lack of oxygen was making my strength ebb as well. My lungs burned and my vision blurred as I strained against the current.

And then, suddenly, someone grabbed my foot. I felt them tug it out of my shoe, and then their arms circled my body and heaved me upward.

I burst through the surface, sucking in air. Relief and exhaustion washed over me at once.

"Whoa!" a deep voice shouted right behind my ear. "That was quite a ride, wasn't it?"

I twisted around to see the face of the man who had saved me. He was a medium-size, muscular guy with a thick beard, dressed in camouflage gear. The hunter.

I figured he was the person I'd seen running toward the gorge as I fell in, as well as the object that had plummeted into the water. He'd jumped in to save me.

He didn't seem the slightest bit worried about having been caught hunting on the FunJungle property, or upset by the ordeal we'd been through. Instead, he was thrilled, cruising on an adrenaline high. Even though I was safe now, and the flow through the lake was gentle, he kept his arms cinched around my body, holding me up.

"You can let go of me now," I said. "I'm okay."

"Hold on a scooch. There's one more surprise in store."

It struck me that the hunter seemed to know an awful lot about this ride, but before I could give it any thought, Old Faithful went off right beside us. A huge column of water exploded out of the lake, shooting fifty feet into the sky. It vented upward for a few seconds, then shut off as abruptly as it had started. The water that had shot out continued raining down on us for a while afterward, though.

Now we floated gently toward the exit dock.

"All righty," the hunter said cheerfully. "That ought to do it. You sure you're all right?"

"Yeah," I said, then thought to add, "Thanks."

"No worries." The hunter let go of me, but subtly kept his hand on my arm as we floated along. "It was probably my fault you ended up in the drink in the first place. I mean, you wouldn't have been up there at all if it wasn't for me, right?"

"Right." I was thrown by the hunter's cavalier attitude. It was one thing to be unfazed—and even a little thrilled—by coursing down the rapids after me. But for a man who had just been breaking the law, he didn't seem concerned at all.

The exit dock was now only twenty feet ahead of us. The FunJungle security guards I had seen arriving earlier had parked their Land Rovers at the end of it and were racing to help us. I couldn't recognize three of them in the darkness—it was possible I didn't even know them—although I could make out the sturdy form of Chief Hoenekker.

The hunter didn't try to get away, or to even make excuses. I figured that maybe this was because there wasn't really any point: His only option for escape was to swim, but security would have easily captured him anyhow. And yet, he still remained chipper and laid-back, even going so far as to wave hello to the guards.

"Hey, guys!" he said cheerfully. Then, to me, he said, "By the way, I'm Jerry."

"Teddy," I responded. "Did you see anyone else up there . . . ?"

"Your friend, you mean? Oh yeah. She scared the bejeezus out of me, coming out of the dark all of a sudden, screaming like a banshee. I almost dropped my dang rifle off the mountain. There she is now."

Jerry pointed to the far side of the giant conveyor belt. I could see Summer bounding down the steps we had gone up only a few minutes before, racing to see if I was all right.

I waved to her to indicate that I was fine, but from that distance, I doubted she could see me. She still had a good ways to go to circle around the loading area and get to the exit dock.

Jerry and I were now at the exit dock ourselves. The current gently butted us up against it.

Hoenekker and the security guards were now waiting for us on the dock. A few other people joined them. They were wearing shorts and collared shirts and had temporary Fun-Jungle IDs on lanyards around their necks. Two had tablet computers and one held a clipboard. I guessed they were part of the design team for the Raging Raft Ride, the ones who had been conducting the tests to see how the water was moving. A middle-aged woman looked to be in charge. She seemed uncertain whether she ought to be relieved that I had survived or angry at me for falling into the ride. Finally, anger won out.

"What the heck were you doing up there?" she demanded. "This is a restricted area!"

"Hey!" Jerry snapped at her, the first time he'd seemed even the tiniest bit upset. "Go easy on the kid, will you? He's been through a lot."

The woman immediately clammed up, looking embarrassed.

The security guards knelt down on the exit dock, extending their hands to us. I grabbed onto one and he easily hauled me up onto the dock.

Hoenekker helped Jerry out. Jerry hopped up onto the dock, dripping water all over the place, and actually smiled at him. "Thanks, Chief."

"Thanks for saving the boy, Jerry," Hoenekker said in kind.

I suddenly felt weak in the knees, and for reasons that had nothing to do with my most recent near-death experience. I understood now why Jerry wasn't worried about Fun-Jungle Security, why he knew Hoenekker, and why he had seemed so calm about trespassing on the property.

He *wasn't* trespassing. The man who'd been shooting at Rocket worked for FunJungle.

ACCUSATIONS

"J.J. obviously wants the lion dead," Xavier Gonzalez said. "There's no other explanation."

We were walking through the halls at school the next morning, heading from science to algebra. Before school had started, I had filled Xavier in on everything that had happened with Rocket, as Xavier was my best friend and a Fun-Jungle fanatic. (Xavier wore almost nothing but FunJungle T-shirts; today's featured a cartoon cheetah and the corny slogan "FunJungle is really Fast-cinating!") Our conversation had been cut short by the start of our class, but Xavier didn't waste a second after the ending bell to start it up again, racing to my side as I walked out of the room.

"There *are* other explanations," I argued.

"Like what?"

"Maybe J.J. only wants to scare the lion off."

That was what Jerry had told me he was doing, but I hadn't been able to ask him any questions about it. Chief Hoenekker didn't want Summer to know the hunter was working for FunJungle at all. "It'd be wise if you didn't share this with her," he'd warned me the night before, while Summer was still running down the mountain to meet us.

"I'm not going to lie to her," I had protested.

"I'm not asking you to lie," he'd said. "Just don't tell her the whole truth. It would be in everyone's best interests." Before I could press the issue any further, he had hustled Jerry into his Land Rover and driven him away. By the time Summer had made it down to the exit dock, they had already been long gone, leaving her with the mistaken impression that Jerry had been arrested.

I had let her believe that, even though I didn't want to. While Hoenekker hadn't said as much, I figured that the orders for secrecy were coming from J.J. McCracken himself.

However, Hoenekker hadn't said I couldn't tell anyone else about Jerry's association with FunJungle, so I had told Xavier. Now, as we wound our way through the crowded halls, my friend said, "They're not trying to scare off the lion. The guy had a gun!"

"Gunshots would scare a lion away."

"So would lots of other things. There's plenty of ways

to make a loud noise without a gun. If someone has a gun, they're trying to *kill* something, pure and simple."

"Maybe the hunter was shooting at Rocket with something else, like rubber bullets."

Xavier stopped at his locker and fixed me with a hard stare. "Why are you defending J.J. McCracken?"

"I'm not defending him. I'm trying to understand what's going on here."

"Face it, you're defending him." Xavier opened his locker. The interior was plastered with photos of wild animals that Xavier had clipped from *National Geographic* magazines. "If all J.J. was doing was trying to scare the lion off, he wouldn't care if Summer knew he'd hired a hunter, right?"

"I don't know." I leaned against the lockers, scanning the halls, making sure that Summer wasn't anywhere within eavesdropping range. "Maybe J.J. thought she'd get upset about seeing anyone with a gun in the park at all." I stood up straight as a thought occured to me. "Besides, we don't even know if the order for secrecy came from J.J. Maybe Hoenekker was the one who hired Jerry, and he doesn't want J.J. to find out. That's why he asked me to keep it secret from Summer."

Xavier considered that while swapping his science book for his math one. "Why would Hoenekker hire a hunter without telling J.J. about it?"

"Hoenekker doesn't have to tell J.J. everything he does.

And he's in charge of security. What could be a bigger threat to the animals at the park than a predator trying to eat them?"

"Good point." Xavier shut his locker and turned to me. "But I still think J.J.'s behind it. Because of the giraffes."

"The giraffes?" I repeated, starting down the hall with Xavier again. "What are you talking about?"

"I'll bet you a million dollars J.J. only hired you to investigate them to distract you from the mountain lion business."

"Are you feeling okay?" I asked. "Because you *sound* completely insane."

"Think about it. The giraffes have been getting sick for weeks. If J.J. was really worried about them, why didn't he come to you before now?"

"He already had his security people working on it. But they failed."

"Even so, he didn't reach out to you until *after* Lily Deakin asked you to help with the mountain lion."

"That's not true. When he invited me to dinner on Saturday night, he had no idea Summer and I had been talking to Lily."

"Oh, I'm sure he did. J.J. always knows what Summer is up to."

"How? She hasn't had a bodyguard in months."

"He doesn't need a bodyguard to keep tabs on her. Did she have her phone with her?"

"Of course."

"Then he could track her on it."

"J.J. has better things to do than tracking his daughter twenty-four hours a day."

"He doesn't have to be doing it actively. There are all sorts of alerts he could set up. Like if she goes out of a certain range, or heads someplace she's never been before, he could get alerted to her movements."

I thought about that. It *did* sound like something J.J. might do. "I suppose."

Xavier asked, "Did Summer take any photos while you were out at Lincoln Stone's place?"

"Yes. She took a bunch of his house. It's hideous."

"Well, there you go. If she posted those to social media while you were there, and J.J. follows her—which I'm sure he does—then he'd know where you were. And the only reason you'd be out at Lincoln Stone's place would be investigating that crime, right?"

"I guess. Though I don't know for sure that she posted anything. . . ."

"Technically, she wouldn't even have to. Any photo Summer takes goes into her cloud account. I guarantee you J.J. has access to it. If a whole lot of crime scene photos started popping up, he'd realize what was going on."

I mulled all that over as we passed the library. The more I

thought about Xavier's arguments, the less crazy they seemed. Summer had definitely taken pictures of the tape outline at the crime scene, as well as Lincoln Stone's horrible house. Less than thirty minutes later, J.J. had invited me to dinner.

"Okay," I conceded, "let's say that J.J. *did* ask us to investigate the giraffes in order to keep us from investigating the lion. If J.J. is really the one hunting Rocket, how does that connect to Lincoln Stone and King?"

"Like this: J.J. knows he has a lion loose on his property and he wants to get rid of it. Well, he can't just hire a hunter and kill an endangered animal. He owns FunJungle, for Pete's sake! The PR would be awful if the public found out. But now imagine that the lion is suddenly a nuisance. It killed the beloved dog of a famous person. And that person is the one who fights for the warrant to hunt it. Now J.J. has the right to have it killed, and the public won't be as upset."

"You think that J.J. McCracken killed King?"

"No!" Xavier exclaimed. "Well, not personally. I'm sure J.J. has lots of shady people on his payroll who would kill a dog for him."

"Um . . . I'm not sure that's true."

"Look, I'm not saying that J.J. knew Lincoln would go on this whole crazy tirade and put a bounty on the lion's head. But if you really think that *someone* killed King and framed the cat for it, who would benefit more than J.J.? The lion's a bigger threat to him than it is to anyone else. It's creeping around *his* zoo at night. Maybe it's been doing this for weeks and we're only finding out now. How long before it kills some exotic animal? Or a tourist? From what you've told me, J.J. couldn't get a permit to kill it until something died. Or got threatened, at least. But if Rocket killed someone else's animal, and the permit is issued, then it's open season. Anyone can take out the cat."

"Maybe. Though it's still not guaranteed that the government will issue the permit at all."

"I bet they will. You said Tommy Lopez's boss didn't even want him investigating this. That his boss was more concerned about politics than her job. Well, who's the most influential person in this area? Not Lincoln Stone. It's J.J. McCracken. If that guy wants the government to do something, the government does it."

"Then why wouldn't he just press the government to let him kill Rocket in the first place?"

"Because then he'd look like a jerk. This way, he doesn't—"

"Gonzalez!"

Xavier cringed in response. We both knew who the voice belonged to.

Our vice principal, Mr. Putterman, was storming down the hall toward us. Putterman was stocky and mean, with a neck so thick it looked like his head went straight into his body. As usual, he was wearing boots and a cowboy hat. Putterman was in charge of discipline at Lyndon Baines Johnson Middle School, and he pursued the task with a disturbing relish. His basic philosophy was that every student was guilty of something until proven innocent.

To my horror—and that of my parents as well—corporal punishment was actually legal at our school. Generally, this consisted of "paddling," wherein Putterman would have the offending student bend over his desk (which was known as "assuming the position") and then swat their butt with a wooden paddle. Apparently, paddling had been practiced throughout much of Texas only a few decades before, but enlightenment had come to most of the state. Somehow, it had escaped my school, though. The philosophy among many parents who had also gone to LBJ Middle seemed to be that *they'd* had to deal with it, so their kids should too.

Putterman didn't paddle kids too often; the fear of it was enough to keep almost everyone in line. But it *did* happen, and Putterman was rumored to enjoy it. His paddle was emblazoned with the words BOARD OF DISCIPLINE, and while it usually hung prominently on a hook in Putterman's office, the vice principal also liked to carry it around the halls, brandishing it menacingly while he looked for trouble-makers. Unfortunately, in Putterman's book, *everyone* was a potential troublemaker; he was often so busy terrorizing decent kids that he overlooked the real problem students.

Which was happening right then. Putterman was bearing down on Xavier, aiming his paddle at the poor kid like a massive pointer, completely unaware that Tim and Jim Barksdale were lurking in the hall directly behind him. The Barksdale twins were idiots and bullies who had caused plenty of trouble for Xavier and me—as well as almost everyone else at the school. At the moment, both of them were mocking Putterman, imitating how he walked while they made dopey faces, and yet, Putterman was so focused on Xavier he didn't even notice them.

Putterman stopped in front of Xavier and jabbed him in the chest with the paddle. "Gonzalez, that shirt does not meet the standards of the dress code for this school."

Xavier was so nervous, he couldn't find the words to defend himself. So I stepped in instead. "It's only a T-shirt, Mr. Putterman," I said, trying to sound as respectful as possible. "T-shirts are allowed at school." I pointed around the hall to all the other kids who also happened to be wearing T-shirts. Many of them glared at me angrily, like I had stabbed them in the back.

Putterman wheeled on me. "Was I speaking to you?"

I shrank back in fear. "No, but . . ."

Putterman jabbed Xavier with the paddle again. Even though he was ostensibly pointing at the shirt, he was poking

Xavier hard enough to knock him backward. "That is a *Fun-Jungle* T-shirt. There is a difference between a regular T-shirt and one that merely serves as an advertisement for a company that has no affiliation with this school. Particularly a company that is merely a carnival sideshow for the display of *animals*." He said this last word the way other people might have said "disease" or "excrement."

Putterman had a bizarre hatred for animals. He often remarked that "the only good animal is the one on your plate." Therefore, he hated FunJungle with a passion, and he couldn't understand what anyone would like about it at all. It was rumored that Putterman hated animals so much because he was really afraid of them. The one place all students knew they were safe from him was the science lab; Putterman never entered it, possibly because our science teacher kept three tarantulas, two turtles, and a bearded dragon in there.

Xavier did his best to answer Putterman, stuttering in fear. "S-s-sorry. I d-d-didn't know that rule."

"Well, you should," Putterman snapped. He then held up the student handbook, which he always kept folded in his back pocket, and announced to the entire hall, "All students are required to know all the rules and bylaws of this school! Failure to conform to said rules will be dealt with harshly!"

Behind his back, Tim and Jim Barksdale continued

mocking him, aping his every move. As Putterman held up the handbook, each of them held up a comic book and shook it wildly. Even I thought this was funny. Around the Barksdales, students struggled to hold in their laughter.

Putterman remained oblivious and returned his attention to Xavier. "I'll let you off with a warning this time, because these rules were only recently amended. But I do not want to see you wearing a T-shirt from *that place* again." He jabbed Xavier with his paddle once more, this time so hard that it knocked my poor friend into a bank of lockers. Then Putterman put the paddle over his shoulder and strutted around the corner.

Xavier was a wreck. His brief encounter with Putterman had made him break out in a cold sweat. He looked down at his shirt morosely. "I can't wear FunJungle T-shirts anymore? All I own are FunJungle T-shirts!"

To make things worse, the Barksdales now swept in. They had been following Putterman down the hall, mimicking his strut, but once he was out of sight, they descended on Xavier.

Until recently, the twins had been so similar in looks and intellect that no one could tell them apart, even their own parents. But over the past few weeks, Tim had developed a volcanic case of acne, allowing all of us to know which jerk was which for once.

"Gonzalez!" Tim said, doing a decent imitation of Putterman's drawl. "I don't like that T-shirt one bit! It has a kitty cat on it, and I'm scared of kitty cats!" He pretended to tremble in fear, getting some laughs from the other kids in the hall.

Now Jim tried to do an imitation of Putterman as well, though he wasn't nearly as good at it. Somehow, his attempt to do Putterman's voice sounded Jamaican. "I hate animals! So I hate that shirt! Now take it off!" Suddenly, he wasn't joking around anymore. He had become his usual bullying self.

Xavier gaped at him, worried. "Take my shirt off?"

Tim loomed over him, having grown menacing himself. He clenched his fists. "Yeah, loser. Take it off."

Around us, the other kids had stopped laughing. They now warily watched the entire exchange play out. I glanced down the hall the way Putterman had gone, wondering why the man never seemed to be around when students were truly misbehaving.

To my surprise, Xavier didn't cave. Instead, he screwed up his courage and stood up to the Barksdales. He swallowed hard and said, "No."

The twins looked to each other. They had obviously expected Xavier would simply give in and do what they wanted. Now that he hadn't, they seemed a bit lost. Finally, after a tense few seconds, they dropped the whole idea of threatening Xavier in favor of taunting him.

Jim pointed to Xavier's cheetah T-shirt. "That's a stupid shirt, Gonzalez. Let me guess. You're one of those tree huggers who thinks mountain lions shouldn't be hunted."

"Our entire government thinks they shouldn't be hunted," I reminded them. "They're an endangered species."

"Well, the government's wrong," Jim told me. "Lincoln Stone says they're bloodthirsty and dangerous and we'd be better off without them."

"That's not true!" Xavier exclaimed, so upset that he overcame his usual fear around the Barksdales. "Mountain lions aren't any threat to us at all!"

"Well, this one won't be much longer," Tim said with a snicker. "My family's going to take it down." He mimed blasting away with a rifle.

"That's right!" Jim whooped. "And then we're gonna get Lincoln Stone's reward money and we'll be rich!"

I frowned at the thought of this. I had never met Tim and Jim's parents, but they were rumored to be excellent hunters with a questionable sense of legality, often trespassing on other people's land in search of game. "It's not legal to hunt that lion yet," I reminded them.

"Says you," Tim taunted. Then he flicked me on the ear with his finger for no good reason and sauntered on by.

"Yeah. Says you," Jim repeated. Then he flicked my other ear and followed his brother down the hall.

Xavier and I watched them go. Our fellow students all took care to leave them a wide berth, knowing the Barksdales would happily give a wedgie or knock the books out of the hands of any unfortunate kid who got too close.

"I wonder how many other people like *that* Lincoln Stone's bounty has encouraged," Xavier said.

"Plenty," I replied.

"J.J. probably didn't even need to hire that hunter," Xavier observed. "Thanks to Lincoln, someone else is going to kill that lion for him."

"There's no proof J.J. was behind this," I said.

"Behind what?" Summer asked from beside me.

I turned to her, startled by her sudden appearance. "Trying to protect the mountain lion," I said quickly. "The whole Barksdale family wants to hunt it down."

Summer glared after Tim and Jim angrily. "Of course they do. Thanks to this bounty, every jerk in the state is going to be after Rocket."

Xavier gave me a knowing glance behind Summer's back, amused that Summer didn't know her own father might be one of those jerks.

Summer pulled her gaze from the Barksdales and turned back to me. "Unfortunately, we've got another problem."

"What?" I asked.

"I just heard from Daddy. The giraffes are sick again."

I winced. "So . . . it *was* the formal couple?"

"No, it wasn't. That's what Daddy wanted to tell me last night, before we saw the hunter and Rocket. They were innocent."

"But if it wasn't them, who else could it be? We watched the giraffes all day yesterday and didn't see anything else suspicious."

"I know. But we obviously missed something. Because somehow, they've all been poisoned again."

WAITING FOR LILY

The bell rang before I could ask Summer any-
thing more about the giraffes or why the formal couple was
innocent, and I had math club during lunch, so it wasn't
until the end of the school day that I could get more information from her. I found her sitting in the shade of an oak
tree on the front lawn of the school, waiting for Lily Deakin
to come pick us up. She had her shoes off and was wiggling
her bare toes in the grass while she read an article on her
phone.

Before I could bring up the giraffes, she asked me, "Did
you know that there's a national park in India that people
have illegally built entire villages in?"

"Yeah," I said. "My father went there to take photos of
leopards for *National Geographic*."

"It's horrible," Summer said. "I mean, here's this preserve that's supposed to protect animals, and people just moved right into it—and the government didn't even stop them. The leopards and all the other animals barely have any space in India as it is. But now they have even less."

"Unfortunately, those people don't have any place else to go," I told her. "They're dirt-poor and there's no other available land around there. They have to live *somewhere*."

"So they should take land from the leopards?"

"No, but . . . these issues are complicated. I read all about it in the article my father took the photos for." I sat down on the grass and pulled my own shoes off. "Why are you reading about this?"

"I'm just looking up stuff on human/wildlife conflict. It's not just happening here, with us and Rocket. It's happening everywhere on earth."

"I know," I said. "I saw plenty of it in Africa. Usually, the animals end up on the losing side."

"It's not fair," Summer groused. "The animals were here first. We took their land. And then we get upset at them for trying to survive any way they can."

A ladybug started crawling over my toes. I picked it up and let it wander across my hand. "How did your father know that the formal couple didn't poison the giraffes?" I asked. While I was pleased that Summer was researching human/wildlife conflict, I was desperate for the news on Operation Hammerhead.

"Hoenekker tracked them down and questioned them. It turned out they hadn't been feeding anything to the giraffes. They were doing a wedding announcement."

"A wedding announcement?" I set the ladybug back down on the ground and let it continue on its way.

"Yeah. Like a save-the-date thing for their wedding. They dressed up and then took a selfie in front of the giraffe. They're going to make it into a card and send it out to all their friends."

"Why a giraffe?"

"Because they really like giraffes. And because giraffes are one of the only animals you can get that close to. They said they were going to write some corny giraffe jokes on it like, 'It's not too long until our wedding. Hope to spot you there.' It's kind of cute, really."

"I guess," I said. Thinking about wedding invitations, I recalled my parents two nights before, teasing me about J.J. McCracken being my future father-in-law, which made me feel slightly embarrassed.

Other students were sitting on the lawn, under the tree, waiting for people to pick them up as well. But as usual, they all were treating Summer differently from everyone else. Everyone was trying to act like they weren't paying any attention to Summer, but they *were* paying attention to her. After all, Summer was famous, and no matter how much she tried to act like a normal teenager, she wasn't. So everyone gave her some distance for privacy, but then kept glancing her way, or interrupting their conversations to eavesdrop on ours.

I asked, "If they were only taking a photo with the giraffe, why were they acting so suspicious?"

"They needed a selfie stick to get the photo right."

"Oh," I said, now understanding. As ridiculous as it was, FunJungle had been forced to ban selfie sticks. It was staggering how many different ways tourists had managed to cause trouble with them. They fell over railings while trying to take photos of themselves. They tried to get close-ups of animals, extending the sticks too far into exhibits, at which point the animals would grab their phones (if they were apes or monkeys) or try to eat them (if they were almost anything else). They would accidentally whack other tourists with them; the FunJungle hospital averaged three selfie stick–related injuries a day. And now that the park was planning to open thrill rides, J.J. knew selfie sticks would only cause more trouble. The Disney empire had already banned them, because tourists kept trying to take pictures of themselves on rides and getting the sticks caught in the machinery. So J.J. had pre-emptively declared them illegal before any damage could be done.

"So they were only hiding a selfie stick?" I asked.

"Yes. The woman had it in her purse. When Marge came charging in, the couple thought she was trying to arrest them for using it. So they ran off and dumped the stick in the garbage."

That made me laugh. "If anyone would tackle a tourist for having a selfie stick, it's Marge."

"No kidding. When Daddy first set up the ban, she was frisking guests for them at the front gates. Hoenekker made her stop it."

"Have you heard how she's doing?"

"Not too bad. They put a cast on her broken leg. She'll only be out of commission another day or two."

I thought back to the chaos Marge had caused at the giraffe feeding area. "After Marge fell into the exhibit, I wasn't paying very close attention to the tourists, were you?"

"No, not really."

"So someone could have poisoned the giraffes then, and we might have missed it."

"There were still a lot of people around then. *Someone* would have seen something, don't you think?"

I shrugged. "This has been going on for five weeks and no one's seen anything yet."

"Plus, Daddy says *all* five of the giraffes are sick today. Not just one or two. But at the feeding areas, you only have access to one giraffe at a time. So how did someone manage to poison all of them?"

"Maybe they came back multiple times. Did you notice if anyone visited more than once yesterday? Or maybe asked to feed more than one giraffe?"

"No." Summer absently plucked some blades of grass from the lawn. "But, to be honest, there were lots of times when I wasn't paying close attention yesterday. I mean, I was trying my best, but . . . being on a stakeout wasn't exactly riveting."

"I know." I picked up an acorn and chucked it at the tree in frustration. "But we were there, right? I mean, if someone had been doing something blatantly dangerous, we would have noticed, wouldn't we?"

"Like what?"

"Feeding the giraffes something that was obviously bad for them. Like candy or garbage."

"Maybe not," Summer admitted. "There were a couple times, when I was there by myself, when I might have been distracted for a while."

"Doing what?"

"Texting friends and stuff."

I couldn't control my annoyance. "So someone could

have poisoned the giraffes during your shift and you wouldn't have noticed?"

"It's possible. I mean, I *thought* I was keeping a good eye on things. But maybe I wasn't. Because someone still poisoned the giraffes."

"Great," I said sarcastically, before I could stop myself.

"What's that supposed to mean?"

"Nothing."

"It didn't sound like nothing. It sounds like you're angry at me."

"You got angry at *me* yesterday," I said testily. "After I didn't run after the selfie-stick people with you. You acted like I'd made a huge mistake and let the bad guys escape. But then you didn't even do the job we were supposed to do in the first place!"

"I *tried*," Summer protested. "But it was boring. You're telling me you never looked at your phone the whole time you were on duty?"

"No."

Summer took off her sunglasses. "Honestly? Look into my eyes and swear you never got distracted."

I met her gaze and said, "I never got distracted."

Only, that wasn't the truth. I *had* been distracted by my phone at times. I had checked my emails and answered some texts and played a few games. But I had never taken my eyes off the giraffes for more than thirty seconds. At least, I was pretty sure that was the case.

I immediately felt terrible about lying to Summer. I had never lied to her before. But I was annoyed at her for slacking off after getting angry at me, and I didn't want to give her any ammunition to argue that I might have slacked off as well. If she had really stopped watching the giraffes for minutes at a time, then all our vigilance on the stakeout had been for nothing.

Summer stared into my eyes for a long time. She seemed to suspect I was lying, but she didn't call me on it. Instead, she finally put her sunglasses back on and said coldly, "I guess you're just a better detective than me."

A car horn grabbed our attention. It was broken, so it sounded like someone was killing a goose. I figured that I only knew one person who drove a car so broken down that even the horn could barely function.

Lily Deakin had arrived. She pulled up into the red zone in front of the lawn and honked at us again.

Summer got to her feet and grabbed her books. "Come on, genius," she said brusquely. "Time to investigate our other case. I'll try not to screw this one up too."

With that, she headed for Lily's car.

I grabbed my bag and followed her, feeling terrible all around. I was frustrated by our failure to catch the giraffe poisoner in the act and worried about J.J. McCracken's possible intent to kill the mountain lion and upset that Summer and I weren't getting along. Nothing about either one of our investigations was going the way I'd hoped.

And things were only going to get worse.

SUSPECTS

"Tommy and I have some exciting new leads in the Rocket case," Lily said. "But we don't have much time to pursue them."

We were driving along a two-lane road through the Texas Hill Country, a little north of school. On both sides of us, barbed-wire fences ran along the shoulder with huge tracts of oak and cedar forest behind them. We were in ranching country, where the properties were enormous and the homes were few and far between. We had seen far more cattle than cars.

Summer was in the front seat. I was in the back, along with a box of 20,000 pamphlets protesting the inhumane treatment of animals in testing drugs for humans. All the windows were rolled down, so hot wind was whistling through the car. The pamphlets fluttered noisily in the box.

"Could we roll the windows up?" I asked. "I can barely hear anything!"

"I'd prefer not to," Lily replied. "My air conditioner conked out yesterday. At least this way, there's a breeze."

Summer sighed with resignation, then asked, "Why don't we have much time?"

Lily said, "Tommy says Fish and Wildlife is under a lot of pressure to make a decision about the permit to kill Rocket. Probably because of Lincoln revving up all his followers. Tommy's been doing his best to slow the process down, and he's not the only one, but—"

"There are other people there who think Rocket might have been framed?" I asked.

"Well, there are other people who think that they should at least take their time to examine all the evidence before saying it's okay to kill a cougar." Lily swerved wildly into the opposite lane to avoid an armadillo that was foraging on the side of the road. "Lots of people, really. But they're not assigned to the case. So the process can only be stalled so long. Which is why we need to find some ironclad evidence to exonerate Rocket."

"Then let's get to it," Summer said. "What are your leads?"

Lily answered, "Tommy got ahold of the video from Lincoln Stone's security system for last Friday night, like you suggested. He knows a guy at the security company. They had to do it on the down-low, because Tommy's boss wouldn't approve even this much investigating. We only have the video from the front gates, but it's enough. Turns out, Lincoln had a couple friends over the night that King died."

"Yeah, we heard," Summer said.

Lily looked at her over the top of her sunglasses, surprised. "How?"

"From Natasha Mason, the mother of the boys we saw near the crime scene," Summer replied. "She said the guests were all drunk and using the firing range."

"She said they *might* have been drunk," I corrected.

Lily said, "Tommy called Lincoln's office to ask about them. He couldn't get Lincoln, but an assistant said Lincoln hosts a poker night every couple Fridays. As far as I know, the assistant didn't even admit that everyone had been out on the firing range. He didn't tell Tommy much of anything, really. He wouldn't even give out the names of the guys who were there. We had to get them by examining the video and running their license plates."

Lily handed her phone to Summer. A video was cued up. Summer shifted the phone to her left side, and I leaned forward so we could both watch it.

The video shifted back and forth between two cameras. One was mounted beside the driveway, so it could record the make of each car that arrived and the license plate number. The other was mounted on the call box by the gate, where the electronic keypad was, and recorded the face of every visitor. The footage was dark and grainy, having all been filmed at night, and Lily's phone was several years out-of-date, so the video quality wasn't very good.

The first person to show up looked an awful lot like Lincoln Stone, except he was considerably heavier. It was like someone had added three rolls of fat to Lincoln's face. He was driving a pickup truck jacked up on extremely large tires. Such trucks were common in the Hill Country. Lots of people liked to go four-wheel driving on dirt roads, especially after it rained, when they called it "mudding."

Summer paused the video. "That's Lincoln's brother."

"That's right," Lily agreed. "His name's Walter. He has some kind of job in Lincoln's media company, but he apparently doesn't do much except screw around and leech off his brother's success."

"Did someone at the company tell you that?" I asked.

"Walter's kind of famous," Summer informed me, then explained to Lily, "Teddy doesn't pay much attention to celebrities." She looked back at me and said, "Walter's the black sheep of the Stone family. He gets in trouble and his brother bails him out."

A pickup truck similar to Walter's drove past us at that

very moment, heading the other direction, chunks of dried mud caked on the undercarriage. It wasn't Walter, though. Just proof that those trucks were hugely popular in the area.

"What kind of trouble does he get in?" I asked.

"Speeding tickets," Summer replied. "Public drunkenness. Bar fights. Sometimes all three in the same night."

Lily added, "Last spring he got busted for shooting road signs."

"So he's broken the law *a lot*," I concluded.

"Every few weeks, it seems." Summer started the video again.

The next person to arrive at Lincoln's home was a woman with long blond hair, driving an expensive sports car. She was disturbingly skinny, with arms that looked as spindly as the legs of a newborn fawn.

"That's a woman!" I exclaimed.

"Wow," Summer said sarcastically. "Amazing sleuthing, Sherlock."

"Natasha Mason didn't say anything about any women being there last Friday," I reminded her.

"She never said she saw who was there at all," Summer reminded me right back. "She only heard them." She looked to Lily. "That's Petra Olson."

"Right," Lily confirmed.

"Who's Petra Olson?" I asked.

"See?" Summer asked Lily. "I told you he doesn't pay any attention to this stuff." She looked back at me again. "Petra is on Lincoln's show a lot. She's even farther out than he is."

"Especially on the environment," Lily added. "Petra thinks the Endangered Species Act should be abolished. She has actually said that it would be no big deal if we wiped out every wild animal on the planet."

I looked back at the grainy image of the woman in the car. She didn't look evil, but I felt a shiver go down my spine anyhow.

The next person to arrive was at least two decades older than Walter, with gray hair and weathered skin. Despite his age, he was driving a sports car as well.

"Is this guy famous too?" I asked.

"Not to me," Summer replied.

Lily glanced at the image on the phone and said, "That's Harlan Briscoe. He's Lincoln's producer. Really, the brains of the entire operation. Lincoln was a nobody when Harlan found him, doing AM radio and speaking to maybe thirty listeners. Harlan made him what he is today."

A semitruck rounded the bend ahead of us. It barely fit on the two-lane road, and we were forced to swerve onto the gravel shoulder to let it pass. There were tarps drawn down over the sides of the truck, hiding what it was carrying, but with our windows rolled down, we could hear muffled squawking. As the truck rumbled past, it left dozens of white feathers fluttering in its wake.

Lily slammed on her brakes so hard I was thrown against my seat belt. The car skidded to a stop on the shoulder, and Lily craned her head out the open window to watch the truck. "Son of a gun," she muttered under her breath.

"What's wrong?" Summer asked.

Lily didn't answer. She was glaring after the truck hatefully. I got the sense she was trying to decide what to do next.

"Lily?" Summer prodded. "Hello?"

Lily snapped back to reality, though she still had a scowl on her face. "We need to take a little detour," she said, then punched the gas.

The tires kicked up a spray of gravel as we swerved back onto the narrow road. We kept going in the same direction we'd been heading, the way the truck had come from, though Lily was now driving a lot faster. We whipped around the bend so hard that I slammed into the door.

I wondered if Lily was going so fast because she was in a hurry to get somewhere, or if she was simply angry and venting her frustration through speed.

"Where are we going?" Summer asked. Though she was trying to sound calm, I could hear a hint of worry in her voice.

Instead of answering, Lily grabbed her phone from

Summer's hands. "I need this back for a moment," she said, then speed-dialed a number and put the phone to her ear.

Summer looked at me questioningly, wanting to know if I had any idea what was going on. I could only shrug in return.

Whoever Lily was calling didn't answer. So she left a message on voicemail instead. "Hey. It's Lily. The Connellys still seem to be up and running. I'm heading there right now to check it out. If you get this, mobilize the troops." She hung up, tossed the phone back to Summer, and muttered under her breath again, "Lousy jerks."

"Lily?" I asked. "What's going on?"

Lily glanced back at me in a way that indicated she might have forgotten I was even there. "It's nothing that concerns you. Just focus on the video. There's one more suspect."

Summer gave me another worried look, but she brought up the video again anyhow.

The fourth person to arrive at Lincoln Stone's was another man, but that was about all we could tell from the video. He sat back in his car so that the camera didn't catch very much of him, and his whole face was cast in shadow. All I could really see of him was his chin and the vague shape of his face. He was driving a pickup truck as well, but it wasn't jacked up on big tires. It was a normal, everyday truck, of which there were probably thousands in the Hill Country. The only thing that stood out was a big dent in the rear fender to the right of the license plate.

"Who's this?" Summer asked.

"We don't know," Lily replied. "I was kind of hoping you might."

"I can barely even see him in this video," Summer said. "Didn't you run the plates on this truck?"

"Yeah, but they came back registered to someone named Cassie Martinez. That driver doesn't look like a Cassie to me."

"And that's all you have?" I asked.

Lily threw the car into another tight turn, leaving skid marks on the road. "Tommy and I are a little shorthanded. He can run the plates, but after that, there's not much we can do. This guy's probably a friend of this Cassie Martinez, maybe even her husband or boyfriend, but short of going and interviewing the woman—which Tommy's not supposed to be doing, or he'll lose his job—we're kind of at a dead end."

"So, were you thinking *we* were going to talk to this Cassie woman?" Summer asked.

"That was the plan." Lily whipped around another corner.

"Maybe we should go do that now," I suggested. I wasn't really in a hurry to question any witnesses. For all I knew, the guy in the car might have killed King and been willing to do anything to protect himself. But confronting him still seemed less dangerous than driving with Lily.

"We'll get to that," Lily assured me. "There's just something else I have to do first. In the meantime, we have three other new suspects in that video."

"They're all friends and business partners of Lincoln's," Summer said. "And one's his own brother. You really think one of those people killed his dog?"

"Definitely," Lily replied. "In fact, they might have all even done it together, Lincoln included. All those people have spoken out about dismantling the Endangered Species Act—and eradicating all natural predators, from lions to wolves to bears. Maybe they cooked up this scheme on Friday night to implicate the lion. You said yourselves the neighbor heard them shooting guns and being rowdy. Probably drinking, too. Way too often, when people get drunk, they come up with stupid ideas that seem like a good idea at the time."

"Like killing your dog and framing a mountain lion for it?" I asked.

"Exactly." Lily swerved onto a narrow road that didn't even have a sign marking it. She hadn't checked her directions once, indicating that she was familiar with the route to wherever we were going.

"I still find it hard to believe someone would kill their own dog for something like this," I said.

"So maybe Lincoln wasn't involved," Lily said. "Maybe one of these sleazy friends of his did it without him knowing. Because they *knew* it'd set him off. They killed the dog, framed Rocket, and then encouraged Lincoln to go on a tirade."

Summer said, "Given what Natasha Mason told us last night, it seems possible that Lincoln could have killed his own dog."

"What's that?" Lily asked, intrigued.

"She said she didn't think Lincoln was a very caring owner," Summer explained. "Seeing as he left a little dog outside when he knew there was a predator around."

"That *is* awfully negligent," Lily agreed. "I wonder if Lincoln might have been an abusive owner. You'd be surprised how many people are. I'm gonna call his vet." She suddenly pulled off the side of the road and turned off the car.

It was a very abrupt stop, given how fast we had been driving to get somewhere. The area where we now were didn't seem any different from the landscape we'd just been racing through, except that the road was a bit narrower. There was still oak and cedar forest on both sides of us, with barbed-wire fence running along each side of the road.

Beyond the popping of Lily's engine as it cooled, the only sound was the distant chirring of insects.

Lily grabbed her phone back from Summer and climbed out of the car. She opened her address book and scanned through it while circling around to her trunk.

Summer and I climbed out of the car too. It was hot on the side of the road. "How do you know Lincoln's vet?" I asked.

"Tommy got the name off King's license," Lily explained. "And given who my dad is, I pretty much know every vet in the area. Melinda Goodwin is a friend. She's one of our people."

"An activist?" I asked.

"No," Lily replied. "But she's on the right side of the fight. Most vets are. If that dog's been abused, she'll know about it." She speed-dialed and, once more, got voicemail. While she left a message for Dr. Goodwin, I noticed something dangling from the barbed-wire fence on the same side of the road where we were parked.

It was an old metal sign, weathered and rusted. At some point, it might have been painted white, but the color had dulled over the years until it was gray. I took a few steps closer so that I could read it.

"Connelly Farm. Private Property. Trespassers Will Be Shot."

Behind me, I heard a metallic squeal. I turned around to see that Lily now had her trunk open. She bent over into it and rummaged around while wrapping up her message to the vet. ". . . so if you have any information about King, I'd greatly appreciate if you could share it."

I ran back over to her. "Is this the farm that truck came from?"

"That's right." Lily hung up, pocketed her phone, and then lifted a pair of industrial bolt cutters out of her trunk. The handles were two feet long and the blades looked sharp enough to cut through almost anything. There were scrapes on them, indicating they had been used many times before.

"Uh, Lily . . . ," Summer said hesitantly. "Exactly what are you planning on doing here?"

"I'm doing what's *right*." Lily slammed the trunk of her car, then strode toward the barbed-wire fence. "You kids stay here. I won't be too long."

The fence only had five strands of barbed wire. Lily easily slipped through them and stepped onto the Connelly farm. Then she set off through the woods with the bolt cutters slung over her shoulder.

I looked at Summer. She looked at me. Neither of us knew what Lily was up to, but we both suspected it was bad.

"We have to stop her," Summer said.

"No," I said. "I'm not doing anything dangerous."

"I'm not saying we should. I'm saying we need to stop *her* from doing anything dangerous." Summer gave me a challenging look, daring me to say no to her again, then slipped through the barbed-wire fence herself.

I stayed where I was, telling myself I was doing the smart

thing, and that I didn't care what Summer thought of me, and if she wanted to get in trouble, that was her business.

It took five seconds for me to crack. Then I scrambled through the fence and ran after the girls.

THE FARM

Lily was slinking through the woods cautiously, but she was still moving fast. By the time Summer and I caught up to her, she was fifty yards onto the property, working her way up a small hill.

"I thought I told you two to stay by the car," she said, though she didn't stop walking.

"What's going on here?" Summer asked.

"This farm is operating illegally," Lily replied. "The government ordered it closed for using inhumane practices, but it appears they've ignored that and continued operating."

"How can they do that?" I asked.

Lily shrugged. "Corporations ignore the law all the time."

As we neared the crest of the hill, I realized I could hear something in addition to all the insects buzzing around. It sounded bizarrely like there was a large party in the distance, with thousands of people chattering away.

"We'll be happy to go back to the car," Summer told Lily, "but you need to come back with us. We can call the police. Or the FBI. Or whoever is supposed to handle this."

Lily said, "If the police or the feds really wanted to handle this, this place wouldn't still be operating. And I can't just sit by while these animals suffer."

We reached the top of the hill. On the other side, much of the forest had been cleared away. Below us, where there had once been a valley full of trees, there were now five long white buildings. Each was about half the length of a football field, thirty feet wide and two stories tall, with low-pitched roofs. They appeared to be made out of aluminum and were painted white, so they were almost blinding in the bright sun. There were windows along the sides, but they were smeared and dingy, as though they hadn't been washed in years. Cooling units sat every few yards along the peaks of the roofs, but even from this distance, I could tell that several were in disrepair and probably weren't working at all.

The party chatter was coming from the buildings, although I now realized that it wasn't human at all: It was the babble of several thousand birds gobbling all at once.

The trunk of a toppled oak tree lay on the ground nearby. Lily knelt behind it, hiding from the view of anyone at the farm. We joined her there, and she began expla[...] farm's layout to us. "Each one of those buildings h[...] to thirty thousand turkeys, although they were only [...] house twenty thousand, tops. The poor birds are all k[...] mass pens with barely enough room to move—and it's prob[...] ably hotter than a sauna in there."

I took a closer look at the buildings and saw the shimmer of heat coming off the roofs. Given how hot it was outdoors right them, I imagined it would be a hundred times worse inside metal warehouses with almost no air-conditioning.

"The farmers are supposed to filter the turkeys' waste," Lily went on, "but they don't. They just dump it right there." She pointed to a pond at the south end of the buildings. Unlike most ponds, no plants were growing around it. There was only barren dirt. However, the surface of the water was covered with a slick of brown algae. "That's basically the poop from a couple hundred thousand turkeys. Lucky for us, the wind isn't blowing this way. Otherwise, we'd be puking our guts up."

As it was, even without the wind blowing our way, I could still get a hint of the stench from the pond. It was bad enough to make my stomach churn.

"This place started out as a family farm," Lily explained. "Raising cattle free-range for generations. But that's a hard business and the family wanted out, so they sold it to the Redwood Corporation."

"Redwood?" I asked.

"Yeah," Lily said. "Sounds nice and natural, doesn't it? But they're one of the worst companies imaginable when it comes to how they treat their animals. One out of every ten of their turkeys in those buildings dies of starvation or disease or heat stroke. And they're not only raising turkeys. They've got facilities like this for cattle, pigs, chickens, and who knows what else all around the country. The company's so big that when the government actually does cite them for poor practices, they can fight it in court for years or even just ignore it. I'm not sure which of those has happened here, but I'm tired of it." Lily peered over the fallen tree and scanned the area around the buildings below.

Despite the size of the operation, there were no humans in sight. I figured that anyone working there was probably someplace air-conditioned and far from the pond full of turkey poop.

"Looks like the coast is clear," Lily observed. "I want you kids to get back to the car right now. I'm serious. If any of my friends show up, tell them where I am."

"Lily," Summer said firmly. "This is a very bad idea."

"I'm sure those turkeys would disagree," Lily said. "If you don't want to be a part of this, you'd better go right now." With that, she sprang over the tree trunk and hurried down the hill.

Summer and I helplessly watched her go. "Think she knows what she's doing?" I asked.

"I hope so," Summer replied. I thought that, given Summer's impetuous nature, she might run down the hill after Lily, but even this seemed to be too reckless for her. She grabbed my hand and said, "C'mon."

Both of us ran back through the woods. We went full-out, not wanting to get caught on the property, and so it didn't take us too long before we saw the road again and Lily's beat-up old car sitting on the shoulder. We quickly slipped through the fence and did our best to act as innocent as possible to anyone who might come along.

None of Lily's friends were waiting there, whoever they might have been.

"So what do you think of our new suspects?" Summer asked. She seemed like she was trying to distract herself from worrying about Lily, but it was worth discussing anyhow.

"I don't know as much about them as you and Lily do," I answered. "But it sounds like any of them could have killed King. Seems like all of them hate mountain lions and hunting regulations. . . ."

"So much that they'd kill Lincoln's dog?"

"Maybe it was an accident." I paced in the shade on the side of the road, laying out what I'd been thinking. "They were all drinking, and they all had guns. What if one of them shot King by mistake? It was dark. King wasn't that big. Maybe someone thought he was a rabbit or something. And then, they wouldn't want Lincoln to know they'd killed his dog. Even if it was an accident. But then, they realize there's a way to shift the blame from themselves *and* get Lincoln riled up about the mountain lions."

"I don't know," Summer said skeptically. "How do you shoot someone's dog without them noticing?"

"Maybe Lincoln was inside when it happened," I suggested. "Or maybe he got too drunk to notice. Once, back in Africa, my dad had some friends visit our camp and they drank so much, one of the guys couldn't get up for an entire day afterward. A whole troop of chimpanzees came right through the camp and he didn't even have any idea it had happened."

"So . . . this person shoots King and then takes off the tail to leave as evidence?"

"Maybe the tail was all that was left after they shot the dog," I said. "They might have been using some really big guns, like the kind people use at game ranches to hunt exotic species. Or maybe they accidentally blew the tail off when they shot King and then just left it behind."

"What do you think they did with the rest of the dog?"

"Dumped the body somewhere."

"Not outside," Summer said. "That would have attracted vultures."

"Okay. Maybe they put King's body in their car and drove it to the dump."

Summer frowned. "I doubt it."

"Really?" I asked. "Because anyone who framed the lion would have had to do something like that with King's body."

"I just find it hard to imagine that a friend would lie like that to another friend."

"Maybe they're not that good friends," I said.

"They play poker every few Fridays. They must be pretty close."

"Not necessarily. Except for the Mystery Man, we know they all work with Lincoln. Maybe they don't like him at all, but play poker to stay on his good side. Lincoln's a jerk."

Summer ran her fingers along the wire of the fence, thinking about that, but she still didn't seem convinced. "What if it was someone else who wanted to hunt Rocket? Like that guy who was lurking around the Wilds last night?"

"Jerry?" I asked, already feeling nervous about where this was going. Apparently, J.J. McCracken hadn't told Summer the truth about his hunter.

"Right," Summer said. "The guy was already willing to trespass to go after a lion, so he'd probably be willing to commit other crimes as well. Like sneaking onto Lincoln's property and killing King and framing Rocket for it."

"That sounds awfully complicated," I said. "There's no

way he could have known that Lincoln would go on the war-path to have Rocket delisted."

"Really? I think anyone who has ever listened to Lincoln Stone would have a very good idea that he'd do that. Maybe Jerry didn't know Lincoln would offer a reward for killing Rocket, but to argue that she ought to be killed? Definitely. Lincoln Stone has claimed that people ought to get the death penalty for jaywalking. So he's certainly going to want the lion that killed his dog dead."

"He was exaggerating about the jaywalking," I said.

"He still *said* it. The man says crazy things all the time. And a lot of his listeners believe every last one of them."

I sighed, knowing this was true. The jaywalking incident had made national news. Someone had walked in front of Lincoln's car as he was driving to work, forcing him to slam on his brakes and spill coffee on his lap, and then he'd come into the radio booth and ranted about how that should be a capital offense. A lot of people made fun of him afterward for being hyperbolic, and even Lincoln had admitted later that he'd gone too far, but some of his core listeners had actually taken him seriously.

This happened with Lincoln a lot. Lincoln spouted off about things all the time; that was his job. Sometimes they were important issues, and sometimes it happened to be whatever had peeved him on the way into work that day.

Lincoln had been known to rail against the cost of postage stamps, people who drove too slow in the left lane on the highway, premade guacamole at the supermarket, and the Dewey decimal system (which he had honestly claimed was a government plot to keep anyone from being able to find the books they wanted at the library).

It was even more unsettling when Lincoln took on serious issues with the same cavalier attitude, shooting his mouth off without thinking about the consequences. For example, he had recently suggested that if illegally crossing into the country was punishable by death, then we'd have much less illegal immigration. Lots of his listeners had really liked that idea, and a few had even gone down to the Rio Grande River with the intent of shooting anyone they presumed to be crossing the border. Lincoln's rants often had consequences like this, because Lincoln generally argued that the government was always wrong, that all other media sources were corrupt, and that he was the only one telling his listeners the truth, so his devoted fans tended to discount anything they heard from the government or other news sources, if they even bothered listening to them at all. To them, anything Lincoln Stone said was gospel.

So it wasn't a stretch to assume that, if Lincoln thought his dog had been killed by a mountain lion, then he would immediately start attacking the Endangered Species Act as a bad idea and claiming the lions ought to be eradicated. J.J. McCracken himself probably knew this, and to me, it seemed more likely that J.J. would think to go after Lincoln Stone's dog than some random hunter might. After all, if J.J. perceived the lion as a threat to his animals or his business, he would have more of a motive than some hunter who simply wanted to shoot a lion.

However, I didn't want to discuss this possibility with Summer. I didn't want to reveal that her father might have hired Jerry and lied to her about it. But I also didn't want to be put in a position where I had to keep hiding that truth from her. So I tried to change the subject instead.

"Who do you think that Mystery Man in the truck was?" I asked. "The fourth suspect?"

Summer absently plucked the barbed-wire fence. "I don't have the slightest idea. All we saw was his chin. It might have even been a woman."

I considered that. My view of the mystery person on the phone had been small and blurry. I had assumed the person was a man, but maybe that was only because they were driving a truck and wearing a cowboy hat. A woman certainly could have done those things. "If that's the case, do you think it could have been Tommy Lopez's boss?"

"You mean the head of the local Fish and Wildlife division?"

"Yeah. I don't even know who that is, do you?"

"I hadn't thought to look it up."

"Tommy's boss has been trying to stop this investigation all along," I said. "What if she was doing that because *she* was the one who killed the dog?"

For a moment, I thought Summer was going to dismiss this as being stupid, but then she said, "Let's see who this woman is." She took out her phone, then frowned at it. "Ugh. I have zero reception out here. How about you?"

I checked my phone. "Nothing. Maybe I can find some coverage, though." I started down the road, holding my phone above my head, hoping to pick up some kind of signal.

I had only gone a few steps before I heard something in the distance, carrying through the hot, still air.

Sirens. They were far-off, but they seemed to be slowly getting louder, indicating they were coming our way.

I looked back at the barbed-wire fence surrounding the Connelly farm. The place where we had crossed still looked ridiculously spindly and low-tech.

Then I looked down the fence. At multiple places, instead of using wooden fence posts, the builders of the fence had used trees. In fact, in many spots, the barbed wire had been strung by the trees for so long that the bark of the trees had grown around it. On one of these trees, there was a small black device mounted right above the top strand of barbed wire.

I looked in the other direction and saw another such device mounted to another tree in the distance.

"Summer," I said nervously, "I think this fence has an alarm system." I pointed to one of the devices.

"Crud," Summer said. "That's a laser sensor. We have them on our property too." She looked up into the trees. "They probably have remote cameras out here as well. So if something trips the alarm, they can see if it's a deer or a trespasser."

"*We* tripped the alarm," I said.

"Only because Lily did it first!" Summer exclaimed. "That was *her* fault, not ours!"

The sirens were getting louder. And now I heard something else, coming from the other direction—from the farm itself. The same cocktail-party chatter of the birds. Only it was getting louder too. And somehow, it sounded angrier than it had before.

Lily Deakin suddenly crested the top of the hill, running as fast as she could. She had abandoned her bolt cutters in her haste. "Get in the car!" she shouted. "We need to go!"

For a moment, I thought she knew the police were coming for us. But then, what she was really running from came over the hill behind her.

Turkeys.

There were hundreds of them, and they were coming fast. I had known that wild turkeys could get quite large, but up to that moment, the only domestic turkeys I had ever seen were on the table at Thanksgiving dinner. These turkeys were much bigger than I had expected. (I would find out later that Redwood had pumped them full of hormones and steroids to get them to grow unnaturally large.) They were also highly aggressive, which was a side effect of the steroids. Wild turkeys can be surprisingly combative, and these guys were all suffering from roid rage.

They came over the hill in a furious, gobbling wave. Their anger wasn't only directed at Lily; they were taking it out on anything that got in their way—including each other. As they ran, the turkeys pecked and clawed each other, and swatted one another with their wings. Others lashed out at bushes and sticks. One launched itself at a cedar tree with such rage that it actually knocked itself unconscious. (Turkeys aren't that smart to begin with, and these drug-addled ones appeared to have few functioning brain cells at all.)

Summer and I raced for the car. We had wandered a ways down the road from it while talking, and while we weren't *that* far, it was still a worrying distance given that a horde of psychotic turkeys was descending on us. We reached it only a few seconds before Lily and the turkeys got to the barbed-wire fence.

I leaped into the back seat while Summer got into the front. Even with the windows down, the interior of the car had been baking in the blazing sun, so the seats were scalding.

In her haste, Lily tried to jump the barbed-wire fence rather than slipping through it, but her foot caught the top wire and she belly flopped painfully into the grass by the side of the road.

Luckily, the turkeys were even less graceful than Lily. Several of the leaders didn't even seem to notice the fence at all and ran right into it, hitting it so hard that they rebounded backward into the flock, taking out several of their brethren. Others attempted to fly over the fence, apparently unaware that domesticated, hormone-bloated turkeys can't fly. They flapped their wings valiantly, but didn't leave the ground and ended up thwacking into the fence as well. The next wave of turkeys promptly ran right into them, squashing them up against the wires.

Lily scrambled back to her feet and ran for the car.

Behind her, a few turkeys managed to get through the wires of the fence. This was entirely due to luck, rather than any mental acuity or problem-solving skills, but the effect was the same. They were past the barrier and free to attack once again.

Lily dove into the front seat. She had badly scraped her arms and knees after flopping over the fence, but if she was in pain, she didn't show it. She might not have even noticed, she was so frightened. Instead, she frantically searched through her pockets for the car keys.

"What'd you do to those birds?" Summer asked worriedly.

"Nothing!" Lily exclaimed, sounding very freaked out. "They came out that angry! You'd think they'd have been *happy* that I freed them, but . . . they don't seem to like humans at all. I guess they've been treated worse than I thought. . . ."

The turkeys were now bearing down on the car, and our windows were still open.

"Lily!" I yelled. "Start the car!"

"I can't find my keys!" she yelled back.

"What?" Summer shrieked. "Where are they?"

"I don't know!" Lily wailed. "I swear I had them in my pocket!"

I looked out the window at the point where Lily had fallen. On the ground, amidst a flurry of approaching turkeys, were her car keys. "You dropped them out there!" I said.

Lily gasped. All the bravado she had shown earlier was gone, erased by the trouble her impetuousness had gotten her into.

Without the keys, we couldn't roll up the windows, and the turkeys were now upon us. It was quite likely that none of them had ever seen a car before, but that didn't stop them from flinging themselves at it furiously. Many clanged harmlessly off the fenders and the doors, but others tried to get at us inside, leaping as high as they could and lashing their heads through the windows. Two managed to somehow clamber up onto the hood and threw themselves against the windshield, making grotesque faces at us as they smeared themselves against the glass.

It felt somewhat like being in a zombie movie, only instead of our car being attacked by mindless brain-eating humans, we were being attacked by mindless, hostile barnyard animals.

I grabbed a thick sheaf of animal welfare pamphlets and whacked a turkey with them as it lunged through the window for me. (I was aware of the irony at the time, but I didn't care; the turkey didn't seem concerned about *my* welfare at all.) The bird toppled back to the ground, gobbling angrily.

The girls didn't have anything to defend themselves with in the front seat. They could only swat at the turkeys with their hands. Lily already had a gash in her palm where she'd been severely gouged by a beak.

"Here!" I said, handing them stacks of pamphlets. "Use these on them!"

"I can't hit an animal!" Lily cried.

"They're trying to peck us to death!" Summer argued. "This is self-defense!" She eagerly grabbed some pamphlets and swatted a turkey so hard its wattle wrapped around its neck like a tetherball. "You need to get those keys!"

"No way!" Lily said, paling at the thought. "I'm not going back out there!"

I brained another turkey with my pamphlets and chanced a look out the window. In the swarm of frenzied birds, I spotted the keys again. But at that very moment, an exceptionally large and moronic turkey plucked them off the ground with its beak—and swallowed them.

"I don't think we're getting the keys back," I reported. "Not for a few hours, at least."

"Oh God," Lily mewled. "My father's going to kill me."

"Not if the turkeys do it first!" Summer exclaimed.

At that moment, however, salvation arrived. A police car skidded to a stop in the sea of turkeys. Their sirens had been wailing all along, but we hadn't been able to hear them over all the outraged gobbling.

The rear window of our car was now being savaged by two angry turkeys, but between them, I could see the police staring in amazement through their own windshield.

A dozen turkeys promptly launched themselves at the police car.

Fortunately, the police had riot gear. While we continued to fend off the turkeys, the police suited up, then emerged ready for battle and armed to the teeth. They didn't shoot any turkeys, but they did stun quite a few with long tasers that looked like cattle prods. The turkeys squawked in shock as the electricity surged through them, and then passed out.

Normally, I would have been upset to see any animal jolted this way, but Summer and I—and even Lily—were relieved.

Eventually, the turkeys seemed to grasp that the police were a more advanced threat than we were and ought to be avoided—or possibly, they were simply exhausted after all their exertion. They fell back, though they still gobbled menacingly, watching us warily with their googly eyes.

The police cautiously approached our car, helped us out, and made sure we were all right.

And then they arrested us.

GROUNDED

I didn't go to jail, but I still ended up in a lot of trouble.

After reviewing the security footage from the Connelly Farm, the police determined that while Summer and I had trespassed, we hadn't done so with criminal intent. After all, we were only kids, and the adult who was with us had abandoned us on the side of the road and gone off to commit a crime. The only reason we had gone onto the farm was to try to talk sense into Lily.

Meanwhile, Lily was locked up right away. We never even got to see her after we were brought to the police station, although we did hear her shouting at some point that the Redwood Corporation was the *real* criminal and that she was only trying to do what was right. "I'm like the Lorax!"

she yelled. "You wouldn't arrest the Lorax, would you?"

My parents were the ones I really ended up in trouble with. They were upset with me for hanging out with Lily Deakin, correctly assuming that the only reason I would do that was to help out with the mountain lion case. Mom felt that Summer and I should have called the police on Lily the moment she went over the fence, so there would be no question of our innocence. Dad didn't quite back her up on this. If anything, he seemed annoyed by the incompetence of Lily's raid and possibly embarrassed that the police had needed to rescue me from a flock of angry turkeys.

So I got grounded.

Summer did too.

My parents never grounded me at home. They couldn't keep an eye on me there, and they knew I could simply go off and wander around in the woods if I wanted to. So I had to sit in my mother's office at Monkey Mountain instead.

All in all, there were worse places to be. The office had much better air-conditioning than our trailer (I probably wouldn't have wanted to wander around our mosquito-infested woods on a day that hot anyhow), and there was a window out into the gorilla exhibit.

Plus, my mother didn't like to stay in her office. In the wild, she could sit still as a stone for hours at a time, watching gorillas—or almost any other animal. In her office, sitting still for five minutes was a chore for her. She knew there were hundreds of primates in the building, and she was far more interested in watching them than answering emails and filing maintenance requests. So she tended to wander off for large chunks of time.

I stayed put, as she had told me to. But she couldn't stop me from investigating further.

In her office, I had a computer with internet access, which was all I needed.

I couldn't help myself. We had new leads in the lion case, and with Lily in jail and Tommy Lopez ordered off the investigation, there wasn't anyone else to look into it. Plus, it wasn't remotely dangerous; I was only collecting information. I was on the computer anyhow, writing a report on the assassination of Archduke Franz Ferdinand, so when Mom slipped out the door, I googled our new suspects.

I found a lot of intriguing information on all of them.

Lincoln Stone's brother, Walter, had a long criminal record. Although he went by "Walter Stone," he had never legally changed his last name from "Turkmeister." (Neither had his brother; "Lincoln Stone" was only a stage name.) The Turkmeisters really had been born in Beverly Hills. They hadn't been rich, but they had been well-off, and yet, even with that leg up, Walter had done poorly in school and been quite a juvenile delinquent. He had been busted several times for underage drinking, public urination, and sneaking into the backyards of famous people to use their swimming pools. Often, he was busted for all three at once.

Walter had never gone to college, shifting between menial jobs and time in jail for stupid crimes. Once his younger brother had become famous, Walter had come to Texas to work for him. While he often claimed to be the "Executive Vice President of Lincoln Stone Enterprises," he didn't seem to do much of anything except back up his brother on various forms of social media. No matter how ridiculous a statement Lincoln made, Walter would happily reiterate it—even statements that Lincoln had quickly admitted were mistaken, like his suggestion that the best way to get rid of old nuclear weapons would be to detonate them. It was as though Walter never had an original thought himself; he simply parroted whatever his brother said.

Thus, when Lincoln had railed against Rocket for killing King, Walter had gone several steps further, saying that all lions in the US should be eradicated. And when Lincoln had said the Endangered Species Act was yet another case of government intrusion in our lives, Walter had gone on to add that it was "a stupid, moronic, and idiotic law." (Ironically, he had managed to misspell all three insults—"sutpid, morronic, and iddiotic"—attesting to who the *real* stupid, moronic idiot was.)

Meanwhile, Walter's newfound job hadn't made him any more responsible. He still got in trouble, usually when he'd been drinking, which seemed to be much of the time. He had made a fool of himself at several public events for his brother, most notably when he decided to moon a rival journalist at the White House Correspondents' Dinner, forgetting that a hundred noted photojournalists were in the room at the time. The resulting photos of his flabby behind had trended all over the internet for the following week. In the past year alone, he had been pulled over for driving while drunk at least four times, but somehow (probably due to his brother's influence) had never ended up in jail. He also had a penchant for shooting inanimate objects; not just road signs, but also mailboxes, pinecones, and his neighbor's drones. He had managed to avoid arrest for all of this as well.

I also found a story about how Walter had somehow ended up with a few World War II surplus grenades and thought it'd be a good idea to try to get rid of the gophers on his property with them. (Amazingly, by all accounts, Walter had actually been sober when he came up with this plan.) Walter hadn't killed any gophers, but he *had* killed his septic tank, creating a geyser of sewage that had also rendered his home unlivable for two months while hazmat crews sanitized it.

Therefore, Walter didn't seem like the type of person who had the mental capacity to start a campaign against mountain lions by killing his brother's dog. However, he *did* seem like the type of person who, after a few too many drinks, might accidentally shoot his brother's dog and then try to pin the whole thing on a mountain lion.

Meanwhile, Petra Olson was far more intelligent. (Of course, one might argue that there were rocks that were more intelligent than Walter.) Petra had authored several books that even her critics admitted were at least well written. I found a few of her editorials online and was impressed, despite myself. Even when she was arguing about something that I completely disagreed with, like gutting the Endangered Species Act, she could be very convincing.

Petra was an avid hunter herself, and I found plenty of photos of her posed over animals she had killed, including grizzly bears, bighorn sheep, and African lions. However, she had always hunted the animals legally and had the proper licenses. As much as I disliked hunting, I knew that many hunters were also ardent conservationists; the problem with Petra was that she didn't seem to care one bit about conservation. She had said, on the record, that she didn't care if the next generation didn't have any grizzlies or bighorns or lions to hunt. "Animals go extinct all the time," she had argued. "There's no tyrannosaurs or brontosaurs anymore and no one complains. If God didn't want grizzlies to go extinct, he wouldn't have given us guns."

So, if Petra had really wanted to kill a mountain lion, she would have been clever enough to manipulate Lincoln Stone into making it legal.

Harlan Briscoe was the toughest to figure out. While Walter Turkmeister was an idiot and Petra Olson was a rabid anti-environmentalist, they both seemed to *believe* the things they said. Harlan merely appeared to say whatever would make him the most money. He was certainly smart and a shrewd marketer—not just anyone could have taken a small-town radio host like Lincoln Stone and made him a huge success—but no one seemed to know if Harlan actually *agreed* with anything Lincoln said.

Harlan had worked in TV and radio for a long time, and he had shepherded other people to fame as well, including a few stand-up comics who had become big movie stars, a Mixed Martial Arts fighter, and Danger Dan, a TV host who traveled the world doing incredibly crazy things like BASE jumping off the Eiffel Tower or scuba diving with great white sharks. Harlan was extremely well respected in the business for finding and nurturing talent. (In fact, a few people observed that, with some of his comics-turned-actors, he could find talent where none had ever existed in the first place.) In all his years in the public eye, though, Harlan had never made a political statement showing that he leaned one way or another. Danger Dan was extremely pro-environment—a lot of his stunts, like the shark diving, were done to show that animals often weren't as bloodthirsty as the public thought— so it was kind of hard to believe that Harlan could work with him *and* Lincoln, but somehow, he did.

So I had a hard time trying to figure out if Harlan would have killed King or not. He didn't seem to have anything against mountain lions or to even care about hunting. He also didn't seem to be the type of person who would get drunk and kill a dog by accident; I got the idea he was far too shrewd and savvy to make such a dumb mistake.

The only thing I could think of was that, maybe, things weren't so good between Harlan and Lincoln. Maybe they'd had a fight, or a disagreement over a contract, and Harlan had decided to lash out.

I still wasn't sure if Harlan would do something like that, but the more I thought about it, it seemed like maybe other people *would*. A lot of people hated Lincoln Stone. Really hated him. After all, Lincoln *liked* saying things that made people mad. When I googled him, I found several lists that counted him as among one of the most despised people in America. (Although there were also lists that included him as one of the most respected people, and both lists seemed to be mostly composed of people who made incendiary political statements for a living.) *What if one of those people had wanted to get to Lincoln?* I wondered. Killing Lincoln, or causing him any harm at all, was illegal. But killing his dog would definitely upset him. And whoever had done it had gotten away. Lincoln thought a mountain lion had done it.

Then again, maybe whoever had killed King hadn't even set out to frame the mountain lion in the first place. Maybe the killer had simply left the collar and the tail behind as evidence that King was dead, and everyone had mistakenly believed Rocket was responsible.

The more I thought about it, both of those scenarios seemed more likely to me than any of Lincoln's associates killing King that night. When you had thousands of people who hated you, there was a pretty good chance that, sooner or later, one of them would do something crazy.

That idea was extremely daunting, though. I wondered how I could possibly even begin investigating the thousands of people who loathed Lincoln Stone, especially when I was grounded.

I only had a few leads:

1) Whoever did it would have to know where Lincoln Stone lived. I knew Lincoln tried to keep that a secret to protect his privacy, but there were probably ways to find out.

2) Whoever did it would have to know that King was actually a bichon frise and not a golden retriever, as Lincoln claimed.

3) Whoever did it had left the mysterious white substance behind on the ground. This was probably the best clue I had—assuming it had actually been left by the dog killer and not someone else—but unfortunately, I still didn't know what it was. Once again, I found myself with the tantalizing feeling that I should have recognized the substance, but for the life of me, I couldn't figure it out.

None of those leads really narrowed my search down at all. So I turned my attention to the two other possible suspects I had.

There was the fourth person who had been at Lincoln's house the night of King's death. The Mystery Guest who had been almost invisible in the security video. All I knew about him or her was that he or she drove a pickup truck that was registered to someone else.

I googled "Cassie Martinez," the name of the owner of the truck. There were a lot of Cassie Martinezes in Texas.

That seemed daunting, so I turned my attention to the suspect I could at least find a name for: Tommy Lopez's boss. I looked up who the director of the local division of Fish and Wildlife was.

Her name was Stephanie Winger. Given her refusal to

investigate the true cause of King's death, I had expected to find lots of reports about her being unfit for her job, but I didn't. Instead, everything I found about her indicated that she was very good at what she did. She had started as a ranger for the service and worked her way up through the ranks. I also found some photos of her, which confirmed she was not the Mystery Guest at Lincoln's. She wasn't built as thick as whoever had been driving that truck. Instead, she was tall and thin. Lots of the photos of her were at events with state senators and the governor, so it seemed possible that she had her eye on a higher office in the future, but I didn't come across anything that suggested she had ever sacrificed her morals for political reasons.

So I had to wonder: Maybe Stephanie Winger was getting pressure to sweep the lion investigation under the carpet herself. Maybe Lincoln Stone wielded enough political clout to get a politician to force Stephanie to do what he wanted. Or maybe the Mystery Guest in the truck *was* a politician. A politician who had accidentally killed King and didn't want anyone to find out. Or a politician who simply wanted mountain lions eradicated.

Which brought me right back to the Mystery Guest again. The best way to find out who he was would be to find the right Cassie Martinez and ask her who was driving her truck the previous Friday night, but my leads to that had disappeared now that Lily had gotten herself arrested.

So had my connection to Dr. Goodwin, Lincoln's vet, who Lily had called right before the turkey incident.

Then it occurred to me that I could probably contact Dr. Goodwin myself. I looked up her name and easily found the number of her practice: Hill Country Veterinary Clinic. I grabbed the phone on Mom's desk and dialed the number.

A pleasant-sounding woman answered. "Hill Country Vet. How may I help you?"

I could hear the yapping of several dogs behind her. Probably pets in the waiting room. "Hi," I said. "I was wondering if I could talk to Dr. Goodwin."

"Are you a client here?" the receptionist asked.

"No. But I have a question for her. She was getting some information for a mutual friend of ours. . . ."

"Information about what?"

"A pet that she takes care of."

"Your friend's pet?"

"No. Someone else's."

"Dr. Goodwin would never give out information about any animal she sees to anyone but the owner." The receptionist no longer sounded quite as pleasant. "That would be unethical."

I tried to explain myself. "This is kind of a special case. . . ."

"It doesn't matter what the circumstances are. It's still unethical."

"But my friend said Dr. Goodwin would tell her."

"Your friend was wrong. Did she actually speak to Dr. Goodwin about this?"

"Er . . . no."

"I thought as much. If you or your friend wants information about someone's pet, I'd advise you to contact the pet's owner directly."

"But . . ."

"I'm sorry. I have other calls," the receptionist said curtly. Then she hung up on me.

I slammed the phone back down in frustration.

Someone coughed behind me.

I spun around to find my mother standing there. "That didn't sound like it had anything to do with Archduke Franz Ferdinand," she said.

For a few seconds, my mind spun, trying to come up with a decent excuse, but then I realized lying would only get me into deeper trouble. "It wasn't," I admitted.

"What were you trying to find out?" Mom didn't sound upset with me for disobeying her. Instead, she seemed intrigued.

"Lily Deakin thought King's vet could tell us if the dog was ever abused," I said.

"Lily was wrong," Mom told me. "No vet would share that information with a random caller. If they suspected a pet was abused, they would probably notify the local Department of Animal Control, but they can't tell just anyone."

I sighed. "Sounds like Lily was wrong about a lot of things."

"But not everything. She thought Lincoln Stone was a piece of work, and he is. I just heard that he's been ranting about Rocket all day."

"What's he been saying?"

"Let's find out."

Mom leaned over my shoulder to activate her internet radio, then tuned into Lincoln Stone's livecast. The moment she clicked on the volume, the room filled with the abrasive, angry voice of the man I had met the previous Saturday.

". . . This cat's still roaming around out there, on the loose, and yet the dimwits in our government still haven't approved the permit to kill it!" he raged. "Apparently, Stephanie Wingnut and everyone else at the imbecilic Fish and Wildlife Service care more about a bloodthirsty predator than they do about the safety of you and your family! That cougar might only be guilty of caninicide for now, but it'll be homicide next. Now, I know you members of Stone Nation, being red-blooded Americans, are smarter than Stephanie and the folks at Fish and Wildlife and everyone else in the government, so you need to make your voices heard. Overwhelm their phone lines! Flood their email inboxes!"

Lincoln went on to give out the phone numbers and emails of everyone he wanted his listeners to call. As he did, it occurred to me that Stephanie Winger was in a tougher position than I had realized. If she hadn't approved the permit to delist Rocket yet, that meant she was doing the right thing, and yet, she was being pilloried for it. That was a lot of public pressure to be under.

Lincoln finished giving out the information and launched right back into his tirade. "Now, that's the absolute *least* you can do. If you're concerned for your safety and that of your family—as any smart person ought to be—then I encourage you to take up arms and protect yourself! Get out there and find that barbaric beast and see that justice is served! Despite the fact that good citizens like yourself have been hunting it for the past few days, that dog-murdering cat is still at large! I know some people might tell you that killing it is against the law, but it's a *stupid* law. And to prove my point, I hereby volunteer to pay *all* legal costs for anyone who shoots that cat. Plus, thanks to a generous donation from the fine folks at Cardiff Gun Shops, I am upping the bounty on that lion's head to one hundred thousand dollars. That's right.

One hundred thousand dollars to whoever kills that cat. I can see my phone lines lighting up right now, so let's take some calls."

Mom turned off the volume on the computer. What little she'd heard had made her look nauseated.

"I guess we're going to get even more hunters here now?" I asked.

Mom nodded sadly, then said, "Let's go for a walk, kiddo."

PREPARATIONS

"I'm not saying your getting involved in this mountain lion mess is a good idea," Mom told me. "But I understand why you want to do it. Honestly, I want to do more too."

Even though night was falling and Mom was done with her work for the day, we hadn't headed straight home. Instead, we were walking around FunJungle, which was a much more interesting and prettier walk than heading along the construction site to our trailer. And there were fewer mosquitoes.

The park had closed, but there were more employees around than usual. The moment the last guests had left, Park Operations had begun to prepare FunJungle for the big anniversary celebration the next day. Already, decorators were hanging banners and bunting, while landscapers were planting fresh flowers. A team of men armed with clippers were trimming all the topiary animals to perfection. On the big lawn in front of Carnivore Canyon, where the main celebrations would take place, the stage was finished. To the side of the lawn, a team of fireworks technicians was setting up a remote launching control center.

"Do more like what?" I asked.

"I don't know," Mom said with a sigh. "I don't want Rocket to be killed any more than you do. I'd like to figure out a way to chase every darn one of those hunters out of here with their tails between their legs. Or to get that idiot Lincoln Stone to admit he's made a mistake."

"If you help me prove that King was murdered, then Fish and Wildlife won't issue the permit to kill Rocket."

"That's not going to stop every knucklehead with a gun from going after that cat. Not when Lincoln has offered such a huge reward for killing her—and volunteered to pay their legal fees, too. I'll be surprised if Rocket survives the night."

"Well, we should at least *try* to do something, right?" I asked.

Mom stared at me for a long while before answering. Then, to my surprise, she smiled. "You're right, Teddy. We should. Tell me what you've got."

So I did. I ran through all the leads I had so far: Walter and Petra and Harlan and the Mystery Guest and Lincoln

Stone himself. I put forward my idea that the Mystery Guest could have been a politician putting pressure on Stephanie Winger, and the possibility that a random Lincoln Stone hater had murdered King just to cause the man grief. Mom listened to all of it thoughtfully, never interrupting me, while we wandered along.

Everywhere we went, decorations were going up, and trucks were rumbling around, moving things into place for the next day's events. Three whole pickup trucks full of fireworks passed us, heading for the launching area in the Wilds.

I saved my suspicions about J.J. McCracken for last. Mom's frown deepened as I laid out this theory for her.

"What's wrong?" I asked. "You don't think it's possible?"

"No, I think it's *extremely* possible," she replied sadly. "J.J. has been worried about Rocket for months now."

"He has?" I asked.

"He's written memos alerting the keepers to make sure all the exhibits are secure against the lion, and I know he had a conversation with Doc and Hoenekker about trying to sedate her and relocate her somewhere else. Doc refused, though."

"Why?"

"First of all, FunJungle doesn't own Rocket, so it'd be illegal. But even if it was legal, there are plenty of dangers for her."

"Like if you don't sedate Rocket just right, you might kill her?"

"Yes, but there's also the question of where you move her. A lot of places aren't suitable for a lion to live, so relocating her there might as well be a death sentence. Humans have moved into a lot of the other places, so you can't put Rocket there without causing more human/wildlife conflict. And the few remaining places that are suitable are probably the domain of other mountain lions. You can't just move one lion into another's territory. They'll kill each other. More lions in this country are killed each year by other lions than by hunters."

"Really?" I asked.

"There used to be a lot more room for these animals," Mom said. "But every day, there's less. There's new homes, new schools, even places like this"—she waved a hand around FunJungle—"and that means fewer and fewer places for lions. Rocket lived here before Lincoln Stone did. And before FunJungle was built. This was her territory first. And now, people are upset at her because she's doing what she must to survive."

"Did J.J. ever suggest trying to kill Rocket?"

"That, I don't know. Although I'm sure that, knowing J.J., he's looked into every option. And the man has a lot of power in this area. He's the number one employer, by far, and every decision he makes has a huge economic impact on the region. The politicians will do anything he wants them to. He could put a lot more pressure on Stephanie Winger than Lincoln Stone could."

"If that's the case, why wouldn't he just ask for the permit to kill Rocket? If he really felt she was a threat to FunJungle, and he's that powerful, he could probably get someone to give it to him."

"That's true," Mom said. "Or maybe . . ." She suddenly seemed unsure about continuing the thought.

"Maybe what?" I pressed.

"Maybe J.J. decided to go after Rocket without bothering to get the permit. After all, I highly doubt he only hired that hunter *after* King died."

I stopped walking, thinking about that. I had seen Jerry at the Raging Raft Ride on Sunday night, only two nights after King had died. He had known his way around the ride quite well for someone who had only started work that weekend. "When do you think he hired him?"

"Honestly, it could have been months ago," Mom said.

"So then, J.J. might not have had anything to do with King?"

"Maybe not. But then again, maybe J.J. had already hired the hunter and then realized he needed a better excuse if he actually killed the lion."

"And then he might have told Jerry to kill King!" I suggested. "He's a professional hunter, after all."

"I suppose it's possible," Mom said, although she didn't sound so sure about it.

We were now close to SafariLand and the giraffe feeding area. A dozen employees were on the roof of the monorail station, hanging banners from it. One proclaimed 365 DAYS OF AMAZEMENT! while the next said WITH MANY MORE TO COME!

A flatbed truck with ZOOM painted on the side pulled up alongside us. Sanjay Budhiraja, the inventor of the fish cannon, was at the wheel. The back of the flatbed was laden with various pieces of his machine. He leaned out the window and said, "Hey, Teddy! How's it going?"

"Pretty good," I said. "This is my mom, Charlene Fitzroy."

"The primatologist?" Sanjay grinned cheerfully. "It's an honor to meet you!"

Mom appeared flattered to be recognized. "It's nice to meet you, too," she said, then eyed the equipment in the back of the truck. "What are you doing all the way out here? I thought you were working with the penguins."

"I am!" Sanjay looked to me enthusiastically. "Teddy, we've made some amazing progress since the other day. The cannon works perfectly, and the penguins love it. So the PR department wants me to put on a display tomorrow for the anniversary celebration. There's a guy in charge, Pete someone. . . ."

"Pete Thwacker," I said.

"Yes!" Sanjay exclaimed. "That's the guy! He's very excited about the fish cannon! He wants everyone to see it. So we're going to get some penguins out on the stage and shoot fish all the way across the great lawn to them, right over the crowd! There's one king penguin, Louis the Sixteenth, who can catch a herring from fifty feet away. We're hoping he can do it for the fans!"

"Are you sure that will be safe?" Mom asked.

"Absolutely!" Sanjay said. "I know it'll be hot, but we're going to have some big tubs of ice out there for the penguins to chill in."

"I meant for the crowds," Mom said. "What if some tourist gets hit by a fish?"

"Oh, I don't think that will happen," Sanjay said reassuringly. "I've already added some safety precautions to the cannon. But Cindy Salerno and I are going to run some tests tonight, once I get everything set up and some of these people clear out. Man, is it always this crowded here at night?"

"No," I said. "This is really unusual. Although there's always a few people here. . . ." As I said the words, I was struck by a thought.

"Is something wrong?" Mom asked me.

"No," I said. "I just had an idea. I need to check something out."

"Well, I've got to get the cannon set up myself," Sanjay said. "Maybe I'll see you guys at the demonstration tomorrow?"

"Sure," I told him, although I was barely focused on him anymore. As Sanjay drove off, I raced to the top of a small rise so I could see the giraffe feeding area.

Night had fallen, but the giraffes were still out in their paddock. The temperature was similar to that of the part of Africa they were from, so there was little sense in locking them up in their building. Although there were a good number of people around, putting up decorations, no one was watching the giraffes.

Mom came up alongside me. "What's going on?" she asked.

"I think we made a mistake with our giraffe investigation," I said. "A big one."

THE TRUCK

"We only did our stakeout during hours when the park was open," I told Summer.

It was Tuesday morning, right before school began. I had tried to reach Summer the whole night before, but she'd had a big report due and her parents had banned her from any texts or phone calls until she was finished. Now we were crossing the front lawn to the steps of the school.

"What's wrong with that?" Summer asked. "That's when all the tourists were at FunJungle."

"Who says a tourist poisoned the giraffes?"

Summer stopped, surprised by that idea. The surge of students heading into school swarmed around us. "What are you saying, that a keeper did it?"

"No, not a keeper. But there are lots of other people

working late at night at FunJungle. And at the same time, it's not too crowded around the giraffes. Or any exhibit. I mean, there's a few security guards on duty, but the park is huge. They can't patrol the whole place at once. Has anyone even looked at the video feeds from Sunday night?"

"I don't know." Summer pulled out her phone. "I'll text Daddy about it, though I don't know when he'll be able to get back to me. He's insanely busy with the big anniversary celebration today."

"I'm sure." I was annoyed I had to be at school that day, rather than at FunJungle, and I knew Summer was too. Fortunately, most of the festivities were going to happen that evening, and her chauffeur was going to take us directly to the park the moment school ended, along with Xavier, Violet, Dash, and Ethan. Summer was wearing a pink dress that her mother had bought specially for the occasion; since Summer was as big a star as any of FunJungle's mascots, the PR department wanted her to be noticed and photographed as much as possible that night.

Most of our fellow students, who all had annual passes, were also heading to FunJungle that afternoon. So were the teachers. The celebration was such a big event that all after-school classes and practices had been canceled that day and no homework was assigned.

"Hey, guys!" Xavier hurried across the lawn to catch up

with us. For the first time I could recall, he wasn't wearing a FunJungle T-shirt. Instead, he was wearing a regular blue polo shirt, and he was acting like it was made of sandpaper, tugging at the collar and wriggling about uncomfortably.

"Nice shirt," Summer observed, really meaning it.

"I *hate* it," Xavier groused. "Stupid Putterman and his stupid rules." The moment he said this, he paled in fear, realizing that Mr. Putterman might be somewhere close enough to overhear him. He swiveled his head around wildly, like an owl homing in on a mouse, before confirming he was in the clear. "The moment I'm out of here today, I'm swapping this itchy thing for something way better." He unzipped his backpack and removed a brand-new FunJungle First Anniversary T-shirt. "Ta-dah! What do you think?"

"It's cool," Summer said, though I could tell that, this time, she didn't mean it. Summer might have loved FunJungle, but she wouldn't have been caught dead in one of their T-shirts. She thought they were ugly and tacky. (I didn't know much about fashion, but I didn't like the shirts much either. Most of them featured garish art and horrid puns like "Iguana go to FunJungle" and "This park sure isn't boaring." The one Xavier was showing us had a lot of mammals and proclaimed "Happy Anni-Fur-sary!")

"My mom got it for me for tonight," Xavier said proudly. "How psyched are you guys for this party?"

"Pretty psyched," I said.

As we started up the front steps into the school, an engine revved loudly behind us. A pickup truck had pulled into the drop-off lane. It looked a good deal like the one the Mystery Guest had been driving.

Summer seemed to realize the same thing. We both stopped to see who was driving it.

The truck was covered with a thin layer of dust, indicating that it had been driven off-road recently, and there was a gun rack in the rear window loaded with four rifles.

The truck jounced up on the curb, nearly clipping a sixth grader, and came to a stop with the engine clanking.

The Barksdale twins leaped out of it. They were dressed for hunting, clad in camouflage from head to toe. It was possible they had already been hunting that morning, as there was fresh mud splattered on the cuffs of their pants.

Xavier groaned. "I can't wear a T-shirt, but those jerks can show up dressed for war? Why doesn't Putterman threaten *them*?"

"Because he's afraid of them," Summer said, then looked to me. "Think it's the same truck?"

I shrugged. "We'd have to see the license plate. And the rear bumper had a dent in it."

Summer immediately started back down the steps toward the truck. I went with her.

Xavier stayed where he was, equally afraid of the Barksdales and getting a tardy. "Where are you guys going?" he asked nervously. "School is about to start."

"We just need to check something out really fast!" I called to him. "I'll meet you in science class!"

Xavier held up his hands, signaling he wanted no part in whatever Summer and I were up to, then slipped through the front doors.

The Barksdales didn't appear to be in any hurry to get to class either. They were still at the front curb. As Summer and I got closer, I could see that both their parents were in the front seat of the truck; it must have been quite a squeeze for the whole family to cram in there, though now that the boys were out, their mother had slid across the seat to the door. "I'll see you out here, the moment after class ends," she told the boys through the open window. "And we'll get back out there!"

"Assuming we haven't bagged that lion already!" their father crowed.

The Barksdale parents were also dressed in camouflage gear. They were locals, having gone to our school two decades earlier, and the rumors around town were that they were no smarter than their sons were. Both had been troublemakers and had continued to be so; they got arrested so often that the holding cell at the local police station was known as "the Barksdale suite." Neither could hold a job for more than a few weeks before getting fired. They were supposed to be good hunters, though; sometimes they *had* to be, as their kills supplemented their food supply. Neither was a fan of rules or regulations. They were avid trespassers, and had often killed things on land they weren't supposed to be on. Recently, Ma Barksdale had shot someone's cow that she had somehow mistaken for a deer.

"Don't you get that cat without us!" Tim protested.

"There's a hundred grand on the line, son," Pa said. "We can't sit around waiting for you."

"In fact, we'd better get going!" Ma exclaimed. "Or someone else'll shoot it before we do!"

"No way! That cat's ours!" Pa Barksdale gave a war whoop and floored the gas, even though there were still lots of kids around. Students scrambled out of the way as the truck leaped back off the curb and peeled out of the parking lot.

I still had time to see the bumper. It had plenty of dents in it—and possibly some blood splattered on it—but the Mystery Guest's had only had one dent. It wasn't the same truck.

The Barksdale twins were coming up the walk now, and they noticed Summer and I were staring after their pickup. They misunderstood *why*, though. They thought we were upset about them going after the lion. (Given, we *were* upset about that, but that wasn't the reason for our stares.)

"Worried about your precious lion?" Jim taunted. "Well, you should be! That thing's gonna be mounted in our house by tonight!"

Rather than take the bait, Summer simply looked around, pretending to be confused, as if she couldn't figure out where Jim's voice was coming from, making fun of the fact that he was wearing full-body camouflage in the middle of town. "Did you hear Jim Barksdale?" she asked me. "I thought I heard him, but I can't see him anywhere."

"I'm right here!" Jim yelled, not realizing that she was joking.

"Jim?" Summer asked. "Are you wearing camouflage or something? Because I can't see you *anywhere*!"

Tim and Jim shared a vacant look, trying to grasp whether Summer was making fun of them, or if their camo gear really was that amazing. Finally, after considering it for a few seconds longer than he should have, Tim seemed to figure out it was the former. "You're making fun of us, aren't you?" he asked.

"Tim?" Summer asked, still looking around blindly. "Is that you? Are you wearing camouflage too? You're blending right in with your surroundings so well." She looked to me. "Can you see them, Teddy?"

"I can't," I said, playing along. "It's like they're invisible."

A lot of the kids who were hurrying to class laughed at Summer's antics—although not *too* loud, as they didn't want to get the Barksdales angry at them.

Tim and Jim turned red around the ears. Neither ever quite knew what to make of Summer, especially when she used humor against them.

"Ha ha," Jim said sarcastically. "You both are hilarious."

Summer squinted at him. "Wait! I think I can see you now! I can sort of make out your face. Yes, I'm sure it's your face, because it makes me want to vomit."

More kids stifled laughter.

Tim glared at Summer. "You're lucky you're a girl," he threatened. "Otherwise I'd punch your face in." Then he hurried off to class with Jim before Summer could tease him anymore.

I was about to head to class myself—it was awfully close to the first bell—when I noticed something across the parking lot.

There was another pickup truck, parked in the faculty area, and now that I saw it, it looked a lot more like the truck in the video than the Barksdales' did. Almost exactly the same.

Summer was still staring after the Barksdales. I grabbed her arm and pointed. "Do you know whose truck that is?"

Summer looked that way. Her eyebrows arched in surprise. "Only one way to find out," she said, and started across the lot.

She moved quickly now, knowing we were racing the clock. Given who her father was, Summer never *really* got in trouble, but she didn't want to tempt fate. I knew I should get to class myself, but it seemed wrong to let Summer do the investigating all by herself.

The last kids were arriving for school, leaping from their cars and hurrying up the steps. I noticed Xavier in the window of the science lab, watching us, obviously worried. He pointed to his watch and mouthed, *What are you doing?*

I held up a finger, indicating I'd be only one minute, which I hoped would be true.

Even though I had been at LBJ Middle School for over a year, I had never been in the faculty parking lot before. There hadn't been any reason, really. As we crossed into it, I discovered that most of the spaces were unassigned, although the closest few to the school were reserved for the administrators. I was surprised to see this type of hierarchy, especially when the reserved spaces probably saved a minute of walking a day, tops. The spaces were marked with plastic signs mounted on spindly stakes; two had fallen over (or maybe had been driven over) at some point and simply lay on the ground at the front of the parking space, waiting for someone to erect them properly once again. This was the case with the one in front of the pickup; Summer and I had to stand over it to read it.

It said: RESERVED FOR VICE PRINCIPAL PUTTERMAN.

Summer and I shared a look of revelation. I thought back to the video, trying to recall if the Mystery Guest inside the truck had no neck. All I could remember about him was that his face had been shrouded in shadow, but that would have been the case for someone who perpetually wore a cowboy hat.

"Is it the same license plate?" I asked.

"I think so," Summer said. "I only remember the first three numbers, though."

So we circled around to the back of the truck. Sure enough, there was a dent in the rear bumper. In exactly the right place.

"Putterman's the Mystery Guest?" I said. "How does he even know Lincoln Stone?"

"I don't know," Summer said, "but he was definitely there. And if anyone would kill a dog, it's that sadistic jerk."

The first school bell rang in the distance. We were tardy.

"C'mon," I said. "We better get to class."

Summer and I hurried around the truck, but someone was blocking our path.

Vice Principal Putterman stood there, legs splayed, arms on his hips, forming a human roadblock. "Oh, you're not going to class," he said, flashing a cruel smile. "You're going to detention."

PUNISHMENT

Putterman hustled me back across the parking lot to the school, seizing my arm in a vise grip. Even though he had also caught Summer, he wasn't holding *her* arm. In fact, he didn't seem interested in punishing her at all. I figured this was probably because he didn't want to pick a fight with J.J. McCracken's daughter; he might have simply had it in for me. He certainly seemed awfully pleased with himself for having nabbed me, even though I had always behaved at school.

"I always suspected you were trouble, Fitzroy," Putterman said proudly. "You might have had all your teachers fooled, but not me. You're getting three days of maximum detention, starting right now."

I gaped at him. Putterman had invented two levels of

detention. The first was regular detention, where you simply sat in a room all day, missing all your classes and "thinking about the error of your ways." It was a bizarre punishment, as it removed you from class and gave you nothing to do, including studying, guaranteeing that you would fall behind in your lessons. And yet, because some students—like the Barksdales—wanted to use their brains as little as possible, they actually *enjoyed* regular detention.

So Putterman had created "Maximum Detention"—or "Max" as it was known—as extra punishment. For this, you didn't merely miss your classes; you also had to stay *after school*. There were two bonus hours of doing nothing tacked on, and you would miss anything you had planned. Like the anniversary festivities for FunJungle.

"I'm getting three days of Max for being tardy?" I asked, incredulous. Putterman didn't like it when kids talked back to him, but I couldn't help it; I had to defend myself. "I would have only been a few minutes late, tops. The Barksdales skip school all the time. . . ."

"I caught *you*, not the Barksdales," Putterman informed me. "And you're not just getting detention for being tardy. You're getting it for being up to no good."

"All he was doing was looking at your truck," Summer argued. "He didn't even touch it. How is that 'being up to no good'?"

Putterman shifted his angry gaze to her. "You'd best be on your way to class, Miss McCracken. This doesn't concern you."

"Teddy didn't do anything wrong!" Summer said sharply. Although she usually didn't like people to know her father was rich and powerful, she was aware that it gave her advantages. No other student could raise their voice to Putterman and get away with it.

Putterman simply ignored her. We reached the front steps of the school and he dragged me up them toward the doors.

I saw Xavier, along with most of my first-period science class, pressed up against the windows, watching me. Even though I was partly in trouble for being tardy, it didn't appear that science had even started yet. Many of my classmates seemed to think it was funny that I'd been busted—or maybe they were simply relieved that someone had gotten in trouble besides them. Xavier appeared to be extremely upset on my behalf. He looked as though he felt he'd failed me somehow.

"Can I call my parents?" I asked. I knew they would never stand for me being treated like this.

"No." Putterman pulled me roughly through the front doors. His tight grip on my arm was really starting to hurt.

"That's ridiculous," Summer said. "Everyone has the right to a phone call."

"This is not a police station," Putterman told her. "This is a school. I am the law here. I have been placed in charge of discipline, and what I say goes."

The school's administrative offices were just beyond the front doors, across the hall from the science lab. Putterman yanked me through the reception area. The school receptionist looked up from her desk as we barged in with Summer on our heels. "My goodness, Mr. Putterman, you're working hard," she observed. "The first bell just rang."

"Mischief never sleeps," Putterman said, then told her, "Make sure that Miss McCracken here gets to class."

The receptionist dutifully stood in Summer's path as she tried to follow us. Putterman shoved me into his office and slammed the door behind him.

The office was small. There was an ugly metal desk, facing two metal chairs. The dreaded wooden paddle hung directly on the wall behind the desk, the focus of the room. To the left of it was Putterman's college diploma. To the right was a framed, personally signed photo of Lincoln Stone. It was far more prominently displayed than the photos of Putterman's wife or children, which were relegated to tiny frames on the corner of his desk.

On the wall by the door was a shelf full of trophies for shooting, indicating Putterman was good with a gun. Alongside them sat a large jar full of contraband items Putterman had gleefully confiscated from students over the past few months: pocketknives, slingshots, gum, tins of chewing tobacco, fireworks, and the like.

Putterman pointed to one of the metal chairs and told me, "Sit." Like I was a dog.

I didn't like that, but I sat anyhow, trying not to annoy him even more. Then, I attempted to reason with him. "Mr. Putterman, I don't know what you think I was doing out there, but—"

"Oh, I *know* what you were doing out there." Putterman didn't sit down himself. Instead, he strutted around his office with his hands behind his back, glaring at me imperiously. "Just like I know that you were at Lincoln Stone's property the other day, snooping around without his permission."

"I had permission from the Fish and Wildlife Service—" I began.

"You see," Putterman interrupted, "Lincoln Stone is a good friend of mine. We met out at a shooting range a while back, before he built his own. He has me up to his place at least once a month. We play cards, shoot guns, have a good old time." The way Putterman said this made it clear he thought I'd be impressed that he was friends with a celebrity. "So when Lincoln saw you on his property with that idiot from Fish and Wildlife the other day, he called me right up and asked if I knew who you might be. And of course, I did. I'm well aware of your reputation for sticking your nose where it doesn't belong."

"I was trying to figure out who killed King," I protested.

"We all know who killed that lousy mutt," Putterman said. "It was a mountain lion, pure and simple . . ."

"Maybe not," I said.

Putterman wheeled on me angrily. "Are you calling me a liar?"

I shrank in my chair under his gaze. "No."

"It certainly seems like you are. And it seems like you think Lincoln Stone is a liar too. I mean, the man *knows* a mountain lion killed his dog. Now, that dog might have been a little pain in the rear, but Lincoln loved it, and he's very upset about it. And yet, here you are, refusing to accept facts as facts, poking around where you shouldn't be, claiming it wasn't a mountain lion at all. Just to cause trouble."

"That's not why I'm doing it at all!" I insisted. "If Lincoln's really upset about his dog, I'd think he would *want* to know who really killed it. . . ."

"Did I ask you a question?" Putterman demanded.

"No," I said. "But—"

"Then you need to keep your mouth shut. You have a serious problem with authority, Fitzroy. You are insubordinate and disobedient and you do not know your place. So perhaps a little discipline is in order." Putterman strode behind his desk, heading for his paddle.

"What?" I cried. "You can't be serious!"

"You see? That sort of outburst is exactly what I'm talking about." Putterman lifted the paddle off the wall, cradling it like a holy relic. "I'm tired of your lip, son. Now I want you to bend over that desk."

I couldn't believe my ears. I couldn't believe this could be happening to me in my own school. I wasn't sure if Lincoln Stone had put Putterman up to this, or if Putterman was simply this cruel and misguided on his own, but I knew I didn't deserve to get paddled. "No," I said firmly. There didn't seem to be any point to following Putterman's rules any longer; it wasn't like I could get into any *more* trouble.

Putterman's eyes narrowed angrily. "What did you say to me?"

"I said no. I'm not getting paddled. I didn't do anything wrong."

"If I say you did something wrong, then you did something wrong. Now assume the position!"

I sprang from the chair, heading for the door, but Putterman had predicted this. He leaped into my path, wielding the paddle like a baseball bat. There was rage in his eyes. For a moment, I thought he might attack me.

There was a sudden commotion outside the door. I heard the receptionist yell, "You can't go in there!" followed by the sound of someone running toward the office.

I thought it might be Summer coming to my rescue. Or Dash or Ethan.

But it was Xavier who burst through the door. He looked nervous and desperate, like he was pretty sure what he was about to do was going to end in disaster—although he seemed relieved when he noticed I hadn't been paddled yet. He held a large mason jar in his hands.

Putterman wheeled on him. "I do not want to be disturbed!" he roared.

"Sorry!" Xavier said. "But there's been an emergency! Violet Grace just got attacked!"

Instead of being concerned, Putterman seemed annoyed that someone else's misfortune had interrupted his torture session. "By what?"

"One of these." Xavier held up the mason jar. The three tarantulas from the science lab were inside it. And there was no lid on the top.

I knew the spiders weren't dangerous. So did every kid at school. Our teacher often let us hold them. But they looked scary, with bulbous bodies and bristly legs and rows of beady eyes.

Putterman yelped and leaped backward, confirming the

rumors that he was afraid of animals. Or spiders, at least. "Why'd you bring them in here?" he squealed.

"I couldn't leave them *there*," Xavier said, doing an impressive job of selling the story. "They're dangerous! One of them bit Violet's hand and now her arm swelled up to the size of her leg!"

Putterman's eyes went wide at the thought of this. He didn't look tough anymore. Instead, he backed away from the jar, trembling with fear. "Get them out of here!" he yelped. "Get them out of here now!"

"But I . . . ," Xavier began, and then pretended to trip on the carpet. "Whoops!" He made an excellent pratfall, stumbling forward, and in the same movement he shook the jar so the three tarantulas launched out of it. Two landed on Putterman's desk.

And the third landed right on Putterman's chest.

Putterman screamed in terror. "Get it off me!" he shrieked. "Get it off, get it off, get it off!" He danced around frantically, trying to shake the spider off himself so he wouldn't have to touch it, knocking over his desk chair and a coatrack. His beloved framed photo of Lincoln Stone tumbled off the wall and broke on the floor.

"Careful!" I warned. "If they bite you, the venom is extremely painful. And toxic."

Putterman screamed again. He somehow managed to

knock the tarantula off himself. It landed on his computer screen. Putterman quickly swung at it with his paddle.

I was worried about the spider, but thankfully, in Putterman's fear, he had completely lost his coordination. He missed the computer by a good two feet, connecting with his desk lamp instead. The lamp sailed right through his office window and shattered on the front lawn.

Putterman didn't seem to care. He was experiencing a full-blown case of arachnophobia, sweaty and hyperventilating in his panic. I almost felt bad for him.

But not quite enough to calm him.

Putterman swatted wildly at the tarantula on his computer once again. This time, his aim was better—although the spider seemed to have sensed danger and had already scrambled away. Putterman drove his paddle right through the computer screen, which exploded in a spray of sparks and crashed to the floor.

Putterman kept on swinging, taking out just about everything *but* the tarantulas. He flattened the photos of his family, destroyed his phone, and swatted a paperweight so hard that it embedded in the wall. On his next swing, he missed the desk entirely and took out his trophy shelf. The trophies came crashing down and busted apart. The jar full of contraband broke open, spilling everything across the carpet.

Finally, Putterman stopped to survey the damage he'd

done, red-faced and panting. The spiders had now hidden for safety, so they were nowhere to be seen, which only increased Putterman's sense of panic. "Where are they?" he asked, terrified.

For a moment, I thought about being honest. But then I remembered that, only a minute before, this man had been willing to paddle me for no good reason. "The biggest one's on your back," I said.

Putterman howled. It was almost inhuman. He spun around wildly, as if he could somehow create enough centrifugal force to fling the spider off his body.

One of the contraband objects that had spilled on the floor was a large rubber ball. Putterman had confiscated it from Dash a week before, because Dash and Ethan had been playing catch with it in the hallway during the changing period. As Putterman spun, he stepped on the ball and his feet flew out from under him. He landed flat on his back atop the array of busted trophies and let loose with another howl, only this one was in pain.

"My back!" he wailed. "I think I threw out my back!" Then, as Xavier and I almost began to feel sorry for him, he glared at us and said, "Don't just sit there, you idiots! I need a doctor!"

Xavier and I happily evacuated his office as quickly as we could.

The entire school administration was gathered outside the door. They had obviously been listening to the chaos in the office, wondering what could possibly be going on in there. Mr. Dillnut, our principal, looked to us expectantly.

"Mr. Putterman fell down and hurt his back," Xavier said. "He needs a doctor."

Instead of calling a doctor, everyone rushed to the office to see what had happened. Xavier and I took advantage of the diversion to continue out of the administrative offices and race back to science class. Both of us were sure that once Putterman healed, we would be in serious trouble, but I was still thankful my friend had come to my rescue and that, for the time being, I had escaped the paddle.

As we slipped into the hallway, Summer came running, her phone clamped to her ear. She stopped, surprised to see us. "I have my dad's office on the line," she said. "Daddy's going to call the principal to get you off the hook."

"That'd be great," I said. "Though Xavier took care of Putterman for now."

"Oh," Summer said. She didn't seem as happy about this as I would have expected.

Xavier looked hurt by her reaction. "You don't think that's good?"

"Of course I do," Summer said distractedly. "It's amazing. It's just that, according to Daddy's office, there's been some bad news. The Department of Fish and Wildlife caved to Lincoln Stone."

Suddenly, I didn't feel so relieved anymore. "You mean . . ."

"Yes," Summer said. "They issued the permit to kill Rocket."

THE GUARD

Putterman didn't cause any more trouble for me.
J.J. McCracken phoned Principal Dillnut himself and then
looped one of his top lawyers onto the call. J.J. laid into the
principal for allowing Putterman to even *think* about paddling me—for something that was really a personal issue,
rather than a school one—and then went on to condemn
the school's whole corporal punishment system as outdated
and barbaric. (Apparently, J.J. himself had suffered some
paddlings back in his days at LBJ.) So not only was I off the
hook—as well as Xavier—but paddling itself seemed like it
was done for at our school.

J.J. had wanted to give Putterman a piece of his mind
as well, but the vice principal was in no position to talk. He
had gone to the hospital in an ambulance, where he'd been

diagnosed with a ruptured disc in his spine, which was going to keep him out of school for the rest of the year.

Xavier didn't even get in trouble with Mrs. Duckworth, our science teacher, despite having left her class without permission—along with a jar full of tarantulas. Mrs. Duckworth claimed to have not noticed Xavier or the spiders were missing, though she had smiled coyly as she said this. I also noticed her smiling as she watched Putterman get loaded into the ambulance, which led me to believe that she—and probably a lot of other teachers at the school—weren't fans of Putterman or his tactics.

As for the spiders, they were recovered by the janitorial staff and returned safely to the classroom.

So I was able to go to FunJungle after school with my friends as planned—although Summer and I still weren't able to go right out and enjoy the festivities. It turned out we had work to do. In addition to getting her father to speak on my behalf, Summer had also managed to track down the FunJungle security guard who had been in charge of patrolling the area near the giraffes on Sunday night: Kevin Wilks. Kevin was working the anniversary party—all members of FunJungle Security were—though he had a break right around the time we arrived at the park.

Summer's driver, Tran, brought Xavier, Dashiell, Ethan, Violet, Summer, and me in through the employee drive-on gate, the same way he drove J.J. McCracken to work. While our friends headed out to enjoy the party, Summer and I found Kevin. He met us in the employee cafeteria, which was located near the administration building and the veterinary hospital. He was sitting at a table by the window, scarfing down a burger and fries before going back to his shift. Summer got free sodas for us. She often got food comped, seeing as her father owned the entire park, and besides, the sodas only cost him about two cents each.

"You worked a night shift *after* helping us with Operation Hammerhead in the morning?" I asked.

"I did have a nap in the afternoon," Kevin replied. "Remember? That's why I couldn't help after Marge went to the hospital."

"I didn't realize you'd be working the whole night, though," I said. "Weren't you exhausted?"

"Nah," Kevin said, though I got the sense he was trying to sound tough for Summer. "I've done this plenty of times. And besides, finding out who poisoned those giraffes was really important. Or, it would have been . . . if we'd done it."

Outside the window, all the actors who portrayed the FunJungle mascots were heading out to join the anniversary party. Since the actors were still in the employee area and it was hard to see where they were going with the enormous heads on, most of them were carrying the heads, so it looked like a parade of enormous decapitated animals. As usual, the actors themselves were a rogues' gallery. The guy who played Eleanor Elephant had so many piercings in his face he probably couldn't have passed through a metal detector; the woman who played Katie Kangaroo was sneaking sips of alcohol from a flask she kept stashed in her marsupial pocket; and Charlie Connor, the little person who played Kazoo the Koala, was smoking a cigar and scratching himself inappropriately. If any small children had been there to see their favorite FunJungle characters in this way, they probably would have started crying.

I told Kevin, "We're thinking the reason that we didn't catch the person who poisoned the giraffes was that we only watched the exhibit during the hours the park was open, and not after the park had closed."

Kevin blinked at me, confused. "So?"

"Someone must have poisoned the giraffes *after* park hours," Summer explained.

Understanding slowly dawned on Kevin. "You mean . . . you think an *employee* poisoned the giraffes?"

"Yes," Summer and I said at once.

"But why would an employee do that?" Kevin asked. "We all love the giraffes!"

I said, "Whoever did this might not have been trying to poison them on purpose. It might have been a mistake.

Maybe they didn't even know they were doing anything wrong."

"You were on patrol in that area Sunday night," Summer added. "Did you see *anything* suspicious?"

"No." Kevin wolfed down a handful of french fries. "I barely saw anyone over by the giraffes at all."

"So you did see someone?" I asked.

"Yes, but only keepers. And none of them would poison the animals, right?"

Summer and I exchanged a glance. The idea of a keeper poisoning one of their own animals seemed impossible. Even by accident. A keeper would certainly know what foods might be dangerous to their charges. But we were running out of options.

"We should probably get their names, just to be sure," I said.

Outside the window, a team of keepers passed with a llama on a leash. As part of the festivities, many animals were being brought out to meet guests. Most were being presented on stages, like the one at the lawn by Carnivore Canyon, at a distance from the audience, but some of the more docile ones like the llama were going to be trotted out in public, where tourists could meet them, pet them—and hopefully learn a thing or two about them. The llama didn't seem the slightest bit fazed by all the activity around it. Instead, it ambled along happily with its keepers like an exceptionally tall labradoodle.

Marge O'Malley followed it in a wheelchair. It was the first time I had seen her since her accident at the giraffe paddock. Her entire leg was wrapped in a cast, so it jabbed out in front of her like the bowsprit of a sailing ship, but it didn't appear to have slowed her down at all. Through the window, we could hear her yelling at the keepers to pick up a few pellets of poop the llama had left on the walkway.

Marge then looked our way, noticed us sitting with Kevin, and pointed to her watch.

Kevin glanced at his own watch and gulped. "Shoot! I'm supposed to be on duty in two minutes!" He quickly crammed the remaining half of his hamburger into his mouth and left the table.

Summer and I grabbed our sodas and followed him.

Summer asked, "You didn't see *anyone* else around the giraffes except for keepers?"

"No one," Kevin replied, his mouth full of burger. "Not this Sunday or any of the others."

"Others?" I repeated, not sure if I had heard him right. Kevin was very hard to understand with his mouth full.

"Yeah." Kevin swallowed a wad of hamburger so big I was surprised he didn't choke on it. "I've been working Sunday nights the past couple of weeks."

An idea came to me as we followed Kevin out into the sun. I didn't like it, but I had to pursue it. "How many weeks exactly?"

"Umm." Kevin screwed up his face as he thought about this. "Five."

Which was the exact number of times the giraffes had been poisoned. I looked at Summer, who had obviously realized the same thing. "Kevin," she said, "have *you* ever fed the giraffes when you're on your shift?"

"Sure," he said happily. "That's one of the best things about it!"

Marge hadn't waited for Kevin to emerge from the cafeteria. She had wheeled off to chastise Charlie Connor for smoking a cigar while in costume. The two of them were arguing in the distance. Charlie called Marge a cow, so in response, Marge ran over his toes with her wheelchair. Charlie then hopped around, howling in pain, and called Marge a whole lot of other things.

Kevin led Summer and me through the employee area, passing the vet hospital.

"What did you feed the giraffes?" I asked.

"Plants," Kevin replied, like maybe *I* was the dumb one. "That's what giraffes eat. They're harpsichords, you know."

"You mean herbivores?" I asked.

"Right!" Kevin said. "That's the word!"

"Which plants?" Summer asked, sounding annoyed now.

"I don't know," Kevin answered innocently. "Does it matter?"

"It might," I said. "Where did you find them?"

Kevin glanced at his watch again. "Over by the giraffes. Could I show you later? I'm supposed to be out on duty already."

"It'd be good to see them now," Summer replied. Before Kevin could protest, she added, "If Chief Hoenekker gets upset that you're not at work, I can call him and straighten things out."

That made Kevin feel better. "Okay," he said, and then led us on through the employee area. We skirted around the back of the Swamp, World of Reptiles, and where the Great Flight Cage was under construction. It still hadn't dawned on Kevin that he might have done anything wrong. Instead, he seemed extremely pleased with himself. "I'd seen so many people feeding the giraffes here," he explained as we walked, "and it always looked like so much fun, you know? So when I started working the late shift around them, I figured I'd give it a try. I found some nice, pretty plants and brought them out, and the giraffes came right up to me and ate them! It was awesome! And the giraffes loved it too. It was like I was giving them chocolate cake or something. This is the stuff right here!" He stopped and pointed dramatically.

We were still in the employee area, near the gate that provided access to the park closest to SafariLand and the giraffes. While some effort was made to beautify the employee areas, not nearly as much attention was paid to them as the tourist areas of the park, where every piece of trash was snapped up within moments of hitting the ground and the landscaping was meticulously cleared of weeds every night. Along the construction fence that surrounded the Great Flight Cage, in a few inches of dirt, some plants were growing. They were weeds, but as weeds went, they were quite pretty, which was probably why no one had uprooted them. They had bright green leaves and large purple flowers, along with berries so blue they were almost black.

"This is what you fed to the giraffes?" I asked.

"Yeah!" Kevin answered proudly. "They love it!"

"Do you know what it is?" Summer asked me.

"Yes," I replied. "It's the solution to our case."

THE CONFRONTATION

"You can't go in there!" J.J. McCracken's secretary shouted.

Summer didn't pay any attention to her, though. She was too excited. Clutching a bouquet of the plants that Kevin had fed to the giraffes, she blew right past Lynda and barged into her father's office.

I was excited too. Otherwise, I might have been more aware of Lynda's unusually alarmed behavior. I had shown up in the waiting area with Summer dozens of times. If J.J. was doing something important, Lynda would calmly ask Summer if she could wait a few minutes; she had never shouted at her before.

J.J. was at his desk when we entered. Pete Thwacker, Fun-Jungle's smarmy-but-effective director of public relations, was seated on the couch across from him. Both reacted with suspiciously startled reactions to Summer's arrival. Normally, J.J. would have greeted his daughter warmly, while Pete might have flashed his made-for-TV grin, but now both looked like deer caught in the headlights of an oncoming car.

Summer didn't catch this. Instead, she held the plants over her head like an Olympic athlete hoisting a gold medal. "Deadly nightshade!" she announced.

"Summer," J.J. said uneasily, scurrying out from behind his desk. "This isn't the best time. I have a million things going on. . . ."

"It's what poisoned the giraffes," Summer told him. "Teddy knew what it was."

My parents had always made it a priority to teach me about the flora and fauna of where I lived. This was partly because it fascinated them and they wanted to share their knowledge with me. But it was also a safety issue. In the same way that a parent raising a toddler in the city would teach their child not to stick a finger in electrical sockets, my parents taught me what plants I couldn't eat around our wilderness camp.

I was now old enough that my parents no longer had to worry about me putting random plants in my mouth, but their fascination with nature remained, and I had certainly inherited it from them. We didn't live in a tent camp, but we were still on the edge of the wilderness, so there were plenty of flora and fauna to study, and it always made sense to know what might be poisonous.

Deadly nightshade wasn't indigenous to Central Texas, but it was a highly invasive species, so I had learned about it. Like many plants, it had been introduced by European settlers and spread rapidly across the country. (Some nonnative plant species, like dandelions, had been so successful that most people didn't even realize they weren't native.) I wasn't an adept-enough naturalist that I had been one hundred percent sure the plant Kevin had found was deadly nightshade, but a quick stop at the veterinary hospital had confirmed it.

Given that J.J. had asked us to find out what had happened to the giraffes in the first place, he didn't seem very intrigued by Summer's revelation. Instead, he appeared far more interested in getting rid of us. "That's very fascinating," he said absently, putting one arm around Summer and the other around me and herding us to the door. "We really ought to discuss it later."

By now, Summer was beginning to realize something was wrong with her father's behavior. "Do you know who fed this to the giraffes?" she asked. "The zebras."

"Is that so?" J.J. asked distractedly, glancing toward his executive bathroom. "I had no idea."

"Yes," Summer went on. "The zebras have been very jealous of all the attention the giraffes are getting and decided to kill them all. But since they don't have opposable thumbs, they had to hire a chimpanzee as the hit man."

"That's very nice," J.J. said, trying to shepherd us out the door.

Instead, Summer dug her heels into the carpet. "You're not even listening to me!"

"Of course I am, sweetheart," J.J. said.

"Teddy and I figured out who's been poisoning your giraffes and how they've been doing it, and you don't even care!"

This shook J.J. back to reality, forcing him to focus on his daughter. "I *do* care," he insisted. "It's just that now isn't the best time. The festivities are about to begin and I have a million things that need to be handled. . . ."

"Kevin Wilks did it," Summer told him. "Your own security guard."

"Really?" Pete asked, jolted into paying attention himself. "Why?"

"Because he's an idiot," Summer replied.

"He didn't *realize* he was doing anything wrong," I clarified. "He thought that the giraffes could eat any old plant . . ."

"Because he's an idiot," Summer said again. "There are a

million signs around this park, telling you that the animals have specialized diets and that you shouldn't feed them. The moron works here and he never read a single one of them."

"He feels really bad about it, though," I said. As dumb as Kevin had been, I didn't want to get him fired. Plus, Kevin felt awful about what he had done. Once he learned that *he* was the poisoner, he had cried so hard and loud that a passing paramedic had stopped to see if he'd been wounded by one of the animals. We had left the two of them together and run off to confirm what species the plant was.

"I hope the press doesn't hear about this," Pete said, far more concerned about FunJungle's reputation than the giraffes. "I'd hate to have the story of our wonderful anniversary celebration marred by the news that one of our own security guards tried to murder our giraffes."

"He wasn't *trying* to murder them," I corrected.

"That's how the media will frame it," Pete informed me. "They love to make things as sordid as possible. They'll claim we have a psychotic animal killer working on our own security staff." He turned to J.J. "If I were you, I wouldn't fire him just yet. Disgruntled employees often go right to the press."

"I'm not doing *anything* about this right now," J.J. remarked, glancing nervously at his executive washroom again. "I have a lot of other things to handle." He looked back to Summer and me. "I really appreciate all the hard work you kids did on this. The party's already underway. Why don't you head down there to enjoy it and I'll catch up with you as soon as I can. . . ."

The door to his washroom flew open and Jerry the hunter walked out. The toilet was still finishing a flush behind him.

Jerry looked momentarily startled to see me there, but then broke into a big smile as he recognized me. "Hey, Teddy! Done any more swimming lately?"

Summer gaped, recognizing him, then wheeled on her father. "What is *he* doing here?"

Normally, J.J. was blessed with the gift of gab, so smooth he could sell sand to Bedouins. But now he found himself tongue-tied in front of his daughter. "Er. Well. You see . . ."

"He's here as a carnivore relocation specialist," Pete said, going into full public-relations mode.

"He's a hunter!" Summer cried. "And a trespasser! He was shooting at Rocket inside FunJungle the other night! Hoenekker arrested him for it! And now he's *here*?"

"Maybe I ought to step outside," Jerry said awkwardly, not nearly as cheerful anymore. "Feels like I'm interrupting something here." He started for the door.

"Stay," J.J. commanded him, and Jerry froze in his tracks.

Summer looked from her father to Jerry, putting things together. Tears welled in her eyes. "Daddy, tell me he's not working for you."

J.J. held his breath for a moment, as though he was considering lying to his daughter, but then said, "Not in the way that you think."

"You hired a hunter?!" Summer exploded.

"A gunman!" J.J. said quickly.

"What's the difference?" Summer asked.

"I didn't hire Jerry here to *kill* Rocket," J.J. explained. "I hired him to chase her away."

"We saw him shooting at her," Summer said accusingly.

"But not with real bullets," Jerry said. "I used rubber ones."

Since this was one of the scenarios I had discussed with Xavier, I felt a slight surge of pride for guessing J.J.'s intentions correctly—and a huge rush of relief that he wasn't actively trying to kill Rocket.

Summer remained annoyed, however. "Rubber bullets would still hurt Rocket if they hit her."

"Well, yes, but that's kind of the point," J.J. said. "We're not trying to make her feel comfy here."

"We need to get her out of the park," Pete said. "And fast."

Something about this phrase struck me as odd, like there was a piece of information I was missing. "Out of the park?" I repeated. "What do you mean?"

Pete winced, like he had revealed something he hadn't

meant to. He looked to J.J., who didn't seem pleased about this either.

"What's going on here, Daddy?" Summer asked.

J.J. sighed and gave in. "I know you've heard that Fish and Wildlife issued the permit to kill Rocket. Well, given that she has a radio collar, they're using it to track her. And it turns out she's somewhere in the park right now."

"Like in the construction area?" I asked.

"No," J.J. said. "In the park itself."

Summer and I both gasped in surprise. Summer asked, "You mean, she's in with the tourists?"

"She's somewhere close to them," J.J. said. "Fish and Wildlife hasn't let me know the exact location. I'm not sure if their tech isn't good enough or what, but they know she's inside the park boundaries. Most likely, she's holed up in a back area or a drainage culvert or something, quiet and away from the crowds. . . ."

"We *hope* she's away from the crowds," Pete put in. "Can you imagine what would happen if a mountain lion got loose during the party?"

I didn't have to. I had seen a tiger crash a party at Fun-Jungle once before. And this party was significantly bigger. "Shouldn't you cancel the celebration?" I asked.

Pete stared at me like I was insane. "Cancel FunJungle's anniversary party right before it happens? Because there's a carnivore loose in the park? I have news crews from around the world here! I have celebrity guests! It would be a disaster!"

"How can Rocket even be here?" Summer wanted to know. "With all these people around? How could no one have seen her?"

"Cats are amazing that way," I told her. "You'd think they'd be obvious, but I've been within a few feet of a leopard and had no idea it was even there. If a cat doesn't want to be seen, you won't see it."

Lynda appeared at the door, holding a sheaf of papers. "I'm sorry to interrupt, J.J., but—"

"I know, I know," J.J. said. "I have six million calls to return and I'm supposed to be at the main stage in half an hour."

"Main stage in twenty minutes," Lynda corrected.

J.J. checked his watch. "Crap on a cracker! Is that the time?" He hurried to where a garment bag hung on a coat hook. "Lynda, I'm not getting to any of those calls today. The rest of you, I apologize, but I have to change while we talk." He looked to Summer. "Your mother talked me into wearing black tie for the festivities tonight." He unzipped the bag, revealing a tuxedo, then stepped behind a potted plant for some privacy and started to change clothes, unbuckling his belt and dropping his pants.

Jerry averted his eyes uncomfortably. "J.J., if you'll just give me my marching orders, I'll be happy to get out of your hair."

"Fish and Wildlife is sending a team here to deal with the lion," J.J. told him. "I can't stop them, but I'd prefer to have you find her first. I don't want them killing an animal on my property. If Rocket's close to the tourists, sedate her. If she's somewhere you can run her off, then do that instead. But for God's sake, use the silencer. I don't want any guests hearing the gun."

"Then we'll *really* have a PR disaster," Pete agreed.

I asked Jerry, "If you could silence your gun, why didn't you do that Sunday night?"

"The sound scares the cat too," Jerry explained, heading for the door. "Maybe even more than getting hit by a rubber bullet does."

"Wait," Summer said, so forcefully that Jerry stopped in his tracks and J.J. froze with his pants around his ankles. "You're going to chase Rocket off the property?"

"That's right." J.J. returned to taking his pants off. He was wearing FunJungle boxer shorts, with little Henry Hippos on them. "That's been Jerry's job here all along. Rocket started prowling around here about two weeks ago. According to Fish and Wildlife, she'd come sniffing around before on rare occasions, but once we filled that fake lake with water for the rapids, she started to act like this was her territory. So I hired Jerry to scare her off."

"But you *can't* chase her off the property now!" Summer argued. "The woods are full of hunters who'll kill her! Or Fish and Wildlife will take her out!"

"Well, I can't let her stay inside FunJungle!" J.J. said, struggling to pull his tuxedo pants on over his cowboy boots. "This is a theme park!"

"Can you imagine how awful the headlines would be if she ate a tourist?" Pete asked, paling as he said this. "Or a celebrity?"

"The lion won't eat anyone," I told him.

"Chasing Rocket out to the wild is condemning her to death!" Summer told her father.

"Well, letting her stay here is condemning my other animals to death," J.J. shot back. "That mountain lion's not a vegetarian! She's got to eat. And if she's lurking around on my property, sooner or later she's gonna kill one of our animals. An endangered one, maybe."

Pete blanched. "What if she eats something endangered and cute? Like a panda?" He seemed even more horrified about this than he did about the lion eating a human.

"Mountain lions don't eat pandas," I said. It probably wasn't true, but I was trying to be reassuring.

"Why not?" Pete asked.

"They don't like Chinese food," I said.

Summer asked her father, "Isn't there any way you can

protect Rocket until Teddy and I can prove she was framed for eating King?"

"How am I supposed to do that?" J.J. was growing exasperated now. He yanked off his shirt so quickly that a button flew across the room and ricocheted off Pete's forehead. "I've got ten thousand animals here and you want me to harbor an apex predator? What am I supposed to do, get the cat to sign a treaty? Have it promise to only eat broccoli until this King thing blows over?"

Summer frowned at him. "There must be something we can do."

J.J. slipped into his tuxedo shirt. He looked as uncomfortable in the fancy clothing as Xavier had in his polo shirt. "Summer, I care about that lion. I do. But I also have a business to run here, and that's hard enough to do on a regular day, let alone *today*. The last thing I need right now is some invasive species getting onto my property." He grabbed his tuxedo jacket and his bow tie and headed out of his office.

The rest of us followed him. Summer stayed right on his heels. "Invasive species?" she repeated angrily. "Daddy, do you have any idea what an invasive species even is?"

"Of course I do." J.J. tried to button his cuffs as he walked. "It's like that deadly nightshade you've got in your hand right now."

Summer looked down, seeming to realize that she was

still clutching the nightshade. In all the excitement, she hadn't even bothered to put it down.

"Or like this lion," J.J. went on. "It's any plant or animal that moves into an area it's not supposed to be in."

"You're right about the nightshade," Summer said. "But you're dead wrong about the lion. This is *her* territory, not ours. If anything, *we're* the invasive species here. Humans are the worst invasive species there's ever been! We've spread all over the world, destroying every place we go, killing all the species that were there first. We've built theme parks and houses and golf courses in the middle of Rocket's territory, and now we're upset when she tries to survive here?"

"Now you're upset I built this theme park?" J.J. asked. "Because I seem to recall you being very excited about it for the entire rest of your life up till now."

"I'm saying that we contributed to Rocket's problem," Summer replied. "So maybe we ought to contribute to a solution."

J.J. reached the elevator, still only partly dressed. His tuxedo shirt was still unbuttoned and his tie dangled undone around his collar. He rubbed his temples with his fingers, like he was fending off a headache. "Summer, it is the biggest night in this park's history. Now is not the time to badger me about this."

"Should I come back tomorrow when Rocket's dead?"

Summer snapped. "Would that be more convenient for you?"

"You know I care about Rocket," J.J. said.

"You *say* that," Summer chided, "but you're acting just like everyone else."

"What's that supposed to mean?" J.J. asked.

The elevator pinged open and all of us crowded into it.

"Poaching isn't the biggest threat to animals," Summer said. "Habitat loss is. Animals are getting crowded out of their own territory all over the planet. And we keep expecting them to survive with less and less—and then getting upset with them when they can't do it. Americans get upset when mountain lions get too close to houses *they* built in the lions' territory. Africans get upset when elephants eat the crops *they* planted where elephants live. In India, people are illegally building entire villages *inside* wildlife sanctuaries! When does it stop?"

Everyone stared at Summer, startled by her outburst. J.J. no longer seemed aggravated with her, though. He seemed impressed. "Where'd you learn all that?" he asked.

"All sorts of places," Summer replied. "I've been doing research on human-wildlife conflict."

"For school?" Pete asked.

"No," Summer said. "Just to know more about it."

The elevator reached the ground floor and we all funneled into the lobby. A young man in a dark suit was waiting for J.J. "Mr. McCracken," he said nervously. "I'm here to take you and Mr. Thwacker to the festivities."

J.J. looked to Summer and me. "C'mon. We'll give you guys a ride." Then he looked to Jerry. "There's a cart for you to drive yourself parked by the loading dock. That way you can keep the gun stowed and the guests won't see it."

"Gotcha," Jerry said. "I'll find it."

"Great." J.J. left Jerry behind and led the rest of us through the lobby of the administration building.

Summer was still upset. "So you're just going to run Rocket off, then?" she asked. "Let her fend for herself against all those hunters?"

"I don't have any other options," J.J. said.

We exited the front doors. A golf cart was waiting for us at the front steps—although, because it was for J.J., it was a fancier golf cart than most. It had three rows of seats, and it was designed to look more like a car, with a black paint job and fake fenders.

"You know who really doesn't have any other options?" Summer asked. "Rocket. She's going to die out there if we don't protect her. Whenever humans and animals end up in conflict, the animals always lose. We're wiping out all our rhinos and bears and hyenas and wolves and pretty soon the only place we're ever going to be able to see any of those animals is in a zoo."

The aide climbed into the driver's seat of the golf cart. J.J. and Pete got into the seat behind him.

Summer and I didn't get in, though. Summer was too angry at her father; she was making a point of not riding with him.

I didn't get in for a whole different reason: I was struck by something Summer had said. I felt like an idiot for not having thought of it before, but now that I had, things began falling into place.

J.J. checked his watch. He still hadn't tied his bow tie. "I've got to move. Are you two coming with me or not?"

"Not," Summer said pointedly.

"Yes we are," I said.

Summer looked at me like I'd betrayed her.

"We need to get out to the party," I said. "And fast."

"Why?" Summer asked me.

"Because I think I know who killed King," I said.

THE PARTY

Summer got into the cart with me. The aide drove as quickly as he could through the employee area. Given that we were in a golf cart, that wasn't very fast. But it was still faster than walking.

Pete was going over J.J.'s speech for the party, which he had written out for J.J. on note cards. J.J. was still trying to tie his bow tie. He kept knotting it wrong, then untying it in frustration.

Summer wanted to know what I was thinking, but I had to make a phone call first. I found the number for the local Department of Animal Control and dialed it.

The employee areas were less crowded than usual. Almost everyone who worked for FunJungle was now out in the park. Many were on duty, but those who didn't have to work that night were enjoying the party.

A woman answered the phone.

"Hi," I said. "Can you tell me if anyone has filed a complaint against a dog in my neighborhood for attacking people?"

"Yes," the woman answered. "If anyone has complained to us, we keep it on file. Can you give me the name of the dog and the address of the owner?"

"The dog's name is King," I said. "It's a bichon frise." Then I gave her the address of Lincoln Stone's house.

I had to wait a bit while she checked the files. We passed through the employee gate into the park. The crowds were enormous. Adventure Road was jammed with people. Even though it was getting late and it was a school night, there were plenty of children; most of them were probably going to stay home from school the next day. Extra food carts had been set up to sell hot dogs and tacos. Mascots, now with their heads on, took pictures with tourists. Bands played music ranging from country to soft rock to zydeco. A large crowd clustered around a keeper holding a twenty-foot-long Burmese python.

The aide driving our golf cart honked the horn. When the tourists saw that J.J. and Summer McCracken were in the cart, they reverently stepped out of the way for us. Many people seemed more excited to see the McCrackens than they were to see the animals. Hundreds of tourists snapped pictures of them, yelling for their attention.

J.J. waved gamely to all of them. "How y'all doing?" he asked. "Everyone having a good time tonight?"

Summer also waved, a fake smile pasted on her face. "How'd you think to check with Animal Control?" she asked me through clenched teeth. "I thought everyone said King was a nice dog."

"Not everyone," I corrected her. "Putterman said King was a pain in the rear. He also called King a 'lousy mutt.'"

The Animal Control woman came back on the line. "It appears there were three separate complaints filed against that dog," she reported.

"Three?" I asked. "Can you tell me who filed them?"

"I'm afraid that's classified," the woman said.

"Can you tell me what the complaints say the dog did?" I asked.

"Yes," the woman replied. And then she told me. Which was all the information I needed.

"Thanks very much," I told her, and then hung up.

"Well?" Summer asked eagerly.

"I think I'm right," I said.

We arrived at the great lawn by Carnivore Canyon. It was a sea of people. The biggest crowd was clustered in front of the raised stage that had been erected the day before. Cindy Salerno was on the stage with a few other penguin keepers and several penguins. Meanwhile, in the middle of the crowd, fifty feet away, Sanjay Budhiraja stood in the bed of his flatbed truck with his fish cannon, launching herring over the guests' heads to the hungry penguins. Given the whoops and cheers, it seemed that everyone was enjoying the show.

"I told you this would be a hit," Pete said to J.J. proudly. "Our polling shows that penguins are the eighth-most popular animal at FunJungle—and the most popular bird by a landslide!"

I saw Dashiell, Ethan, Violet, and Xavier by the flatbed, eagerly watching Sanjay load the cannon. There was no time to say hi to them, though.

A VIP area was cordoned off close to the side of the lawn, reserved for special guests who had paid an exorbitant "party fee," celebrities, and FunJungle animal keepers. (One of the perks of the VIP area was that it allowed you to mingle with keepers.) This area was slightly less crowded than the rest of the lawn, and instead of having to wait in long lines to pay for food, there was a buffet.

The guard stationed at the entrance to the VIP area immediately recognized J.J. and unhooked the cordon for all of us to pass through. By now, J.J. had his tuxedo shirt buttoned, but he still hadn't managed to knot his bow tie. In exasperation, he yanked it off and threw it into a trash can.

I figured my parents were somewhere in the crowd, but at the moment, I was looking for someone else. I scanned the sea of faces, spotting plenty of keepers I knew, the center for the San Antonio Spurs (who was easy to find as he was a good six inches taller than anyone else), and a few actors from TV shows. To my surprise, I also saw Lincoln Stone. He was chatting up a B-list actress who mostly did horror movies.

Summer saw him too. "What's *he* doing here?" she asked indignantly.

"He paid his VIP fee," Pete replied, then escorted J.J. toward the main stage. "You'll be making your speech right after the penguins," he said.

It occurred to me that, with his short stature and his tuxedo, J.J. looked a bit like a penguin himself.

As he disappeared into the crowd, shaking hands and welcoming guests, I spotted who I *was* looking for by the buffet and hurried over. Summer ran along behind me.

"Hi," I said to Natasha Mason. "Can I talk to you?"

Natasha, like most of the keepers, was still in her work clothes. She was trying to wrangle Grayson and Jason, who had entirely loaded their buffet plates with candy. They had obviously eaten a lot of it already. Their faces were smeared with chocolate, and they were so amped on sugar I could practically hear them buzzing.

"Hi, Teddy!" Grayson said exuberantly. "They have chocolate-covered caramel apples here!" He held up a half-eaten one to show me. It was half the size of his head.

"I'm busy with my family right now," Natasha said. "Could it wait until tomorrow?"

"No. It's urgent," I said. Then I lowered my voice and told her, "I know you killed King."

Natasha had pale skin to begin with, but it turned out she could go even paler.

By my side, Summer gasped, surprised by my accusation, but she didn't interrupt the moment.

Natasha didn't deny what I had said. She took a few seconds to collect her thoughts, then said, "Let's discuss this away from the children." She tapped the shoulder of a tall man who was loading his plate at the buffet. "Hon, can you watch the children for a bit?" she asked. "A work thing has come up."

The man turned around. He looked at Summer and me curiously, probably wondering how we qualified as "a work thing."

"This is Summer McCracken, the daughter of the Fun-Jungle owner," Natasha said as a way of explanation. "And Teddy Fitzroy, whose mother works with primates. Kids, this is my husband, Mason."

"Mason Mason?" Summer asked. "Really?"

Mason Mason didn't get a chance to respond, as his sons had run off to the dessert buffet again and he had to go after them.

Natasha led us away from the buffet to a space where there weren't so many people. She still seemed pale and confused about what to do next.

On the stage, Cindy Salerno was introducing a king penguin named Louis the Sixteenth to the crowd. "Louis has proven to be quite adept at catching herring in the air," the keeper said. "Would anyone like to see him?"

A cheer went up from the crowd.

"How did you know . . . ?" Natasha began, but then didn't seem sure where to go with that question.

"You left something behind when you tried to make it look like King had been eaten," I said. "A tiny bit of wolf poop."

Natasha blinked at me, startled. "You know what that looks like?"

"I know what *hyena* poop looks like," I said, then turned to Summer to explain. "They're one of the few animals in the world that have white poop. Because of all the bones they eat. But wolves are another."

"Oh!" Summer exclaimed, understanding. "That's what tipped you off! When I mentioned the hyenas!"

"Right," I agreed. "For days, I've been trying to remember what that white stuff we found at the crime scene reminded me of. Now I know: dried hyena poop." I turned back to Natasha. "You must have stepped in some wolf poop at work. It dried on your boot, and you left it behind at the crime scene."

"And that was the only evidence you had?" she asked.

"No," I said. "Your boys also made a big deal about telling me how nice King was. But it turns out, King *wasn't* very nice. Lincoln's own friends didn't like him very much. And when I called Animal Control, it turned out you had complained to them about the dog before. Three times."

"He attacked my sons," Natasha said, still sounding angry about it. "King might have been little, but he was mean as a wolverine. Once, Grayson had to get stitches from him. Grayson was minding his own business in our yard and King ran right under the barbed wire and bit him on the leg. And that jerk Lincoln still let him run free. So I called Animal Control to complain, to see if maybe they could force him to keep the dog inside. Or keep it on a leash. But they couldn't make him and he wouldn't do it."

"So *that's* why you killed King?" Summer asked. "To protect your kids?"

Natasha glanced nervously at her family. Grayson and Mason were ignoring their father and stuffing their faces with more candy.

I suddenly understood. "It wasn't you, was it?"

"No," Natasha said softly. "I had told the boys to be ready to protect themselves. In case King tried to attack them again."

"The croquet mallets," I said, remembering that one had what I had *thought* was dried paint crusted on the end. I now realized it had probably been blood. "They weren't only for mountain lions."

There was a distant whump as the Zoom cannon launched a fish over the crowd, followed by a huge cheer as Louis the Sixteenth caught it.

"Grayson left his sneakers out on the back porch last Friday night," Natasha explained. "He'd gotten mud on them. But I wanted him to bring them inside overnight, because of scorpions."

I understood that. You couldn't leave your shoes outside at night in Central Texas because scorpions might crawl into them. Then, when you put them on, they'd sting your feet.

Natasha went on. "All Grayson did was go out on the porch to get them, and that awful little dog was out there. Lincoln and his idiot friends were off shooting their guns. We could hear them. And they'd been drinking. They probably didn't even know the dog was out. Well, King came running up, barking and snarling at Grayson, scaring him to death. And he'd already been attacked by the dog once, so . . . The croquet mallet was right there. He was only trying to protect himself. He didn't even hit King that hard. . . ." Natasha sniffled sadly. Even though she hadn't liked the dog, she was obviously still upset by its death.

"So you made the death look like a lion kill to protect Grayson?" I asked.

Natasha nodded sadly. "He felt terrible. He still does. He even wanted to tell Lincoln what he'd done, bless his heart . . . but I couldn't let that happen. Lincoln is awful. He terrorizes my sons even when they haven't done anything wrong. If he knew Grayson had killed his dog . . ." She shivered at the thought of what Lincoln might do. "I knew Rocket had been around, and I knew Lincoln knew about her too. So I thought I'd make it look like King had been eaten. I snuck over the fence onto his property and laid out the scene."

"But you made mistakes," Summer said.

"On *purpose*," Natasha said. "I thought if I didn't leave some things behind, like King's collar and a little fluff from his tail, Lincoln might never figure it out. I wanted him to be convinced a cougar had done it—and not one of my boys. Only, I never . . ." Her voice hitched, like she was about to cry. "It never occurred to me that he'd go on a crusade against Rocket. I thought he'd just have a funeral for King and move on."

Out on the lawn, the fish cannon display was wrapping up. Louis the Sixteenth caught his final herring to massive applause. It was almost time for J.J.'s speech.

I said to Natasha, "So that's why you tried to point the finger at someone else the other night? You were trying to protect Rocket?"

"Yes." Tears welled in Natasha's eyes. "I never meant for any of this to happen. I didn't want Rocket to be killed, but I also didn't want Grayson to get in trouble. I figured, maybe if people thought one of Lincoln's idiot friends had killed the dog, it would cast enough doubt for Rocket to be left alone. . . . But now I've heard that the permit has been issued to kill her." She broke down and sobbed.

I had a good idea what was upsetting her. The woman worked with wolves, which had been unfairly vilified and nearly hunted to death all over the world. And now, because of her actions, the same thing was happening to an innocent mountain lion.

On the central stage, Pete Thwacker strode to the microphone and flashed his million-dollar smile. "Hello, everyone!" he said. "I'm Pete Thwacker, head of public relations at FunJungle. Is everyone having a good time tonight?"

The crowd cheered back enthusiastically.

Summer told Natasha, "You still might be able to save Rocket. But you'll have to admit the truth. It's the only way."

"I know," Natasha sobbed.

"My dad can protect Grayson from Lincoln," Summer assured her.

Onstage, Pete Thwacker said, "Now, here's a man who needs no introduction at all. . . . So I won't give him one!"

There was a smattering of polite laughter.

Pete looked upset that his joke hadn't gone over better, but he soldiered on. "Ladies and gentlemen, the founder of the FunJungle Family Adventure Park, Mr. J.J. McCracken!"

A chimpanzee walked out onto the stage, wearing a tuxedo and holding note cards.

The audience laughed much harder at this than they had at Pete's joke.

Then J.J. McCracken walked out, pretending to be flustered. He glared at the chimp and said, "What do you think you're doing, buster?"

The chimp made a face for the crowd, then handed the note cards to J.J. and walked off the stage.

The crowd loved it.

I could see my mother at the edge of the stage, helping out with the chimp. He leaped into her arms, allowing J.J. to have the attention to himself.

"That guy looks a lot better in his monkey suit than I do in mine," J.J. said, getting more laughs. He then launched into his speech, but I didn't really listen. Something else had caught my attention.

Stephanie Winger, the head of the local Department of Fish and Wildlife, was shoving through the crowd in the VIP area. Four Fish and Wildlife agents followed her. They were all carrying long, thin metal cases. Tommy Lopez was in the rear, moving the slowest. He looked awful, like it made him sick to be there.

A lot of guests seemed to be under the mistaken impression that the agents were FunJungle characters, like the mascots. They nudged their children excitedly. "Look!" one exhilarated father told his kids. "It's the animal patrol!"

Lincoln Stone noticed the agents too. Their presence intrigued him enough that he abandoned the B-movie actress to follow them.

The actress looked very relieved to not have to talk to Lincoln anymore.

I had a bad feeling about the agents' arrival, and Summer and Natasha obviously did too. Without saying a word to one another, we followed them as well.

On the stage, J.J. McCracken was welcoming all the guests and thanking them for being a part of the FunJungle adventure.

Stephanie Winger found who she was looking for: Chief Hoenekker. He was at the part of the VIP section closest to the stage. A lot of guests weren't paying much attention to J.J.'s speech; it wasn't nearly as interesting as penguins or flying herring were, so they had taken the opportunity to go to the buffet, the bar, or the Porta-Potties. But up near the stage, people were watching J.J., and Hoenekker was watching the crowd.

Hoenekker saw the Fish and Wildlife agents approaching and frowned, clearly not happy to see them. He abandoned his spot and moved away from the most crowded area so that he could talk to Stephanie Winger away from the guests.

The least crowded spot, by far, was around the control panel for the fireworks display. Another cordon separated it from the rest of the VIP area, probably so no guests would push any buttons or trip over any of the electrical cables. A lone guy in a FANTASTIC FIREWORKS T-shirt sat before the panel, running through a series of safety checks. Hoenekker slipped under the cordon.

"Hey!" the fireworks guy snapped. "This is off-limits!"

"Can it," Hoenekker told him, flashing his badge.

The Fish and Wildlife agents slipped under the cordon too. So did Lincoln Stone.

Summer, Natasha, and I stopped at the cordon; we could see and hear everyone on the other side just fine.

Hoenekker glared at Lincoln. "Get out of here," he said. "This doesn't concern you."

"Oh yes it does," Lincoln said.

Before Hoenekker could argue with him, Stephanie Winger interrupted. "Chief, we need to talk. It's urgent."

The tone of her voice made Hoenekker forget about Lincoln. "What's wrong?"

"We've been triangulating the location of T-38," Winger said, referring to Rocket by her official number. "As you know, her collar has been indicating that she has been inside the park for the last twenty-four hours. As we get closer to it, we can pinpoint its location with more and more accuracy. But our current readings are causing us some concern."

"Why's that?" Hoenekker asked.

"Because they're indicating that T-38 is out on that lawn," Winger replied.

We all looked to the lawn, which teemed with people. The crowd was so thick we wouldn't even have been able to see a mountain lion in it. But we certainly should have seen people *reacting* to a mountain lion.

"That's not possible," Hoenekker said. "Your readings must be wrong."

"That's what we thought at first," Winger answered. "But we've checked them a dozen times. The cat is out there. We've heard that some theme parks have tunnels underneath them, so all the characters and employees can get from place to place without being seen. Lions like to hole up in dark areas, like caves or dens. So we figure she might be in one of those."

"There's no tunnels underneath this lawn," Hoenekker said. "Though there's some back in Carnivore Canyon." He pointed to the area beyond the stage.

Stephanie Winger shook her head. "That's not where the signal is coming from. Our tech might not be the most up-to-date, but it's not that inaccurate. And it's telling us the lion is somewhere out there. . . ."

She pointed to the lawn again, only this time, as she did it, understanding dawned on her. Concern creased her face, because she'd realized where Rocket probably was.

The other Fish and Wildlife agents seemed to realize it too, as did Hoenekker and Natasha and Summer and I.

Only Lincoln Stone didn't. "Where the heck's the lion?" he demanded.

"I think she's under the stage," said Stephanie Winger.

THE HUNT

The central stage where J.J. McCracken stood was raised three feet above the ground, so there was plenty of room for a mountain lion under it. A black tarp draped over all the sides, hiding the area below the stage from view of the crowd, so it would have been dark and sheltered, like a large cave or den. It was also in an area free from people with guns, it was close to the water source of the Raging Raft Ride, and there was plenty of prey around. To a cougar on the run from hunters, it might have looked like a nice, safe place to bed down.

So it was conceivable that Rocket had gone to sleep under the stage, unaware that, once daylight came, thousands of people would be surrounding her hiding place. And while Rocket might have been agitated by the presence of all those people, she probably would have stayed put, where she felt secure, rather than emerging into the daylight where everyone would see her.

"She's *there*?" Lincoln Stone asked, pointing at the stage, at once shocked and excited.

Stephanie Winger told Hoenekker, "You're going to have to evacuate this area right away."

Hoenekker groaned at the thought, but obviously knew it was the right thing to do. "All right," he said, "I'll clear the crowd, but I need your people to stand down until that's done."

"Fine," Stephanie agreed. "Though I'll have my agents get prepared, just in case T-38 needs to be contained." She nodded to her team.

The four of them set their metal cases on the ground and opened them. Inside each was a rifle. The rifles were in pieces, which were nestled in foam. The agents set to work assembling the weapons behind the fireworks control panel, where they were hidden from the crowd.

Tommy Lopez looked even more miserable.

Hoenekker pulled out his radio and spoke to his own agents. "Attention all FunJungle Security, we have a Code Green at the main lawn. The mountain lion is underneath the central stage. I repeat, the lion is underneath the stage. I need a sedation team in position immediately—"

"A sedation team?" Lincoln interrupted. "That cat needs to be killed."

"Not by any of my people," Hoenekker told him.

"It shouldn't be killed at all!" Summer announced. "It didn't eat your dog, Mr. Stone! And I can prove it! Listen to your neighbor!" She turned to Natasha Mason expectantly.

Everyone else turned to Natasha as well. She swallowed hard, then told the truth. Almost. She changed it slightly to protect Grayson. "*I* killed King," she said. "The dog came onto my property Friday night and attacked my son. It was an accident. I was only trying to fend him off with a croquet mallet and I hit him too hard with it. The lion had nothing to do with King's death. She's completely innocent."

Almost everyone was startled by this reaction—except Lincoln Stone, who appeared enraged by it. Instead of being angry at Natasha for killing King, however, he seemed more upset that his crusade against the cougar had been revealed to be a farce. "That's a load of bull," he said dismissively.

The Fish and Wildlife agents didn't seem nearly as sure. They had all assembled their rifles, and now they looked to their boss to see what she thought.

"Can you prove this?" Stephanie Winger asked Natasha.

"I have King's blood on a croquet mallet," Natasha said. "I didn't mean for the lion to get blamed. Please don't kill her because of my mistake."

Stephanie Winger took a moment to weigh the situation. Which was a moment too long for Lincoln Stone.

"You don't really believe this story?" he asked. "It's just a last-ditch scam to protect the lion!"

"If there's evidence . . . ," Stephanie began.

Lincoln didn't wait for her to finish. "You idiots are like every other branch of the government," he sneered. "Totally useless. Guess I'll have to handle this myself." He suddenly snatched the rifle from Tommy Lopez and started for the stage.

"Hey!" Tommy yelled, grabbing Lincoln's arm.

"Get your lousy hands off me," Lincoln said, and drove the butt of the rifle into Tommy's stomach so hard it sent him reeling. Another agent tried to catch Tommy, but couldn't hold his weight, and they tumbled into the fireworks control panel. Tommy's arm smacked a row of buttons.

"No!" cried the fireworks operator.

It was too late. The buttons instantly sent a wireless signal out to the rows of canisters Summer and I had seen by the Raging Raft Ride.

Lincoln was storming out of the VIP area with the rifle. On the stage, J.J. McCracken was wrapping up his remarks. Mom still stood to the side with the chimp. Pete Thwacker was by her side. Dad was at the front of the crowd, taking publicity photos.

The canisters were all loaded with fireworks and their charges were primed. Now a dozen of the charges detonated, blasting the fireworks upward. They soared high into the sky behind the main stage—well before they were supposed to—and exploded.

The crowd oohed and aahed with excitement.

To Rocket, however, they probably sounded like gunshots.

The cat was certainly already on edge after being surrounded by so much noise all day, and the crack of the fireworks was the last straw for her. As Jerry had told us, the noise of a gun was probably even scarier to a mountain lion than being hit by a rubber bullet. So Rocket bolted from her hiding place, dashing through the tarp that draped the front of the stage.

She emerged onto the lawn from directly below J.J. McCracken, right in front of the crowd. Her sudden appearance, in tandem with the fireworks, was so dramatic that most people thought it was part of the show—just like the gag with the chimpanzee had been. A few tourists yelped in surprise, but the majority applauded enthusiastically.

Rocket paused, startled to find herself facing so many humans, unsure what to do next.

She was a healthy, impressive lion, with muscles that rippled beneath her gorgeous fur coat. The radio collar around her neck was a slim hoop of black plastic, which probably contributed to the audience's belief that she wasn't dangerous; with the collar, she looked like an enormous pet cat. Some idiots in the front row even tried to pet her, until Dad blocked their path.

Virtually the only people who realized the lion was a threat were the FunJungle employees and the chimpanzee, who shrieked in fear, leaped from Mom's arms, and scrambled up into the stage's lighting grid. Pete Thwacker fearfully attempted the same thing, only his attempt to climb wasn't nearly as graceful, and he ended up tumbling to the stage and landing flat on his back. The audience mistook this for part of the show as well and laughed.

J.J. watched the whole display, goggle-eyed, unsure whether or not to warn the crowd or pretend like it was all an act. All he could think to say was, "Nice kitty. Nice kitty. Stay." Like maybe Rocket really *was* a pet.

The entire audience might have continued calmly watching the show had Lincoln Stone not charged up onto the stage with his stolen rifle. "That's not a zoo lion, you pinheads!" he shouted at the crowd. "That's the one that killed King!"

Now it dawned on people that the lion wasn't part of the show. Those who recognized Lincoln took his warning seriously. Those who didn't know him thought he was a deranged lunatic. Either way, everyone started to run—only no one knew which way they should go. So the lawn was suddenly chaos.

Lincoln aimed his rifle at Rocket.

I lunged at the fireworks control panel and pounded as many buttons as I could. Out in the Wilds, dozens of fireworks blasted off at once. It sounded like a barrage of gunfire, which startled Rocket into running again.

Before Lincoln could shoot, the lion fled into the panicked crowd, disappearing into the mayhem.

Even though there were people everywhere, Lincoln still took aim at the cat. His finger twitched on the trigger.

But then Mom body-slammed him. Mom wasn't that big, but when she was angry enough, she could take down a silverback gorilla. She and Lincoln tumbled to the stage.

Lincoln didn't shoot, but he kept hold of the rifle. He raised it to club Mom with it, but the chimp came to her aid. The chimp was still too afraid to descend from the lighting grid, but he saw Lincoln as a threat to Mom, so he dropped his tuxedo pants and urinated on him.

Lincoln scrambled away, spluttering in disgust, and tumbled off the stage.

Fireworks were still exploding in the sky. Hysterical guests were overturning everything that got in their way. Buffet tables were upended. Landscaping was trampled.

Porta-Potties toppled with unfortunate guests inside them. Charlie Connor, the actor playing Kazoo the Koala, was bowled over so hard that the head of his costume flew off. While small children shrieked at the sight of their favorite cartoon pal getting beheaded, the head rolled away and took out the actor playing Zelda Zebra.

Pete Thwacker seized the microphone and did his best to do damage control. "There is no need for alarm!" he told the frantic tourists. "I assure you that everything is under control. Please walk calmly toward the exits and do not panic. . . . Waaaugh!" He shrieked in terror as the Burmese python slithered past, then made yet another failed attempt to scramble up into the lighting grid.

A team of keepers raced past in pursuit of the escaped python.

Through it all, Rocket was on the run. I climbed a Chinese elm tree and saw her sprinting off toward the Wilds. "She's heading out of the park!" I yelled to Summer over the noise.

"We can't let her leave!" Summer yelled back. "If she does, someone will shoot her!"

I spotted Kevin Wilks close by, clutching a sedation rifle. He was apparently part of Hoenekker's containment team. I didn't feel I could count on him to do anything with the gun except shoot himself in the foot, but someone I thought I *could* count on was close by.

Tommy Lopez was staggering to his feet, recovering from Lincoln's sucker punch. I leaped down from the tree to his side and asked, "Can you help us sedate Rocket?"

"Sure thing," Tommy gasped. "But she's moving awfully fast."

"Leave that to me," Summer said, and she ran off into the crowd.

I led Tommy over to Kevin. Kevin probably should have been doing some sort of crowd control, but he wasn't the greatest at thinking on his feet—or thinking at all, really. Without direct orders, he was merely standing there, looking worried.

"This is Tommy Lopez," I told him. "He's from Fish and Wildlife, and he needs your rifle."

"Okay," Kevin said, and handed it over.

The rest of the Fish and Wildlife agents, along with Stephanie Winger, had run off after Rocket as well. I had no idea if they were still planning to shoot the cat or not.

Natasha Mason had split too. I saw her heading in the opposite direction that Rocket had gone, herding her family to safety. Grayson and Mason seemed far more upset that they had to abandon the dessert bar than they were about the lion.

I looked back toward the stage. Lincoln Stone was no longer there. I had no idea where he'd gone.

Mom was still onstage, though, coaxing the chimp down into her arms.

The crowds were thinning out on the lawn. Most people seemed to have fled for the exits, though many had headed in various other directions, and a few had stayed behind to do things like gather up spilled candy and loot abandoned taco carts. Somehow, the actor dressed as Eleanor Elephant had climbed up a tree. He perched on a branch, looking bizarrely like the title character in *Horton Hatches the Egg*.

The llama galloped past, pursued by two keepers.

A flatbed truck pulled up next to us. It was the one that Sanjay Budhiraja had been shooting fish from. The fish cannon itself and several ice chests full of seafood still sat on the back. Dad was at the wheel, with Sanjay and Summer crammed into the passenger seat beside him. "C'mon!" Summer yelled to Tommy and me. "Rocket's getting away!"

There was no time—or space—to climb into the front seat, so Tommy and I leaped onto the back of the flatbed.

Before Dad could drive off, Dash, Ethan, Violet, and Xavier raced up and jumped on with us. Xavier needed a little extra help, but he made it.

"You think you can have all the fun without us?" Dash asked.

Ethan pounded on the roof of the truck and said, "Let's go!"

Dad hit the gas and raced across the lawn in pursuit of Rocket. The lawn was now clear enough of people that Dad could drive relatively quickly, but a lot of things had been left behind that got squashed underneath our tires: abandoned plates of food; commemorative souvenir soda cups; a chocolate fountain from the dessert buffet; the disembodied mascot head of Kazoo the Koala.

Those of us in the back stood, hanging onto the cab, keeping an eye out for Rocket. The fish cannon was strapped down well, but the ice chests weren't. They were skidding around with us, and every time we hit a bump, frozen herring would fly out.

We roared past the stage. Mom was comforting the chimpanzee, who had finally deigned to come down (although Pete Thwacker had finally managed to climb up into the lighting grid and looked like he planned to stay there). J.J. McCracken was simply staring at the ruins of his party, in shock.

Ahead of us, the lion was racing past Carnivore Canyon, heading for the Wilds, moving at a good twenty miles per hour.

A FunJungle Land Rover skidded onto the walkway behind her. My friends and I caught a glimpse of the man behind the wheel.

"That's Lincoln Stone!" Violet shouted.

I figured Lincoln had stolen the Rover from a FunJungle employee. He looked like a man possessed. He tended to ignore facts when making his arguments much of the time, and now he wasn't about to let them get in the way of avenging the death of his dog.

Dad gunned our engine to go after him, but as he did, someone moved into the path ahead of us, blocking our way.

It was Mr. Putterman. He was in a wheelchair, with a back brace as well. He stared us down defiantly, determined to help Lincoln.

"Putterman!" Ethan yelled. "Get out of the way!"

But Putterman didn't move. Dad had no choice but to hit the brakes. On the narrow path, there was no way around Putterman, leaving Lincoln free to pursue Rocket without us.

But then, with a rebel yell, Marge O'Malley zoomed into the road ahead of us in her own wheelchair. She bore down on Putterman, her broken leg pointing in front of her like a knight's lance, and slammed directly into him. It was like wheelchair bumper cars. The force of Marge's strike sent Putterman careening backward along the path, which dipped downhill toward the Australian section of the park. Putterman quickly picked up speed, screaming in fear, then crashed into a railing so hard that his wheelchair upended, flipping him over into the wallaby exhibit. He slammed to the ground and was instantly beset by curious marsupials.

"My back!" Putterman screamed, obviously having reinjured his ruptured disc. "Someone help me! I can't move!"

A wallaby is probably the most gentle animal that exists, but Putterman didn't know that. I certainly wasn't going to take the time to tell him. In fact, I did the opposite. "Careful, Putterman!" I yelled. "Wallabies are vicious and bloodthirsty!"

"And they can smell fear!" Xavier added.

Putterman wailed in terror as the adorable little creatures bounded to his side and sniffed him.

Marge rolled out of our way, having cleared our path, and saluted.

"Thanks!" Dad yelled to her, and hit the gas once again.

Unfortunately, we had lost a lot of ground. Rocket and Lincoln were now far ahead of us, already at the construction site.

Rocket sprang over the wooden fence without breaking stride. She simply leaped to the top, then bounded down on the opposite side.

Lincoln didn't slow down either. He plowed straight through the fence and continued after the lion.

In the wallaby exhibit, one of the animals gave Putterman a friendly lick. "Somebody save me!" Putterman cried. "It's trying to eat me!"

We bore down on the hole that Lincoln had left in the fence. The flatbed was wider than the Land Rover, though. Dad hesitated a moment, but Summer told him, "It doesn't matter if you break it! My dad will understand!"

Dad sped up again while those of us in the back took cover. The flatbed took out a few extra feet of fence on both sides, leaving a trail of splintered wood in our wake.

Instantly, the landscape turned to dirt. We raced along it through half-built buildings and dormant construction vehicles. Ahead of us, Rocket was still on the run, but the cat was tiring and now Lincoln was gaining on her. Rocket juked left and right a few times, trying to shake her pursuer, but Lincoln stayed behind her.

A gunshot rang out. A bullet sparked off a cement mixer just behind Rocket. The cat yowled and scurried onward.

I spotted four people in camouflage gear racing through the framework of the Black Mamba roller coaster.

"That's the Barksdales!" Xavier shouted.

Indeed it was. In addition to their forest camouflage clothing, they all had taped twigs and branches to themselves. In the woods, this might have hidden them. However, in the barren construction site, where there was no greenery at all, it made the family stick out. There really wasn't anything *more* noticeable than four human-size bushes running through a half-built theme park.

While the rest of his family raced ahead, Pa Barksdale scrambled up a large hill of sand to try for a better shot at Rocket.

"He's going to kill her!" Violet exclaimed. "She doesn't have any cover!"

Which was true. Rocket was out in the midst of a wide, flat expanse of open ground.

Ethan asked Tommy Lopez, "Can you shoot that guy with a tranquilizer dart?"

"No way," Tommy said. "Sorry, but the amount of sedative in here will kill him."

I looked after Rocket helplessly. Lincoln Stone was bearing down on her with the Rover, the Barksdales were coming, and the poor cat had no way to defend herself.

But *we* had a way to defend her.

Before I could even think about what I was doing, I grabbed the launch tube for the fish cannon and fired up the generator. "I need you guys to load this for me!" I yelled.

"With what?" Dash asked.

"Fish!" I exclaimed.

My friends immediately leaped to work. By now, half the frozen fish had tumbled out of the ice chests, so we were up to our ankles in seafood. Dash, Ethan, Violet, and Xavier snatched up the fish and dropped them into the loading area while I held the tube as steady as I could.

Pa Barksdale had reached the top of the sand hill. He was taking careful aim at Rocket.

I blasted him with a fusillade of frozen fish. My aim was off at first—it was hard to balance in the back of a moving truck—so my first salvo came in low. I stitched the hill with a school of capelin, leaving them embedded in the sand like fence posts.

It was enough to startle Pa Barksdale, though. His shot went wide and he hit the Land Rover instead. The front tire blew, throwing the SUV out of control.

Pa apparently thought we were shooting real ammunition at him, because he turned from Rocket and aimed his gun at *us*.

So I made my next shot count. I pegged him right between the eyes with a herring.

Pa flew backward and tumbled down the hill, splatting face-first in a foundation of wet cement.

Meanwhile, Lincoln was struggling to steer the damaged Land Rover. A person who was thinking clearly probably would have stopped the SUV, but Lincoln was determined to go after Rocket no matter what. He didn't brake at all, so as his front tire deflated, he lost command of the Rover and it skidded into a row of Porta-Potties. The latrines burst apart one after the other, coating the Rover—and Lincoln, who had the window down—in human waste. The Rover finally spun out in the middle of a pool of filth.

Lincoln wasn't done yet, though. If anything, being covered in feces made him even *more* determined to get Rocket. Roaring with anger, he leaped from the driver's seat with his rifle and set after Rocket on foot.

Meanwhile, the remaining Barksdales were still coming in from the side.

I leveled the fish cannon at them. My friends kept loading seafood into it.

I fired at the Barksdales. I was getting better at aiming the cannon now. My first blast cut them off at the knees, pegging them with flying fish. They went down hard, crashing to the ground, their rifles flying from their hands.

"Let us off!" Dash yelled. "We'll handle them from here!"

Dad slowed down enough for Dash, Ethan, and Violet to leap from the back of the truck. They quickly snatched the Barksdales' rifles off the ground.

"That's mine!" Tim Barksdale shouted, starting to get to his feet.

"Stay down or you'll get a swordfish up your butt!" Violet said with menace that surprised me. It was an empty threat—I didn't have any swordfish—but it worked. Tim lay back on the ground, and all the Barksdales raised their hands in surrender.

Dad hit the gas again and we sped on after Lincoln and Rocket.

The lion was now almost out of energy. Her speed was flagging. Even worse, she had run into a dead end.

She had reached the end of the construction site and arrived at FWAP, the FunJungle Waste Appropriation Plant. The area was bound on three sides by concrete walls to hide it from view, as it was hideously ugly. The factory itself was basically a two-story-tall, foul-smelling metal composter. Dump trucks filled with animal poop would drive up a concrete ramp to drop their loads into the top; the poop would then be combined with other refuse and composted for weeks before coming out the exit chute into other trucks, which would haul it off to local farms. The composter was surrounded by fetid piles of moldering garbage, which reeked so bad we all had to clap our hands over our noses.

Lincoln followed Rocket into the FWAP, smelling pretty terrible himself. He was limping after wrecking the Rover, but he forced himself onward, clutching the rifle in his poop-smeared hands.

The smashed-up Rover blocked the entrance to the FWAP, so Dad had to stop the truck. From the flatbed, I could see everything that was happening within the concrete walls.

Rocket seemed to realize she was cornered. She turned to face Lincoln and backed toward the composter, teeth bared.

Lincoln cocked his rifle.

I raised my fish cannon at the same time. "Lincoln!" I yelled. "Drop your gun!"

Lincoln didn't even look at me. "This lion's going down," he said. "She killed King. She deserves what's coming to her."

"She didn't kill King!" Summer yelled. "Your neighbor did!"

"I'm not bluffing!" I warned Lincoln. "I have a fish cannon and I'm not afraid to use it!"

Next to me, Xavier stood at the ready, his hands full of frozen fish.

Tommy Lopez was taking aim at Rocket too, only he was using the sedation rifle.

Lincoln Stone was a lot closer to Rocket than we were, though. The cat was only fifty feet ahead of him.

Even though Rocket probably could have easily killed Lincoln, she didn't attack. Instead, she kept backing away, hissing.

Lincoln raised the rifle and took aim.

I fired first. After all, I'd warned him, fair and square.

The first herring nailed him in the right shoulder, spinning him toward us. The next caught him square in the chest. Lincoln staggered backward, but doggedly kept his hands clutched on his rifle.

Rocket saw her opportunity to escape and ran for the exit behind us.

Lincoln tried to shoot the lion, even as he was tottering, so I hit him once more.

The third fish was the largest one yet, a bluefin tuna that appeared to have been tossed in with the other fish by mistake. It caught Lincoln in the face with a wet *thwap* and sent him reeling onto the loading platform. Lincoln's gun discharged straight up, blowing out the cap that plugged the compost chute.

There was an ominous rumble, and then the poop of a thousand different animals, which had been cooking in the hot sun for days, poured down the chute onto Lincoln's head.

Lincoln was buried up to his neck in a pile of reeking compost. His arms and legs were pinioned to his sides, so he couldn't move, and given the way he screamed in disgust, I figured a lot of the stuff had gotten into his mouth as well.

Rocket was running toward us, using the last of her strength to escape, when Tommy Lopez fired his rifle. The dart caught Rocket in her rear haunch, and the sedative quickly went to work. Rocket yelped and tried to keep running, but her back end quit on her. She wobbled a bit, then sat down, gave a confused whine, and collapsed in the dirt. Within seconds, she was sound asleep.

"Is she going to be okay?" Xavier asked, concerned.

"She'll be fine," Tommy said. "And she's a lot safer here than she would be out there." He nodded toward the woods beyond the construction site. "At least until we can get that permit to kill her revoked."

He picked up his radio and called Stephanie Winger. "Boss. This is Lopez. Rocket is neutralized. The lion is down."

"Good work, Tommy," Winger replied. She sounded relieved. "Bring her in."

I peered over the edge of the truck at Rocket. She was breathing hard after all her exertion, but she seemed fine otherwise.

Sanjay Budhiraja whooped with excitement. "That was amazing! I never thought of this possibility for the Zoom! Humane self-defense! It's a whole new marketing angle!"

Summer climbed out of the truck and joined me on the flatbed. She took my hand as we looked down at Rocket. "Isn't she amazing?" she asked.

"She sure is," I said, although I wasn't only talking about Rocket.

In the FWAP, Lincoln Stone was struggling impotently to get out of the pile of poop. Finally, he screamed with exasperation, "Could you idiots get me out of here?"

"Sure!" Dad yelled back. "But, being idiots, it might take us a couple hours to figure out how to do that."

"That's not funny!" Lincoln screamed.

It was funny to everyone else, though. Even to the Barksdales, who Dashiell, Ethan, Violet, and Xavier were marching down the road at gunpoint. Despite their annoyance at being captured, the Barksdales burst into laughter at the sight of Lincoln writhing around in disgust, up to his chin in animal waste.

"You look like a dinosaur ate you up and pooped you out!" Pa roared.

Tommy leaped off the flatbed and knelt by Rocket's side. "C'mon," he told us. "We can't leave her here."

The rest of us joined him. Even though I had been close to thousands of animals at FunJungle, it felt different to be so close to Rocket, who was still wild. She smelled of musk and grass, and her body was so warm from activity that I could feel the heat just being near her.

"I'm sorry I called you idiots!" Lincoln wailed in the distance. "Please come help me! This is disgusting! If you don't get me out of here soon, I'm gonna puke!"

We ignored him.

"Anyone know where we can take Rocket so she'll be protected for the next few days?" I asked.

"The next few days?" Summer smiled knowingly. "I think I know how to protect her for a lot longer than that."

Epilogue

THE REFUGE

Two weeks later, I found myself standing by the scrub oak forest at the edge of the FunJungle parking lot. A new stage had been erected, significantly smaller than the one for FunJungle's anniversary, only big enough for five folding chairs and a podium. J.J., Kandace McCracken, and Summer sat in three of the chairs. Stephanie Wilder sat in the fourth, and our local state congresswoman was in the fifth.

Despite the McCrackens' fame, the crowd for the event was the smallest I had ever seen at FunJungle. Xavier, Dash, Ethan, and Violet were there, along with my mother and my father, who was taking photos. Beyond us, there were only a few dozen people, mostly fans of Summer who were there to see her, rather than caring about what the ceremony was for. (Tommy Lopez had wanted to come, but he'd had an emergency at work; someone had tried to smuggle a shipment of elephant ivory through the port at Galveston, and he'd been called in to help make the bust.)

Pete Thwacker was pacing behind me, putting on a good face, though I knew he was upset. He had invited dozens of news stations, but only the local ones had shown up.

"We should have promised them an animal," he muttered under his breath. "If we'd put a panda or a baby tiger on that stage, every major network would be here. We didn't even get Houston, for crying out loud."

"This isn't about pandas or tigers," I reminded him, echoing what Summer had told him over and over.

"It doesn't matter," Pete groused. "If you want a crowd, you need an animal. If Summer was holding a koala up there, the photos would make the front page of every paper in Texas."

I knew Summer didn't want to do that. In the days leading up to the ceremony, Pete had repeatedly proposed that Summer be cuddling everything from an aardvark to a weasel, but she had refused, not wanting to distract from the point of the ceremony. J.J. had respectfully conceded to her wishes, even though I could tell he was annoyed by the size of the crowd too.

It was ten minutes past when the ceremony should have begun, and it was hot in the parking lot. Heat rose off the asphalt in waves so thick the main gates of FunJungle shimmered in the distance.

J.J. looked at Pete impatiently. Pete scanned the parking lot, as if hoping to see news crews from the major networks suddenly arriving, then frowned and nodded to J.J.

J.J. stood and approached the podium. Most of the small crowd stopped talking to watch him, although a small gaggle of Summer fans continued to take selfies with Summer in the background. "Good afternoon," J.J. said. "I'd like to welcome everyone here, and the distinguished members of the press, for what I feel is one of the most important announcements I have ever made: the establishment of a new wildlife refuge to protect local species."

Summer beamed proudly as her father said this. After all, the refuge had been her idea.

Starting the day after we'd rescued Rocket, Summer had begun to pressure her father about the huge plot of land he owned around FunJungle. Instead of paving it all to build more theme parks and resorts, she wanted him to simply leave it wild. J.J. wasn't about to admit this to the crowd, but he had balked at the idea; he still had dreams of an entertainment complex that would rival Disney World.

Summer had been extremely upset by this. "The whole point of FunJungle isn't to make money," she had argued while her family and I were having dinner. "It's to protect animals and educate people about them, right?"

"Er . . . sort of," J.J. had said weakly. It was clear that he really thought it was to make money.

"Well, we shouldn't be doing that at the expense of our local animals," Summer said. "Isn't it hypocritical to tell our guests that people in India and Africa need to be setting aside more land for tigers and elephants if we're not doing the same thing for our own mountain lions?"

"She has a point," Summer's mother agreed.

"Besides," Summer continued, "you already have one theme park. How many more do you need?"

"I was kind of thinking four might be nice," J.J. admitted.

"And where's Rocket supposed to live, then?" Summer asked pointedly.

J.J. couldn't even meet her gaze and looked down into his mashed potatoes.

At the time, Rocket was in one of the quarantine areas at the FunJungle veterinary hospital. She was fully recovered from being sedated, but no one had felt it was safe to let her go free again; there had still been too many hunters out there looking for her, hoping to cash in on the reward Lincoln had offered. The quarantine area wasn't very big, but there was nowhere else to put Rocket. She had paced and yowled incessantly throughout her first day there.

J.J. McCracken was one of the shrewdest business negotiators on earth, but the one person he couldn't say no to was his daughter. He had *tried*. Originally, he'd argued that the whole purpose of buying the land was to develop it, and that making it a protected area would be a serious financial strain for him. So Summer had stopped talking to him. She didn't say a word to her father for three whole days, and every time he'd texted her, she'd simply responded with: We have plenty of money already.

On the third day, J.J. had cracked and agreed to the refuge.

The fact that FunJungle needed some good public relations was an additional factor. Thanks to Rocket's crashing the party, FunJungle's anniversary celebration had received far more press than it might have otherwise, but Pete Thwacker had pointed out that this wasn't exactly the press they had hoped for. "Despite all the hard work everyone at FunJungle does to care for the animals," he told J.J., "this park is starting to get a reputation as a place where chaos occurs on a regular basis; it wouldn't be a bad idea to make a big gesture where you put a charitable cause ahead of your ability to earn money."

However, the refuge alone wouldn't have been enough to protect Rocket. There was still a permit for hunting her and a bounty on her head. Luckily, Lincoln Stone's behavior at the anniversary party had worked against him.

After all, Lincoln had really been the one to start the panic at the party, not Rocket. (In retrospect, many guests realized they *should* have been frightened by the unplanned arrival of a mountain lion, but since Rocket was wild and not an escaped animal, most didn't fault FunJungle for her being in the park.) Lincoln had argued that he had been looking out for the safety of the guests when he'd taken the stage with the rifle. However, an investigation by local law enforcement had revealed that Lincoln had been informed Rocket hadn't killed King and yet he'd tried to shoot her anyhow. So he had been arrested for reckless endangerment.

Once he got bailed out of jail, Lincoln had steadfastly defended himself on his radio and TV shows, claiming that Natasha Mason's story wasn't true; it was all part of a left-wing conspiracy against him. But there was plenty of evidence to back up Natasha's claims, and Lincoln had made many enemies among his fellow broadcasters who were thrilled to have a story that made him look foolish and dangerous: Inciting a panic at a popular tourist attraction filled with families was a PR disaster. So was ending up neck-deep in animal poop. Lincoln's image took another hit when it was revealed that King was actually a bichon frise, not a golden retriever as he'd claimed—and furthermore, a vicious bichon frise that often attacked his neighbors' small children. Lincoln's show was yanked off the air on TV and radio networks across the country. He didn't lose *all* his stations, but he lost his political clout. Stephanie Winger admitted she had made a mistake in issuing the permit to kill a mountain lion and rescinded it.

J.J. didn't mention any of this on the stage, though. Instead, his speech was far more focused on the issues at hand: "Animals need open space," he was saying. "And they're running out of it everywhere on earth—even right here. As much as I want people to visit FunJungle, I certainly don't want that to be the *only* place anyone can see a mountain lion."

Summer grinned as her father said this. She had written those lines for him.

A pickup truck with FUNJUNGLE VETERINARY HOSPITAL stenciled on the sides pulled up to the edge of the parking lot fifty yards away from us. A large shipping crate sat in the cargo bay. Kevin Wilks guided the truck in with a pair of orange batons.

Kevin was no longer in FunJungle Security. Hoenekker had planned to fire him, but before he even got the chance, Kevin had walked into his office and surrendered his badge. Kevin felt miserable about poisoning the giraffes and claimed he didn't deserve to wear the uniform of a FunJungle security guard. He still needed work, though, and promptly asked Hoenekker if there were any other jobs at the park. Hoenekker had directed him to parking lot operations, which was the least popular division at FunJungle; the job entailed standing in the parking lot and directing tourists to spaces. No one liked it because the parking lot was broiling on hot days, and the tourists often got confused and nearly ran over the employees on a regular basis. You did get a free Parking Patrol baseball cap, though. Kevin leaped at the chance and seemed to be enjoying himself. At the very least, he hadn't accidentally poisoned anything.

Meanwhile, Marge O'Malley was still bucking to get herself back on the security force. Her manhandling of the poor tourists during Operation Hammerhead was a strike against her, but her assistance in taking out Putterman to help us go after Lincoln Stone—in a wheelchair, no less—was considered a plus. Hoenekker was still reviewing her case.

Under Kevin's guidance, the veterinary truck swung around and backed up to the edge of the parking lot, so the rear gate faced the woods.

"Habitat loss is the number one threat to wild animals today," J.J. was saying. "Far more than poaching or hunting, and it is a threat in which all of us are complicit. Every house we build, or farm we get our food from, or road we travel, is on land where wild animals once roamed."

Natasha Mason was on the far side of the small crowd,

Grayson and Jason by her sides. Lincoln Stone had threatened to sue Natasha for caninicide. But since there was a record of Natasha filing multiple complaints about King, and Lincoln had done nothing to restrain his dog, Lincoln didn't have much of a case. His lawyers pointed out that suing would only make his bad PR situation even worse, so he had begrudgingly dropped the lawsuit.

The Mason family had still felt terrible about what Rocket had gone through—and what I had endured as well to protect the lion. As an apology, they had made a donation to the World Wildlife Fund in my honor—and bought us a bug-zapper for our house.

J.J. was already wrapping up his speech. Pete had advised him to keep it short and sweet, given that it was sweltering in the parking lot and no major news organizations were covering the story anyhow. "I'd like to thank all of you for coming out here today for this special occasion," J.J. said. "And now I'd like to invite Stephanie Winger from the Department of Fish and Wildlife to do the honors."

There was polite applause as Stephanie approached the microphone.

Down along the parking lot, Doc Deakin climbed out of the passenger side of the veterinary truck, walked to the back, and dropped the tailgate.

My parents had told me that Doc had posted bail for

Lily, who was now awaiting trial at home. Lily was hoping to avoid prison and get mandatory community service instead. Doc hadn't told my parents any of this; as far as they knew, Doc hadn't said a thing about his daughter to anyone.

Doc had a little more to say about the giraffes. Knowing what they had been poisoned with made treatment much easier. Nightshade was bad for them, but it could have been much worse. Charcoal had been mixed into their food for the past two weeks to help them purge the toxins from their systems, and now they seemed to be in perfect health. Daily giraffe feedings for the tourists had resumed. Meanwhile, J.J. McCracken had ordered his grounds crew to eradicate every single bit of deadly nightshade growing on the FunJungle property.

Stephanie Winger was saying something nice about J.J. and his commitment to the environment, but it appeared most people were already losing interest in the presentation. We were all wilting in the heat. I felt bad for Pete Thwacker; in addition to dealing with the small crowds, he also had to wear a three-piece suit.

"They should have done this ceremony in the Polar Pavilion," Dash whispered to me.

"This ceremony doesn't have anything to do with the Polar Pavilion," I whispered back.

"Who cares?" Dash grumbled. "It's air-conditioned."

The Polar Pavilion had been even more crowded than usual lately. The fish cannon had been a bigger hit than expected. So many people were crowding the penguin feeding times that J.J. had asked Sanjay Budhiraja to think of other places a cannon could be used at FunJungle. A new Zoom was going to be unleashed at the sea lion pool within the next month, and using one to fire raw meat into the carnivore exhibits was under consideration.

Doc climbed up into the bed of the pickup. The young vet who had driven the truck posted herself nearby with a sedation rifle.

I knew Rocket was in the shipping crate, though most other people didn't. Of course, Pete had wanted Doc to make the release of the lion closer to the podium, where the news crews could film it. Doc had refused, claiming the crowd would make Rocket skittish. "You don't want a reporter getting mauled on live television, do you?" he'd asked.

Pete had turned greenish at the thought of this and decided it was a bad idea.

Rocket wouldn't really have attacked anyone, but I could definitely understand her being on guard around people, given how she'd been treated by them lately.

"Sadly, this park alone won't guarantee the lion's safety," Stephanie Winger was saying. "Lions need room to roam, and wildlife corridors to connect those areas. If we keep carving up the wilderness, we might as well be stranding these animals on separate islands and condemning them to extinction. But at the very least, this is a start. A good-size refuge is far better than no refuge at all. So, without any further ado, I would like to officially consecrate the Summer McCracken Wildlife Refuge."

Everyone broke into applause, louder this time, as we were excited for this moment—and pleased that the ceremony was almost over.

Summer wasn't clapping. Instead, she sat in her chair, stunned by the name of the refuge, which had been a secret until now.

That had been *my* idea. I had suggested it to J.J. at dinner one night, while Summer was in the bathroom. Up until then, J.J. had been thinking about simply naming it the McCracken Wildlife Refuge. "That kind of sounds like it was named after *you*," I had argued. "It was Summer's idea. You should name it after *her*."

"That's a wonderful suggestion," Kandace had said, and after that, there was no way J.J. could argue against it. Not that he would have. He seemed to like the idea anyhow.

Now, on the stage, Summer leaped to her feet and hugged her parents. Then J.J. escorted her to a ceremonial ribbon that had been strung between two trees at the edge of the parking lot.

In the truck, fifty yards away, with far less ceremony, Doc lifted the hatch on the shipping crate.

A few seconds passed, and then Rocket sprang out off the back of the truck.

It happened so fast no one else but my parents even seemed to notice it. Rocket was merely a blur of tawny fur.

While Summer cut the ceremonial ribbon, the big cat raced into the forest and vanished from sight.

Rocket Is Not the Only Mountain Lion in Danger!

Habitat loss is a threat to mountain lions throughout their range. In fact, habitat loss is the single greatest threat to animals all over the earth. Wherever there are humans, animal populations are losing ground to cities, towns, and farms, and the more we expand into their territory, the greater potential there is for human/wildlife conflict. As the human population keeps growing on earth, the issues of habitat loss and human/wildlife conflict are only going to get worse.

At first, this might seem to be an unsolvable problem: After all, we humans need places to live and food to eat. But there are still things that you can do.

At the most basic level, be aware that you are sharing this planet with other creatures. Even in our biggest cities, there are still wild animals. You can take care to reduce the potential for human/wildlife conflict around your home by not leaving food out where raccoons or opossums can get into it, or not letting your cat run free so that it kills local birds. (A Smithsonian study estimates that outdoor cats kill between 1.4 and 3.7 billion birds a year.) If you're venturing into the wilderness, be prepared for the possibility of running into wild animals and learn what to do when that happens. (And please, if you're hiking in mountain lion territory, don't let your dog off leash.)

On the larger scale, many organizations are working to develop ways for us to live in harmony with animals. My friends at the World Wildlife Fund are developing ways to keep elephants from destroying crops in Asia and Africa, and to keep polar bears from raiding garbage dumps in the Arctic. Meanwhile, the fine folks at the Nature Conservancy are buying land to set it aside for threatened animals. If your community is building new roads and schools, you can get involved and pressure your leaders to make sure that they are providing wildlife corridors to allow animals to still move about with as little human contact as possible. Because habitat loss is occurring everywhere, there is no single solution to the problem—but that just means that anyone, anywhere, might have an idea that helps. Even you!

Check out the WWF at wwf.panda.org or the Nature Conservancy at nature.org to learn more about these issues and what you can do to protect wildlife and have a positive impact on the natural world!

Acknowledgments

With this book, I set a record for the number of people who helped me do research. I am hugely indebted to the following people:

Seth Riley from the National Park Service, who tracks and studies mountain lions in Southern California, and who taught me all about these amazing animals, how they come into conflict with humans, and what we can do to prevent it.

John Lewis, Connie Morgan, Candace Sclimenti, Mike Bona, and Joshua Sisk at the Los Angeles Zoo, who showed me around behind the scenes and answered all my questions, no matter how bizarre they were (particularly the questions about giraffe vomit).

Linda Henry from SeaWorld, who was a font of information about penguins.

Steve Jeffries, the California manager for Garden State Fireworks, who taught me how all those amazing displays work.

Jay Sonbolian, Katy Henry, and Amanda Prager, who

connected me to the fine folks I just mentioned.

Barney Long, Nilanga Jayasinghe, and Giavanna Grien, who do incredible work in species conservation for the World Wildlife Fund, and who are coming up with and implementing brilliant ways to counter human-wildlife conflict around the world.

And my wife's dear friend, Todd Deligan, the co-inventor of the fish cannon (yes, it really exists!) and former vice president of Whooshh, which manufactures said cannons (yes, that's really the name!).

Then there are the amazing people who have made these books happen in the first place:

Liz Kossnar, my excellent editor; Justin Chanda, my enthusiastic publisher; and Lucy Cummins, the greatest cover designer on earth.

Jennifer Joel, agent extraordinaire, and her clever niece Lexington Satnick, who came up with the title for this book.

Rose Brock, my study-guide guru and occasional interviewer; Sarah Mlynowski, the fairy godmother of festivals; and James Ponti, the funniest fellow author anyone could ever tour with.

And all the amazing, devoted librarians, book store owners, and store employees who have promoted my books over the years.

Finally, there's my family:

My parents, Ronald and Jane, who have supported my desire to write throughout my life.

My sister, Suz; my brother-in-law, Darragh; and my niece, Ciara, who are my biggest cheerleaders.

My late wife, Suzanne, who always supported everything I did.

And last but certainly not least, my children, Dashiell and Violet, who give me ideas, help me edit, and provide the best sounding board any author could ever ask for. I love you!